The Sixth Rider

The Sixth Rider

Max McCoy

A DOUBLE D WESTERN
DOUBLEDAY
NEW YORK LONDON TORONTO SYDNEY AUCKLAND

A DOUBLE D WESTERN
PUBLISHED BY DOUBLEDAY
a division of Bantam Doubleday Dell Publishing Group, Inc.
666 Fifth Avenue, New York, New York 10103

DOUBLE D WESTERN, DOUBLEDAY,
and the portrayal of the letters DD
are trademarks of Doubleday, a division of
Bantam Doubleday Dell Publishing Group, Inc.

Library of Congress Cataloging-in-Publication Data

McCoy, Max.
The sixth rider / by Max McCoy.—1st ed.
    p.   cm. —(A Double D western)
    1. Dalton family—Fiction. 2. West (U.S.)—History—1848–1950—
Fiction. I. Title
PS3563.C3523S59   1991
813'.54—dc20   90-48093
CIP

ISBN 0-385-41495-1
Copyright © 1991 by Max McCoy
All Rights Reserved
Printed in the United States of America
April 1991
First Edition

For my father

You would have me, when I describe horse-thieves, say: "Stealing horses is an evil." But that has been known for ages without my saying so. Let the jury judge them; it's my job simply to show what kind of people they are. I write: you are dealing with horse-thieves, so let me tell you they are not beggars but well-fed people, that they are people of a special cult, and that horse-stealing is not simply theft but a passion.

—ANTON CHEKHOV
from *Letters,* 1890

The Sixth Rider

One

WE RODE INTO TOWN from Indian Territory, with our hats pulled low and our dusters buttoned tight over our six-guns. I was bone-tired from the trail—from sleeping on the ground and having cold biscuits and scalding coffee for breakfast—but the closer we got the faster my blood started pumping. Cimarron must have recognized familiar territory, because he went into a trot and I had to rein him back so as not to get ahead of the others.

There were six of us, counting me.

Bob and Grat and Emmett had these phony black mustaches and beards tied to their faces, but there was no need to hide mine, since nobody could recognize me now. Dick Broadwell and Bill Powers had no need for disguises, either, because they weren't known in these parts.

Near the old cheese factory at the section line we met a couple in a farm wagon. Bob touched the brim of his hat, natural as you please, just like we were on our way to Sunday School. A few hundred yards on we passed a couple of business types in a buggy, and they took in our dust-covered clothes and the Fish slickers and bedrolls tied behind saddles and our Winchesters hung butt-first from the pommels. I heard one remark, "They must be marshals up from the Territory."

Bob laughed. I could feel their eyes on our backs long after we passed.

As we came up to the old green clapboard farmhouse with the rickety red barn out back, Cimarron tried to amble over to the lane going to the house, but I pulled him up short. My brothers came up alongside and we sat there a moment, looking over the old homestead. Nothing was true, not the barn or any of the posts, and although it had been empty only a few years it was all coming down from its own weight. Pa never

had been much with a hammer. There were weeds and vines everywhere. The land was doing a pretty good job of reclaiming what we had
never made our own.

"I sure wish Ma was in there baking a pumpkin pie for us," Emmett
said. It was just like him to be thinking about food.

"It would be a damn sight better than your biscuits, that's for sure,"
Grat said.

Everybody laughed except for Bob, who sat there a moment real still
and then swung down off his horse and waded across the weeds in the
ditch to the house. He unbuttoned his trousers and made water. His
back was to us, but we could hear the sound of it and see the stream.

We reined up at the Hickman place on Eighth Street, at the edge of
town proper. Bob took out his gold watch and flipped it open, the
morning sun glinting from his diamond ring. By that time my heart was
thumping like I'd run a footrace.

"Right on time," he said and slipped the watch back into his vest
pocket. He nudged his horse over to mine and laid a hand on my
shoulder. "Little brother, are you ready?"

"I feel like making a withdrawal from a Yankee bank," I allowed,
trying to be brave like him and Grat, although my insides felt like they
had turned to ice water. I looked over at Emmett, who at twenty was
three years older than me, and I thought I saw the gleam of something
in the corner of his eye, but he quickly looked away.

"You know what to do," Grat said impatiently, "so do it." A wisp of
blond hair had fallen out from under his hat onto his forehead, which
looked strange with the black beard and mustache.

I nodded and spurred Cimarron on. I took the first alley that would
take me around to the south end of the Plaza, while Bob and the others
continued at their leisurely pace down Eighth Street. I fought an urge to
look back over my shoulder.

My job was to come in from the south to reconnoiter the Plaza and
see how many customers there were in the banks. I was to tie Cimarron
at the hitch in front of the dry-goods store. When everything looked
clear, I was to give the signal for the others. One man walking across
the Plaza wouldn't attract attention, but six would.

That was the plan, anyway. But I found out that a sidewalk crew had
the brick pavement all dug up in front of the dry-goods store, and there
was nowhere to hitch our horses as Bob had planned. I looked the
situation over and tried to decide where Bob would want the horses,

now that his first choice was out. I reckoned it would be someplace out of the way, but easy to get to from both banks.

The Plaza was a cobblestone triangle surrounded by dirt streets. The Condon Bank Building, which was just a couple of years old, was wedged like a big piece of pie between Union and Maple Streets. The point of the pie ended in the bank office, with a two-story cast-metal front with frills and ornamentation and other such nonsense poking toward the center of the Plaza. Beneath this metal facade was a covered porch and thick glass picture windows which made it easy to see in. Just across the way to the west was the First National Bank, a one-story affair with bay windows on either side of the door. The rest of the Plaza was rounded out by a couple of hardware stores, a drugstore, a shoe-maker's shop, newspaper office, and Long & Lape: furniture and under-takers.

The hitch post on Eighth Street behind the Condon Bank was as good a place as any to leave Cimarron. I dismounted, but left the Win-chester in its scabbard. My coat covered my old .45 Colt and beaded holster.

I strode as confidently as I could onto the Plaza. The morning sun felt good on my face, although it was still cold enough to see your breath. The hardware stores were already open and there were some folks doing business, but from what I could tell I was the only armed man on the Plaza. I sauntered over to the front of Rammel's Drug Store and pretended to eye the patent medicines. Then I walked casually down the sidewalk to the First National and peered in through the bay window. The bank had just opened, and I didn't see anybody but a clerk behind the counter.

I crossed the street to the Condon and peered through the big win-dows and saw they already had a customer at the cage. So I leaned against one of the metal posts, trying to be as natural as I could. When the farmer left the bank I strolled out to the well in the center of the Plaza. I gave one last glance to make sure nobody had walked into the First National. Then I gave the sign that Bob had devised—I took off my sweat-stained hat and wiped my brow with a bright red handker-chief.

No sooner had I replaced my hat than the gang marched out of an alley to the west, in the direction of the livery stable and the city jail. I didn't like the looks of that alley. It was too far from the banks.

Bob and Emmett were out front, dusters open now, and I could see the tips of their carbines sticking out from under the fringes. Grat, Powers, and Broadwell followed close behind.

I started to fall back, but Bob wheeled around and laid a hand on my shoulder. "I've changed my mind," he said, "I want you to go with Grat." Then, under his breath, he said to me, "Keep an eye on him."

Bob was the leader, so I nodded and walked double-quick to catch up with Grat as he entered the front door of the Condon Bank.

The teller had his head down in the books and didn't look up when the door opened. We fanned out in front of the counter. Grat pulled himself up to his full six feet, two inches and roared, "God damn it all! Get your hands up, because we aim to rob you."

Powers and Broadwell had their carbines out, and took up positions on either side of the door. With all the artillery at the ready, I didn't even bother to draw my Colt. I don't think I could have held it still if I had.

The teller's hands went into the air as his face went white. The head cashier came out of a back room to see what all the commotion was about, and Grat pointed the Winchester in his face and told him to get his hands up.

"Hand over all your cash and reserves," Grat said. "Be smart about it if you'd like to keep that head on your shoulders."

"Is that you, Grat?" the cashier asked as he hiked up his hands. His name was Charlie Ball and he, like the rest of the town, had grown up with the Dalton boys.

"Sonuvabitch," Grat muttered as he tore off the false beard and dashed it to the floor. From beneath his coat he took a two-bushel grain sack and threw it at Ball, who caught it in midair.

Grat went behind the counter and kept Ball at gunpoint while he slowly emptied the counter and drawers of the petty cash used to start the day's business.

"Dammit, Grat," Powers called from the front. "Go for the goddamn safe, that's where the gold will be. Forget about the drawers. This is taking too damn long."

"I'm in charge here," my brother shot back. "Okay, what about the safe? Let's look lively."

Grat herded Ball back toward the vault. Ball swung the big iron door open and they both stepped inside. Grat asked him what was inside three canvas bags on the floor, and Ball told him: silver.

"Silver?" Grat whined.

Ball nodded.

"Put it in."

Ball began digging handfuls of silver dollars from a canvas bag and dumping it into the grain sack. Grat ordered him to work faster. But when Ball tried to pour the silver into the flimsy sack, silver dollars spilled out and rolled across the floor.

"Hurry up," Powers called back. "What the hell is taking so long?"

Ball took his time picking up the strays and putting them back into the grain sack. I wanted to tell Grat to forget it, to just take the damn canvas bags, but it wouldn't have done any good. Grat was in charge and that was the way it would stay.

"Ask him what's in the back of the safe," Broadwell shouted back. "And for God's sake, hurry! There's some people starting to gawk at us."

"What's back there?" Grat asked, indicating the inner door.

"Nothing," Ball said. "Oh, some change, pennies and nickels and that sort of thing. No gold."

"Open it."

Ball hesitated and I could see the wheels working.

"I can't," he said too quickly. "It's on a time lock."

"What the hell time does it open, then?"

"Half past nine."

"What time is it now?"

Ball fumbled with his pocket watch and peered at it down the length of his nose.

"Twenty after," he said, and snapped the watch shut.

Grat's eyes got kind of wild-looking, and he glanced around as if he were expecting Bob to give him advice. I tried to tell Grat it was a lie but I was told to shut up. Grat asked him how much money was on the books when they closed last night.

"Four thousand and some odd dollars," Ball said. "You've got it all, right there in your sack. You've cleaned us out."

Grat smiled for the first time. The grin stretched from ear to ear and showed his strong white teeth. "You're lying," he said. "I think there's gold in there. Goddamn it, I ought to put a ball through you right here and now."

"Please," Ball said, showing his palms. "Don't do that. There may be some gold in there. But it's locked, see?" Ball grabbed the handle and gave a grunt. "It's not time for it to open."

"We can wait ten minutes," Grat said, and sat down in a chair behind the counter, rifle across his lap.

"You're going to get us all killed," Powers said, wild-eyed. "We can't wait ten minutes in here. There's people already looking in through the windows out there. What do you want me to do, shoot them? Damn it, we've got four thousand dollars in the bag. Let's get the hell out of here."

"I say we stay," Grat said. "I came here for gold and I ain't gonna leave here without it."

Powers was right, any fool could see that. But none of us would leave without the others. So there we sat. Although it was October, the sweat ran down our faces and puddled beneath our short ribs. When the front door swung open, jangling the bell above it, we damn near jumped out of our skins.

It was an old man, and he made it halfway across the floor before he noticed the rifles. Bewildered, he stopped.

Broadwell took off his hat and introduced us properly.

"This here is the Dalton gang, sir," he said. "That big fellow behind the counter is Grat Dalton, who escaped from a jail in Fresno, California, so he could come back and pay his respects to his hometown. We're engaged in making a little withdrawal here, and we would count it as a personal favor if you'd be so kind as to take a seat on the floor over there behind that desk." Broadwell pointed gently with the business end of the Winchester to make his point.

The old man nodded and shuffled over to the spot indicated, and sat down.

"Thank you kindly," Broadwell said.

"What've you got in your pockets, grandpa?" Powers asked.

"Leave him be," Grat murmured. It was enough.

"Any sign of the other boys?" Grat asked.

"No," I said, peering through the window to the east at the First National. "I can't see anything stirring."

Another customer came in, a kid from the dry-goods store looking to change a ten-dollar note, and Broadwell urged him to take a seat next to the old man.

Feeling like we had enough company for a while, Broadwell walked over and set the bolt on the front door. Holding the Winchester in the crook of his arm, he had just bolted the door and turned back to us when we heard the crack of a rifle and the *ting!* of the slug as it made a hole in the glass. Broadwell's Winchester clattered to the floor. I thought he had dropped it out of surprise until I saw his hand clamped over his left elbow and the blood between his fingers.

"Boys, I'm hit," he said, and walked back to the counter. "I believe my shooting arm is done for. If I don't make it out of here with you all, I want you to know it was an honor to have rode with you."

My heart dropped somewhere down around my stomach, because I realized Powers was right: Grat had killed us all.

Another slug knocked a quarter-sized hole in the thick glass, then another, and soon hell itself was raining in through those big picture windows. There must have been an army hidden out there in the doorways and the rooftops of the Plaza. Slugs came in two and three at a time, smacking against the floor and the walls and the desks, scattering paper everywhere.

"They're handing out guns at the hardware store," Powers said.

"Is there a back way out?" Broadwell asked.

"No," Ball said.

Defeat crossed Grat's face.

"I do believe those people are crazy and mean to kill somebody," he said. "Charlie, get yourself and your people back into that vault for your own good."

Grat, Powers, the bleeding Broadwell, and I hunkered down behind that mercifully thick counter and tried to study our situation, but it was hard to think with all the lead raining in.

"I don't aim to go back to prison," Grat said.

Broadwell smiled and said, "My Pa lives in Hutchinson and he's a good man. When this is over, won't you tell him where to fetch my body? I haven't seen him in five years."

It was the first time Broadwell had ever spoken of his kin.

It was clear we were going to have to fight our way out, even though none of us had yet fired a shot. Grat dumped most of the silver out of the grain sack and just kept the notes to make it lighter. Broadwell was attempting to get the Winchester up to his shoulder, but couldn't quite manage it without an elbow. Powers was breathing like a locomotive, his eyes were wild, and he was either cussing or praying under his breath—I don't know which.

I closed my eyes and rested my head against the counter. I felt old and used up, like a watch that doesn't run anymore or a deck of cards with a couple of faces missing. I was scared, but at the same time kind of relieved, because it had finally come down to this. The trail had ended and I knew that I wasn't going to swing at the end of a rope. Then I thought about Jane and how she would hear how I ended, and I was sick, like my insides were already busted up.

I opened my eyes and found myself staring at the back wall, into the face of a big clock that was ticking away like nothing at all unusual was going on around it. The time was nine forty-five, and I knew the sonuvabitch had lied to us about the time lock. Below the clock was a calendar pad with the date: Wednesday, October 5, 1892.

Then a stray round hit the clock and time stopped.

It was my birthday. I was seventeen.

"The horses are out that door and down the alley to the right," Grat said. "It's the only way out of here. And if we can't make the ground, by God, let's at least die game."

Grat made his move and the rest of us followed, jumping over the counter and making for the door. The Colt sprung into my palm easily, just like it always had.

Two

THEY SAY THAT THIRTEEN is an unlucky number, and I reckon I'm living proof, because it all started on my thirteenth birthday. I didn't pick up a gun and start robbing banks. But my head was so filled with tales of the James and Younger gangs—we were Youngers on my mother's side, and distant cousins of the Jameses, although a lot of folks accused us of making that up—that it's a wonder I didn't. Start robbing banks, that is. Colonel Elliott always said that impressionable minds ought to be shielded from the glorification of outlawry. Considering the spell that brothers Bob and Grat had me under, I was a goner from the start.

I was living with Mama in Coffeyville at the time, and come to think of it, I was the thirteenth child in a Protestant Irish family of fifteen. Our Pa was a damn good fiddler and even a better drunk. With the help of Colonel Elliott, a lawyer from back East who had purchased the *Coffeyville Journal* the year before, Mama had divorced him. Pa just drifted around the countryside after that, sleeping in barns and stables or wherever some kindhearted family would take him in.

I'll save the rest of my family for later, because if I started a rundown of all my brothers and sisters, it would sound like a chapter out of the Good Book, with all the begetting our Mama and Pa did. Some say it would have been a whole lot easier on everybody if she had divorced him a mite earlier. *Quien sabe,* as the cowhands say.

I recall that on the afternoon of my thirteenth birthday, me and Johnny Williamson were down on the banks of the Verdigris River target practicing. It was our usual after-school routine, and we were giving the cans and bottles hell. At least I was.

I was practicing my fast-draw just like my brother Bob had shown me: gun arm straight out in front of me, palm down, with a nickel balanced on the back of the hand. On my hip was an old converted Navy in a cutaway holster, tied down with a piece of rope. My legs were firmly planted, knees slightly bent, and my attention was focused through narrowed eyes on a green medicine bottle sunk into the soft earth of the riverbank, thirty paces away.

"Are you going to say it?" I asked through clenched teeth.

"I just wanted to make sure you were ready," said Johnny.

"Any time between now and sundown would be fine."

Johnny let the muscles in my arm ache for another fifteen seconds or so, then shouted:

"Draw!"

My right hand whipped down, leaving the nickel suspended in air for an instant. My palm found the butt of the revolver and snatched the gun forward out of the holster. At the same time my left hand cut across in a chopping motion, and by the time the barrel was in business position the fleshy edge of my hand caught the spur of the hammer and tripped it backwards.

The gun boomed and the medicine bottle exploded, but not before the nickel hit the ground.

"You're still too slow," Johnny laughed.

I cussed and holstered the Navy. It had started out as a percussion revolver, the kind where you had to load each cylinder with power and shot and cap the nipples, but it had been converted to accept cartridges. It may have seen service in the war, but its history was uncertain. Pa had took it and some other rubbish in exchange for a horse. When I finally talked him out of it, I bragged to my friends that Jesse James had carried it while he was riding with Quantrill. The way a Dalton sees it, it wasn't exactly lying, because for all we knew old Jess *had* carried it.

"Don't you think you've practiced enough?" Johnny whined.

"I don't expect a man can be too ready," I said.

"From what I've seen you're getting worser instead of better. That nickel is ahead of you every time," he said. "Why don't you just admit you're licked and give up?"

"I wouldn't talk that way if I were you," I said, and randomly aimed at a snapping turtle sunning himself on a log down the river a piece. I changed my mind at the last minute and switched to a branch on the log, neatly clipping it off at the base.

"That's girl shooting, holding it out in front of you and aiming like that," Johnny said, just to show he wasn't impressed. "Anyway, when are you going to let me shoot?"

I handed him the Navy—there was one round left in the chamber—then trotted out and set up another bottle amid the remains of the others I'd busted. Then I ran like hell because I'd seen Johnny shoot before.

He missed by a yard and commented dryly that the gun was shooting a little low and to the right.

I reloaded, and told Johnny it would be the last cylinder for the day. I just had to try to beat that nickel one more time.

I shook out my hands and wrists and closed my eyes. I got a picture in my mind of that can, and then let the rest of my mind go blank, not letting myself get tensed up over trying to beat the nickel. I remembered what my brother Bob had told me—don't aim, don't try, just *be* the gun. Finally I said "okay" and extended my arm, the nickel on the back of my hand.

"Draw!"

I was the gun.

The can jumped in the air before the coin hit the ground.

I hooped and hollered and fanned the Navy, emptying the rest of the cylinder at the can, making it dance this way and that. It felt good. I had been practicing since early that summer, and I had the callouses on my palms to prove it.

I took off the holster and placed it and the gun in a burlap sack. I slung the sack over my shoulder and we made our way up through the brush of the riverbank to the road. The sun was low in the autumn sky, and Johnny and I cast long shadows as we walked toward home.

Johnny Williamson and I had been best friends since Pa had moved us into the little green farmhouse just outside Coffeyville, perched on the state line just above Indian Territory. Pa had taken a shine to the Verdigris Valley when he wandered down here in '63 to buy horses on the old Osage Indian Reservation. The Osage were busy stealing them from their rebellious red brothers to the south. Pa wasn't a Union man, but the Federals were buying anything with four hooves and he figured he might as well make a little money from the situation.

I don't remember what it was like before we moved to Coffeyville, but what memories I do have aren't much worth talking about. Just the kind of thing that gets you sad and does you no good at all, like watching Pa rolling around on the floor drunk and raving about the devils that were after him.

I truly envied Johnny Williamson, because he had a father who stayed with them and who never touched a drop and who worked hard all day. Old Man Williamson was mean as hell all right—I think he'd sooner take a harness strap to Johnny's behind than sit down to dinner —but at least he was a real father. All I had was a washed-up old drunk who would decide to be kind every once in a blue moon, which just made everything harder, because you really couldn't hate him. Lord, he always looked so old and stove-in. By the time I turned ten, he was already in his sixties.

I was thinking about all that as Johnny and I reached the home place, about how I wished I was Johnny instead of being me. Ordinarily Johnny and I would have hung around outside, by the fence talking, or throwing hedge apples behind the barn until it was plumb dark, but tonight was different. Mama always made sure we had something a little special to eat on birthdays, and you could count on one of her good pumpkin pies this time of year. So I said so long for now while Johnny lingered by the fence, knowing that Mama would see him there and invite him in later for a piece of pie. He always said my ma made the best darn pumpkin pie in the county.

I slipped in the door quietly and crept up the stairs to my room, where I hid the sack with the gun in it underneath the bed. Mama had forbidden me to take it out unless my brothers were with me, because right after Pa gave it to me I was showing it to Johnny and it went off when he dropped it on the floor. It put a hole in the parlor wall. That was the last time I had loaded it up full. From then on, I left the chamber under the hammer empty, like Bob had told me to do in the first place.

I sprinkled some water from the basin on my face and brushed my hair down with my hands, and knocked the river mud as best I could off my clothes and boots. I slipped back downstairs and came back in the door like I'd just got home.

"Mama," I called, even though I already knew she was in the kitchen.

"Where have you been, Samuel?" she asked, as she whipped up a batch of mashed potatoes. "Supper is almost ready. Go call your sisters to the table. And go tell Johnny he can come in and have a piece of pie with us. I saw him out by the fence. I declare, that boy has a better nose on him than a bloodhound."

"Yessum," I said.

Leona and Nannie were sewing by the light of a lamp in the corner of the parlor. I told them it was supper time. Then I went to the door and waved for Johnny to come in.

"About time," he said, sniffing. "I was about to freeze out there."

"Did you tell your folks?"

"Hell, no," he said. "Papa won't mind. It means more food for him."

"Come on back to the kitchen," I said. "Wash your hands in the sink, or Mama will have a fit."

The girls were already bellied up to the table. Minnie Johnson, our sixteen-year-old cousin from Harrisonville who had gotten into some kind of trouble and had to leave, was also there. Mama had told me to be watchful around her, but I didn't know what she meant. I asked her to explain it, but she wouldn't.

"Did you tell your folks you were eating with us?" Ma asked.

"Yes, ma'am."

"That's a good boy."

"I'll just have a small slice of pie, if that's all right with you, Mrs. Dalton."

"You must eat a meal with us. There's plenty to go around."

"Yes ma'am, if you insist."

"I do. It's Samuel's birthday today. His presents are there on the sideboard."

Mama was just putting the chicken on the table—we may not have had red meat very often, but the coop out back supplied plenty of eggs and chicken dinners—and I hadn't seen a spread like that since Christmas. There was corn and carrots and biscuits, and the pies were cooling on the sill. Mama clasped her hands and lowered her head, and I asked God to grant her brevity.

"Oh, Lord," she began, "We thank Thee for this bounty before us, and for the togetherness we share this evening, and for the occasion of Samuel Coleman Dalton's birthday. May he grow up to be a true and honest and reverent man. We ask Thee to watch after the older boys who can't be here tonight because they are enforcing the law and doing Your will in the wilderness of the Indian Territory. We ask that You watch over the grown boys who are trying to make homes for themselves and their families in California. We ask—"

"For a slice of Mama's pumpkin pie!" a voice roared from the window. Grat's smiling face peered in.

"Amen!" said Mama, as she looked over her shoulder.

Grat was a big man, twenty-eight years old, six feet tall and with the muscle to match. Like all of us Daltons, he was blond and blue-eyed.

He came through the door and swept Mama up with one arm as easily as another man might pick up a child. In the other hand he held his rifle. Behind him was Bob, shaking the trail dust out of his clothes. Bob was about twenty at the time, strong but not nearly as big as Grat, and something of a dandy. Both wore revolvers on their hips and tin stars on the pockets of their flannel shirts.

"Samuel Cole," Bob called out to me, "we left our horses at the post. Would you mind taking them to the barn and brushing them down? They've had a hard ride."

"Let him eat his supper," Mama pleaded. "It's his birthday."

"Oh, I forgot. Well, Sammy, do it for us anyway. I see you've already got your plate set, so I'll just sit down in your spot and keep your chair warm while you're at it."

I got up reluctantly from the table. I was so hungry my stomach was talking to me.

"One other thing," Bob said as I reached for the latch. "There's an extra mount out there. A blood bay with a jagged patch of white on his forehead."

"Yeah?" I asked, not getting it.

"He's yours, boy. Happy birthday."

He was a beautiful horse, fifteen hands high, with a patch of white on his forehead that looked for all the world like a thunderbolt. I took the horses into the barn, unsaddled my brothers' mounts, and gave them some oats and brushed them down until their coats shone. I was still brushing my horse down when Bob came out to the barn, picking his teeth.

"There's supper left for you," he said.

I nodded, then stammered my thanks for the horse.

Bob waved it off. "We all went in together. Frank too. You're going to be a man soon and we reckoned it was time you had a horse of your own. Take care of him. Treat him right and he'll be the best and truest friend you got. That's the thing about horses. They're better'n a lot of people in this world. They always have time to listen to your problems, they never lie to you, and if you're in a pinch they'll die for you trying to get you out of it. All they ask in return is that you feed them and show a little affection once in a while. That's more than I can say for most women."

I nodded as if I understood.

"What're you going to name him?"

"Cimarron," said I.

It was a Spanish name for that which is wild and untamed, and I had taken a fancy to it from seeing it in the dime novels.

We went back to the house, where Mama had a plate warming for me in the oven. Johnny was still there, listening to Grat's story about what it was like to be a riding deputy for Parker, the hanging judge. Grat had been wounded in the arm the month before while serving writs on some rustlers down in the Territory, and he showed us the scar. It was puckered and all purple-looking, but Grat said it was nothing because it hadn't hit the bone.

"That'll teach you to duck next time," Bob said and laughed.

After I cleaned my plate and polished off two slices of pie, Mama gave me the presents that had been waiting on the sideboard. The first one, from Mama, was done up in white paper with a red ribbon. It was a New Testament, with a black leather cover and Jesus's words printed in red. I was sort of embarrassed because I avoided going to church with Mama and the girls whenever I could. It made me uncomfortable to sit in those hard pews, sweating like a sardine, and try to be sociable with all those people who during the week didn't have the time of day for us Daltons.

"You're nigh to being a grown-up man," she said. "I wanted you to have something to live your life by. I wish your Pa had found the Good Book instead of corn liquor. When you read it, I want you to think of me."

Mama started to cry, and my eyes got a little blurry too. I couldn't bear to tell her how I really felt, so I thanked her and kissed her on the cheek and told her I'd keep it with me always.

The girls had made me a few foolish things, but they were already in bed, so I didn't have to fuss over them as much. Nannie had sewn me a handkerchief with my initials in the corner—SCD—and Leona had knitted a pair of socks. One of them was longer than the other but I pretended not to notice.

Minnie, who was still up because she was all of sixteen, then made a big show of handing me my present, which came in a little wooden box. I opened the lid. It was a straight razor.

"I reckoned it was time you had one," she said. Then she leaned over and gave me a hug that was a little more than cousinly, and before she let go she whispered in my ear, "I've got another present for you later."

I turned red as a beet and thought I was going to die for lack of air. Everybody laughed again and Bob slapped me on the shoulder—nobody heard that last part Minnie said to me—and Mama put out the coffee cups on the table for us boys.

"Johnny," she said, "don't you think it's time you ran on home? It's getting awfully late. I do believe it's nearly ten."

Bob whipped out his pocket watch. He just loved for somebody to mention the time. "Matter of fact," he said in a studied voice, "It's a quarter past."

Johnny looked miserable and got up from the table. I knew he was going to get a thumping for being out all night. He thanked Mama for the supper and the three pieces of pie he ate, and wished me happy birthday. Then he grinned evil and added, "You shot real well today."

"You boys haven't been out playing with that infernal gun, have you?" Mama asked straightaway.

"See you tomorrow," Johnny said and slipped out the door. He just couldn't resist getting me in trouble.

"Oh, Mama," I said, trying to defend myself. "We weren't hurtin' nothing. It was just a little target practice. And I beat the nickel this time."

"I've told you about that—"

Bob held up his hand gently and Mama stopped. Bob smiled and said quietly, "He's growing up, Mama. I know he's the youngest boy and he'll always be the baby to you, but a man's got to know how to ride and shoot. It's just the natural order of things."

Mama never could argue with Bob. None of us could.

"All right," she said. "But, Samuel, you make sure you're with your brothers the next time you want to target practice."

"Did you really beat the nickel?" Bob asked.

"You bet," I said.

"Good," Bob said. "Tomorrow, you can show me how you did it."

The conversation at the table kind of petered down to nothing after that. Bob and Grat sat there with their eyes heavy because the trail was catching up with them. They had been on the road for three days straight.

Minnie said good night and went on upstairs to her bedroom where the other girls were already asleep. I looked away when she brushed past me so I wouldn't blush again. Grat and Bob got up and stretched— Grat's knuckles brushed the ceiling—and they bid Mama good night. She said again how good it was to have her boys sleeping under her roof again.

Mama suggested they all sleep up in my room, which used to be their room, but Grat said that they were so tired of sleeping out in the cold they'd rather bed down on the kitchen floor, as close to the stove as they could.

Bob nodded.

"I remember how the wind whistles through the walls up there on the north side," Bob said. "If you don't mind, we're going to be a little antisocial and stay where it's warm. Beds kill my back these days, anyhow."

I waved and walked up the stairs, lugging my presents with me. I was sort of relieved, because I had gotten used to sleeping by myself. Part of it was that I could stay up and light a candle and read if I wanted. I kept Ned Buntline and the others hidden with the Navy under my bed. But I was too tired for it that night. I stripped down to my long johns and blew out the flame and slipped under the quilt. I was fast asleep when somebody laid a hand on my shoulder.

I let out a little grunt in surprise, but Minnie put a finger to her lips. She placed a candle on the table beside the bed.

"It's just me," she said. "I don't bite."

"What're you doing here?"

"I told you I had another present for you," she said and smiled, then ran her tongue around her lips to wet them. Minnie was kind of pretty, with long dark hair and big brown eyes, and skin that was real fair and burned easily when she was out in the sun. I had sort of been noticing things like that about girls lately, especially when it came to Johnny's big sister, Jane. But I didn't even have the courage to say hello to Jane when I saw her walking to school in the mornings, and here was Minnie in her sleeping gown sitting on the bed with me.

"Mama would have a conniption fit if she knew you were in here," I said.

"What your Mama don't know won't hurt her," Minnie said, and just like that kissed me full on the lips and pressed herself against me. I had never kissed a girl before, but I had been thinking a lot about it. I never imagined it could be like that. I had the idea of both people puckering up and just giving each other a little peck. But Minnie was working her mouth every which way against mine, and once I even felt her tongue rake against my teeth. She tasted warm and salty, and she was wearing the most wonderful-smelling perfume. She put me in a real embarrassing condition and I gathered the quilt up around my lap.

Minnie giggled and said it was time she made a man out of me. She pulled her flannel nightgown clear up over her head, threw it on the floor, and sat there beside me buck-naked. She seemed to glow all over in the candlelight, and I'd had no idea her tits were so big beneath her clothes. I have to admit they were certainly lovely. I wanted to kiss them, but all I could do was reach out and cup one in the palm of my hand. The pink part felt warm and hard, and she grabbed my hand with both of hers and closed her eyes and sighed.

"Minnie, we shouldn't," I finally managed, and pulled my hand away. She shifted position and I could see a lot of silky black hair in the place between her legs. I was powerful curious about it all, but powerful scared, too.

She reached down into my long johns and grabbed me. I thought I was going to pass out.

"My, you are big for your age," she purred. Then we got into sort of a wrestling match, with her trying to climb into bed with me and me wanting her to, but trying to keep her out just the same. She landed on the wood floor with a big thump, and one hand rubbed her behind while the other rubbed her eyes. She was crying. A big tear rolled off her chin and streaked her chest.

"I'm sorry," I said, "I like you a lot, I truly do, but—"

"Just hush up," she said, as if she were speaking to a child. She found her nightgown and struggled into it, not taking any notice that it was inside out. "I thought you were growed up, but I guess I was wrong. I'll just have to find me a real man."

She left, closing the door behind her so hard I thought it was going to wake up Mama. I blew out the candle quickly so there wouldn't be any light showing beneath the door.

I sat there in the dark for a long time, feeling rotten about how I'd hurt her feelings, and feeling rotten because I had wanted to take advantage of her. I don't know whether I felt worse because I had wanted to or because I hadn't actually done it. I felt guilty, too, because in the middle of all that wrestling around with her I had messed my long johns.

Bob was right. Horses were simpler.

Three

MINNIE WAS SITTING with Bob the next morning at breakfast, and didn't give me so much as a "how do you do" when I took my place at the table. I usually took my time with my eggs, because I hated school and was never anxious to get there, but this morning I ate quick and said goodbye.

It was still early. The sky was filled with red and gold to the east, and in the west a few stars lingered. It was also damned chilly. I went to the barn to check my horse first, and after that I waited at the end of the lane, stamping my feet and rubbing my hands, hoping to catch sight of Jane. I had made up my mind that this was the day I'd say hello. Only she never came out. I guessed she must have been sick or something. When I got to school I was ten minutes late and had to put up with a licking from the old witch of a teacher. I acted bored through the whole thing, which only made her flail harder with the switch, and I yawned when she was finished. My behind was still tingling at lunchtime, but I'd be damned before I'd let on that she hurt me any. I don't know why people in authority always have to see you squirm before they are satisfied enough to lay off a body.

The whole episode put a damper on the rest of the day. Even though I could read and 'cipher as well as any of them, I just played stupid so I wouldn't have to get up from my seat. It didn't count for much, anyway, unless you were a banker or lawyer or storekeeper's kid like Lucious Baldwin. Then they put you in the front row where they could make over you easier, even though you might be dumber than dirt and couldn't write your name in the snow.

On my way home from school I saw a handbill tacked up on a telegraph pole. "NOTICE," it said, "TO ALL MARKSMEN. The Coffeyville Rifle Club will host a Rifle Competition—$1.00 Entry Fee. Grand Prize: Winchester repeating rifle." I tore the handbill down and stuffed it into the pocket of my coat.

Bob was waiting for me when I got home, and said he wanted to see me shoot. I started to go upstairs for the Navy, but he said that we would use his revolvers. We went out behind the barn and set up some cans on the fence. I strapped on his heavy gun belt carrying the .45 Colt he packed at the time. I cleared leather a few times to get a feel for the gun. It was a little heavier than the Navy, but also had a shorter barrel and came up faster. Its balance was different—not nearly as nose-heavy as my old gun.

Instead of a nickel, Bob placed a silver dollar on the back of my hand and told me to draw when ready. I told him I was used to somebody shouting for me to draw, so he waited a few seconds and gave the signal.

I pulled and fired. The shot was high.

"No," Bob said. "Don't fan the gun. That just makes you shoot wild. Cock it with your thumb as you're pulling and you'll be a lot more accurate."

"That's not how I learned," I said. "Give me a minute. This .45 is a lot different than the Navy."

I pulled the gun a few more times, twirled it, returned it to the holster. I had to readjust my aim for the short-barreled Colt. Actually, I didn't aim at all; I *pointed,* like you do when shooting birds on the fly with a shotgun. When I felt I had the feel of the gun down at last, I replaced the silver dollar on the back of my hand and nodded. I narrowed my eyes and felt myself running down my arm into the gun.

"Draw!"

The Colt flashed out and boomed, punching the can backward while the dollar was still a foot off the ground.

"Damn good for fanning it," Bob allowed. "But what about the second and third shots?"

"Set them up," I said, and Bob placed a row of three cans on the fence.

I waited until Bob was clear, then took a deep breath and let it out slow. I pulled and fanned—Bam! Bam! Bam!—and all three cans jumped off the fence.

Bob slapped me on the back.

"That's pretty fine shooting," he said, taking the Colt and pushing the spent shells out with the ejector rod. "But there are three things that count in a gunfight. The least of those three is speed, and you've got that. The second is accuracy, and you've got that one, too. Do you know what the third and most important one is?"

"Luck?" I ventured.

"No, it ain't luck," Bob said, reloading the gun. "It's keeping your wits about you. The man who comes out on top is the man who stays calm and thinks his shots through. Cans don't shoot back; men do. A lot of good and quick shots have died because they went to pieces when facing another man with a gun."

I nodded.

"There are a few other things that can help. Ever heard of the road-agent spin? It's done like this." He showed me how, when handing the gun butt-first to someone, you could spin it and come out with it cocked, ready to do business.

"Of course," Bob added, "my preference for just about any kind of scrap is a Winchester. It's hard to beat that kind of power and range." Bob was a natural shot and fired his rifle from the hip most of the time, not having to aim.

"I almost forgot," I said, and drew the handbill from my pocket.

"A Model 86 Winchester rifle in .44-40," he said, and his eyes lit up. "Why, that competition's tomorrow. I think I might enter. What do you think, Samuel?"

"I reckon you could use a new Winchester."

"I reckon you're right," Bob said, and his eye caught Minnie rounding the corner of the barn. "Give me back my leather," he said. "Lesson's over for today, pard."

I moped over to the Williamsons', hoping to find Johnny, but found Jane chopping wood instead. I thought it was a peculiar activity for a girl who was too sick to go to school that day.

"Howdy," I said.

She said hello and then I realized, like an idiot, I didn't have anything else to say. So I asked her where Johnny was.

"He's in the house," she said, taking a breather and leaning on the handle of the axe. With a calloused hand she wiped a wisp of hair away from her brown eyes.

I nodded and stood there for another minute, not wanting to see Johnny anymore. I felt kind of peculiar being around Jane.

"I hope you're feeling better," I said, finally.

She looked at me funny.

"I haven't been ailing."

"Well, I noticed you weren't at school today," I said quickly. "I just thought . . . you know, that you were sick."

She sagged a little there on the axe handle, and wiped the back of her hand across her eyes. They were tearing up something awful.

"I'm not going to be going to school anymore, Sammy," she said and looked away. "Papa thinks I'm old enough now to stay home and help with the farm. Times are tough, and he said I'm going to have to start carrying my own weight. Pa said there's no sense in girls going for book-learning, anyhow."

She perched a log on the stump, drew the axe back, and put all of her weight into it. Only, she didn't hit it square—it angled off the top, sending vibrations up the handle and shooting splinters back at her. She dropped the axe like it was hot, and clenched her hands together, then she felt a splinter that had stuck in her cheek. A little trickle of blood was tracing its way down to her jaw. She sat down on the cold ground, hugging her knees close to her chest, and started to bawl like a baby.

I knelt down next to her and lifted her chin up, and as carefully as I could, plucked the splinter out of her cheek. I told her how sorry I was, and how it wasn't any of my business and I didn't mean anything by asking. But that just seemed to make her cry harder. Then I didn't know what to say, so without thinking I just reached out and put my arms around her shoulders and held her tight against me, and she buried her head against my coat.

"I was just worried about you," I said at last.

I got up and put that damned log on the stump and cleaved it into two, then four, and tossed the pieces on the woodpile. There was a knack to splitting wood and I didn't think a grown man ought to expect a girl to do it for him. I went ahead and finished up the rest of it, stacked it real neat, and drove the axe into the stump and left it there.

Jane was still on the ground, but she had stopped crying. She was just watching me. I guess it had taken me twenty or thirty minutes to finish up, and I don't know how long she'd sat there watching. I felt embarrassed and more than a little foolish, since I had made her cry in the first place.

"I'll just see Johnny later," I told her, and started off toward home.

"Sammy?" she asked. I stopped and looked back over my shoulder. "Thank you for asking about me."

"You'd better get inside," I said. "It's turning mighty cold tonight."

She got up, brushed her skirt off, and tugged at my coat until I turned around. She gave me a sisterly peck on the cheek. I was glad I was so flushed from the work already.

Old Man Williamson came up to the house from the barn about that time, and I knew he'd seen Jane kiss me, but he didn't say a thing. His face was long and his eyes were hard. He was so tired he just sort of dragged his feet along. He passed by us without a word and went into the house, for his supper, I reckon. Jane followed after him.

I trudged back home.

Pa came around that evening while I was out in the barn brushing Cimarron down for the fourth time. I was puzzling over a brand on Cimarron's flank, an obscured Circle R or something similar, when Pa slipped in the door and was up on me before I knew it. His cheeks were hollow and his eyes were sunk way back in their sockets, giving his head the appearance of a living skull. His hair was wild and there were bits of I don't know what in his beard. His breath was foul enough to knock a horse down. I had to turn away when he spoke.

"Son," he said.

"Pa," I said.

"Your horse?" he asked, running a practiced hand down a foreleg to check the muscles and bones.

"Yeah. Birthday present from Bob and the boys."

"Birthday, eh?" he asked, cocking his head to one side. "How old are you now, Samuel? Twelve?"

"Thirteen."

"I'll be damned. My youngest son is almost a man hisself. I think that calls for a drink," he said. "You got any?"

"No, Pa. You know I don't drink."

"Maybe you could loan me a couple of bucks to go downtown to the drugstore and get my prescription filled. What do you say, Sammy?"

"I'm flat busted."

The disappointment on his face was painful to see. He ran the back of his hand across his forehead, and in the light from the kerosene lamp it shone slick with sweat. He let out a long sigh, the wind whistling through his ruined front teeth. He glanced around the barn and saw the other horses in the broken-down stalls.

"Your brothers still here?"

"In the house."

"Your Mama . . ."

"There too."

Pa winced and held up his hand.

"Do me a favor, Sammy. Run up to the house and tell Bob his poor Pa is out here and wants to talk to him. No, tell Grat. Grat's here, ain't he?"

"Yep."

"Tell Grat."

"When I'm finished," I said, and continued to brush down Cimarron.

"I'm hurtin' something terrible," he said.

So I threw down the brush and marched up to the house to fetch Grat. Bob was at the kitchen table talking with Mama, and they stopped all of a sudden when they saw me. I thought I saw the gleam of a tear in her eye before Mama looked away. I found Grat in the parlor, with his faro outfit spread out on the floor in front of him.

"Pa's in the barn," I said. "He's looking for someone to buy him some liquor."

Grat nodded and started putting the cards back into the wooden box with the Royal Bengal Tiger painted on the top.

"You gonna buy him some?"

Grat nodded.

"How? I thought you was broke too."

He just shrugged and said he'd find a way. Grat ambled through the kitchen and I followed behind, and when Mama looked up I said Grat was going to help me in the barn with my horse.

"Samuel, could you sit down for a bit?" Mama asked.

I told Grat to go on and I'd catch up.

I sat at the big oak table—the one that Bob often joked had seen everything but intercourse, and the way his eyes shone when he said it I wasn't too sure about that, either—and Mama poured me a cup of coffee. I spooned some cream and sugar in it, and Bob said I should get used to drinking it black, because that's the way it was on the trail.

"Have you given any thought to your future?" Mama asked.

I sipped at the coffee and thought for a bit before I answered, as if I was weighing my options. Truth was, I was trying to think of something to say, because I didn't have a clue as to specifics. Before I could get out with anything, Bob broke in.

"You're old enough to know how things are here," he said, scratching a match on the table and lighting a cigar. "You know Mama has had a tough time of it here. It's never been easy on her feeding such a brood, and now that Pa is gone, it's been even harder. You're big enough to start learning to make a living."

I nodded.

"We thought it might be a good time for you to go to Fort Smith and help your brother Frank and his wife. Naomi's heavy with child and it won't be long before she can't run the farm by herself. You know Frank's gone for weeks at a time riding for Parker in the Territory, and he can't afford to give that up because it's the only cash money they have. If you were to help out for a year or two with them, and learn farming along the way, it would be best all around."

"I haven't given much thought to farming."

"Our older brothers, Hank and Littleton, are doing all right for themselves out in California. Bill, too."

"I'd rather be a cowboy," I said.

Bob shook his head.

"The big outfits and the railroads have put most cowhands out of business. Besides, it's a miserable life. Ask Emmett—he'll tell you what it's like freezing your tail off in a line shack during the winter. But if that's what you want, I'll see you get hired on somewhere, maybe down at the Turkey Creek with Em, in two or three years. I know you're big for your age, but right now, you're just a mite green. You'd be in better shape once you work on the farm for a spell."

"Grat's a posse man for Frank. Couldn't I learn that?"

"The pay's worse than punching cattle. Two dollars for every writ you serve, and you're likely to get your head blowed off in the bargain. If you kill somebody in self-defense, you've got to bury them out of your own pocket. But if that's what you want, I reckon Frank might hire you on for his posse, after you've filled out some on the farm."

The coffee was going cold in my cup. I was too big to cry and too hurt to laugh. From what I'd seen of farming, up before dawn and work till dusk, I wanted no part of it. I thought of Williamson trudging home with that burned-out look in his eyes. Besides, what farmer had ever made a name for himself, like old Jess had?

Mama reached out and gripped my hand, hard.

"You know I love you, don't you, Samuel? You don't have to go if you don't want to. We'll manage somehow. I can't stand the idea of you being homesick."

"Homesick?" I blurted out. "It ain't that at all. I'll miss you something awful, I reckon, but I've already made up my mind that I'm not gonna stay here in Coffeyville another damn minute. It's just, well, I never saw myself as a farmer or a store clerk or truck like that. I want to be like Bob and Grat, I want to see a chunk of this country. I want a name for myself, Mama."

Mama closed her eyes tight and clasped her hands under her chin and started praying, right there, asking the Lord why there was so much of Pa in this one, too.

"Will you teach me to ride and shoot?" I asked Bob. "Teach me to read sign and sleep out under the stars and be free, like in *Buffalo Bob's Weekly?*"

"Them's just fairytales," Bob said. "It's not like that out there and never was. You should learn farming. Frank needs your help. How can you turn your back on him, with a wife about to drop a calf and him away most of the time?"

"How can you turn your back on me?" I asked. Now I was having a hard time holding the tears back. "I ain't got no Pa here to teach me those things I ought to know, at least no Pa that I'm not ashamed to be around. You're the closest thing I ever had to one. I want to be like you."

Bob reached out all of a sudden, and I put my hands in front of my face because I thought he was going to hit me. Instead, he grabbed me by the shoulders and pulled me out of the chair to him and hugged me tight like I was five years old.

"You're a real Dalton, that's for sure," he said. "You're about the best little brother anybody ever had. But I'm shooting straight with you on this, you hear? Frank needs a hand around his place. If you'll go and help him for just a year, I'll teach you everything I know, God help your young soul."

"You promise?"

"I said so, didn't I? You go with Frank and take care of Naomi and the farm and I'll drop around when I can. Is it a deal?"

"It's a deal," I said. I could stand a year of farming if I knew Bob was waiting for me when it was over.

"Then you'll be riding with me by year after next."

Mama shook her head but knew I'd be better off with my brothers than if I was to strike out on my own. She prayed again and asked God to watch over the Dalton boys. I reckon He already knew we'd need it.

Late that night, I heard footsteps outside. I got out of bed, went to the window, and pulled back the curtain. Minnie and Bob were threading their way, hand in hand, to the barn.

Four

IT WAS LIKE A CARNIVAL at the rifle competition the next morning. There were flags and streamers and a band playing, and a long table laid with red, white, and blue bunting and a big hand-lettered sign that commanded, "Register Here." We tied our horses at a picket line they had run along one side of the meadow—I had saddled Cimarron with an old army contraption that Pa had left in the barn—and we walked across the dew-covered grass to the table.

Bob pulled a silver dollar from out of his vest and plunked it down. "Name?" the man asked, without hardly looking up from his pad.

"Robert Dalton."

He scratched the name in.

The man handed over a number, and asked Bob to pin it on his back so the judges could see it during the shooting. I used a straight pin to put it on the back of his coat. Grat didn't seem interested in a number.

The man said the match would start in another half hour or so.

Bob nodded, and looked around the meadow to find something to pass the time. Grat complained that there was nothing to drink, and Bob reminded him that this wasn't the Territory—Kansas had been voted dry as a bone, and the only place you could get liquor now was at the drugstore, for "medicinal purposes." Coffeyville didn't have any saloons anymore, but it suddenly had plenty of drugstores.

Then Bob spied Tackett's photographic tent, and he declared it was time for a Dalton boys portrait. Tackett was doing a land-office business, because the shoot was just like a big family reunion, and we had to wait in line for a little bit. When it was our turn, he situated us in front of a backdrop painted with a forest scene. The tent faced east to catch the light of the sun, which still wasn't too far above the trees. There were some stumps for us to sit on. Tackett put me and Bob in front, because we were the smallest. He tucked a blanket around us to hide our pants, which were wet from walking across the meadow, and plastered with seeds and leaves and such. Bob held his Winchester 73 in the crook of his arm, and Grat swept his coat back a little so the butt of his Colt would show. I didn't have a gun so I opened my Barlow knife and held it in my fist.

Tackett scurried back behind the camera, which looked like a big box on a coatrack, with a water glass stuck square in the middle. He ducked behind a cloth in back of the box and kept saying "Don't move, Don't move" while he fiddled with things. Then we heard something like a watch mechanism click, and Tackett ducked back out again and slid the plate from out of the back. He said the picture would be ready by the time the match was over, and that we could pay him then. He handed the plate off to an assistant who ran inside the tent with it, and called for the next group.

When the match finally got underway, they set up a string of six paper targets with big bull's-eyes one hundred yards downrange, and called out for numbers to line up and fire five shots apiece. Most of the shooters did tolerable well, placing most of their shots near the center. A few managed to get one or two dead center. But Bob easily put all five shots right in the black, so close it was hard to tell the individual holes the slugs had made.

When the first round was over, they tallied up the scores and straightaway eliminated two thirds of the sixty or so contestants. Bob, of course, made the first cut. Then they set the targets up and had the shooters step up again six at a time. Bob stepped up and fired all five shots from the carbine without even taking the gun down from his shoulder. He just shot and cocked, shot and cocked, like it was the easiest thing in the world, and when he was done he just turned and sauntered off, not acting the least bit interested in his score. All of the shots were in the black again.

Then, for the first time, I noticed this tall German fellow, Number 13. He was intent—his eyes were hard when he shot. He took his time placing each round. He would aim the gun a little high at first, and then let the barrel just float down slightly to where it was dead center, then he would squeeze the trigger. Methodical, I guess Colonel Elliott would have called it. This fellow would then stand like a hawk, waiting for the others to finish, until they fetched his target up to him and he could have a gander at it. He was the only man I ever saw who was as good a shot as my brother Bob.

After an hour or so of shooting, the field had been narrowed down considerably. There were three others in addition to Bob and the German, but it was clear to everybody where the real contest was. Grat was getting excited, and said he reckoned it was time for him to go to work. He stood up and took some greenbacks out of his pocket and said, loud enough for just about everybody to hear, "I've got twenty dollars here that says Bob Dalton can whip that German. Are there any sporting gentlemen here?" There were, of course, and before the next round began he had five takers at twenty bucks apiece. I swear, Grat's eyes shone like Pa's did when he had a new bottle.

I learned from a gentleman sitting next to me—who had bet against Bob—that Number 13's name was Kleohr, and that he was the Coffeyville Rifle Club's crack shot. He owned a livery stable in the alley by the city jail. He'd been hired to take the place of a Union conscriptee, and had moved to Coffeyville after the war.

After the other three had shot, and were obviously out of the competition because none of them got all five shots in the bull's-eye, Bob stepped up to the rail. He wasn't acting quite as cocky as he had before, but he was still smiling. He slipped the five rounds into the receiver of the Winchester, shrugged his shoulders to loosen his coat, then brought the rifle up and sent five shots downrange. A man with a little telescope was checking the targets, and he announced that all of Bob's shots were in the black. The crowd let out a little cheer, and Bob gave a wave and stepped back to let Number 13 have his chance.

The German had been sucking on a big pipe while Bob shot, and now he tapped the ashes out against his heel and stepped up to the rail. His shots came at such regular intervals, about ten seconds apiece, that you could have set your watch by them. And, I'll have to give him this, he was a sportsman—he left the lever down on his rifle with the breech open after he was finished, to show the chamber was empty. The man with the telescope announced another perfect score, and the crowd cheered again.

Now it was just the two of them, and they stepped up and shot two more targets. Every round was in the black, but they were getting a little wider spread than they had been at first. There was a little conference between the judges, and they decided to move the targets back to one hundred fifty yards.

It seemed like Bob and the German were just getting warmed up, because they turned in another dead-solid perfect round.

There was another conference, and the judges hemmed and hawed around—by this time it was past noon and they must have been hungry —and they moved the targets back to two hundred yards. That was a pretty far piece for a short-barreled saddle rifle. At that distance there's quite a bit of drop; you got to aim above the mark to hit it. It's kind of like pissing off the top of a barn, trying to send every last drop in a teacup on the ground. Grat wasn't feeling nearly so confident now, I could tell. But Bob just took it in stride, stepped up to the rail, and punched five holes in the black. The judges had to push the crowd back, because they had surged forward to slap Bob on the back and such. Thing was, that lanky German did the same damn thing with his clock-work shooting.

The judges decided to switch around and let the German go first, and I saw right off this bothered the man. But, he tapped out his pipe and stepped up to the rail and knocked off four shots, and I could tell by his rhythm they all found their mark. The wind came up then, stirring the tops of the trees and sweeping along the meadow, and he paused for a fraction of a second in his routine in an attempt to compensate; his last shot barely grazed the edge of the bull's-eye. When the spotter hollered it out, a murmur swept through the crowd.

Bob had the most peculiar look on his face, like it had been him that missed. He stepped up and sent four shots sailing like he really didn't care what he hit, then he stopped.

"Four in the black, Mr. Dalton," the man with the telescope said. "You have one more shot left."

Grat was rocking back and forth. He had a hold of my shoulder with one of his hands, and he was squeezing so hard I thought he was going to pinch it off. "He's got him, he's got him," he kept saying.

Bob smiled and aimed real careful and touched off his last round. You could have heard a pin drop, the crowd got that quiet waiting for the result.

The spotter peered carefully at the target, then handed the telescope to a friend for a double-check. He was stretching it out for all it was worth. He finally stood up and said, "It's not quite in the bull's-eye. It's a tie."

Everybody started gabbing like a bunch of hens, and Grat smacked his forehead with his fist. Hard. "I'm going to kill him," he moaned. "Sammy, I'm going to kill that bastard. He did that on purpose. I know him too damn well. Sonuvabitch. I have this money on pawn from the Gold Room Loan Agency."

Grat was right. Bob couldn't resist an opportunity to grandstand. Bob shook his head and laid his rifle down, then addressed the crowd.

"Folks," he said, "I bet we could be here all day and not settle this. I'm damned hungry—pardon my language, ladies—and I'll bet you are too."

"I'm hungry," I agreed.

Grat punched me so hard he knocked me off my stump.

"I'll be the first to admit that I've met my match," Bob said. "I haven't had the pleasure of seeing a finer marksman anywhere than Mr. Kleohr. If it's all right with him, I'd like to settle this thing real quick."

Bob took a silver dollar from his pocket and held it up.

"Would you care for heads or tails?" he asked the German.

Kleohr looked more than a little shocked. In his eyes I saw him thinking of what it would be like to miss again. His mustache twitched, and he tapped on his pipe. I think he must have been caught up then in Bob's grand gesture. Both of them could walk away winners, even though just one would get the rifle.

"Heads," Kleohr said.

Bob tossed the coin high into the air, and everyone followed it up and then back down. Bob snatched it in his fist, slapped it on the back of his left hand, and snuck a glance.

"Heads it is!"

The crowd cheered, the brass band started up, and the judges pressed the Model 86 Winchester rifle with the thirty-inch barrel into the German's hands. Grat was moaning like a sick calf. I don't think anybody but me saw Bob slip the dollar back into his pocket real quick, without giving anybody a chance to see it.

Bob shook Kleohr's hand like they were old friends.

Men started clawing around Grat, demanding their money, but he protested that it was a draw. They were quick to point out that the bet had been that Bob would beat the German, and that hadn't happened. I thought that Grat was going to open up with his fists and take them all on at once, and he probably would have if Bob hadn't told him to pay them. Grat was wiped out, but Bob said he'd make it up to him.

We packed up, and on the way back to the horses Bob stopped at Tackett's tent and give him the silver dollar—the one he'd used in the toss and the last one he had to his name—for the photograph. He grinned from ear to ear, not at all like somebody who was broke and who'd been beat out of a brand-new Model 86 Winchester rifle.

"Look at that, boys," he said, holding the picture out in front of him so we could take it all in. "Just look at it and try to tell me that folks won't *remember* us. Jesus H. Christ, it is one beautiful day."

Five

PA DIED THAT WEEKEND. He was found on the road to Vinita, a jug of whiskey at his side. He finally managed to drink himself to death.

Strange, but it didn't seem real when Mama first told me what had happened. Oh, I heard the words and knew what they were supposed to mean, but in my heart I believed that Pa would be back around any day now, slinking around the barn and asking for money to buy some liquor. It was only when my brother Frank came back for the funeral and we put on our Sunday-go-to-meeting clothes and stood beside a little pile of dirt that it seemed awful final.

The last time I had seen Frank was at a barn dance near Dearing with Bob and Grat, and, as usual, Frank was keeping the boys in line. Frank was different than my other brothers. He wasn't religious or anything— he was always scoffin' at Bible thumpers, and every other word he said usually had four letters—but he was solid. Frank was every bit as big as Grat, but he didn't get mad like Grat did, and he wasn't like Bob at all because there wasn't a bit of show-off in him. Frank was all serious, and didn't laugh much, not like the others did. His mustache drooped and his blond hair was already gray at the temples. Others thought it was his work as a deputy marshal that made him look old, but I reckoned it was just what happened when a man got nigh onto thirty.

I recall that Bob and Grat were really whooping it up at that dance. Grat had already drained the flask he carried with him and was taking pretty regular nips from a little brown jug that was passed around. Grat was a bit awkward when he was sober, but the more he drank, the bigger his feet got. That didn't stop him from begging a dance from the prettiest girl there.

There was one fellow sitting on a bale of hay along the side of the barn, and from the way he watched Grat swing this little redheaded girl around, I figured it had to be her beau. He was a healthy boy, a farm lad. His eyes were smoldering and his cheeks were red, and I could tell he was trying to decide whether to call Grat out or not. When Grat's rough hands got just a little too free, he decided he'd had enough. He shot up like a rocket, strode across the floor, and jerked the girl away.

"You're with me, Brigitte," he said.

Grat jerked her back. "I think she'd rather stay with me and dance," he said with a big stupid grin on his face. "Run along home—I'll take good care of her, I promise."

The farm boy swung a big haymaker that Grat could see from a mile off, and he blocked it with his left arm and drove his right fist deep into the boy's stomach. All the breath went out of him, like a bellows.

Frank stood up from where he had been sipping whiskey out of a tin cup, and walked over to Grat. Frank drew Grat's coat back, snatched away the revolver, and stuck it into his own belt.

"If you're going to fight, I want the damn knife, too," Frank said.

Grat cussed but took the seven-inch hog sticker from its sheath down inside his right boot. Frank tossed me the knife, underhanded and butt-first, and I caught it and drove it into the wall behind me.

"I think you're too drunk for me to stop you from fighting," Frank said, "but I'll be goddamned if I let you ruin this dance by spilling any blood. And if that boy can catch his wind and get back up, I hope he whips hell out of you, because it would teach you a lesson."

The farmhand was up on one knee now, and about ready to lunge, but Frank touched him on the shoulder and said, "Take it outside, son." So he and Grat made for the door and went at it in the dark, rolling and hitting and kicking and cussing.

Brigitte rushed out to see, saying as she went, "I never had two men fighting over me before." Everybody else followed, and the music went with the fiddler. I tried to sit still, but couldn't stop fidgeting.

"Go ahead and watch," Frank said. "Just don't get any ideas. You'll be damned near as big as Grat in a few years, and I hope you're not as stupid. Just remember that no matter how big you are, there will always be somebody who can whip you. Save your fighting for when it counts."

Frank didn't get his wish, because Grat beat the living hell out of the farm boy that night. But I never forgot how Frank had laid things out for me to where they made sense. He was also the only one that Grat, or Bob for that matter, would tolerate giving their guns to.

So it was natural that, after we got back from the funeral, I asked Frank his opinion on the thing that had been troubling me most.

"Where do you reckon folks go when they die?" I asked.

Frank thought a minute and said, "I can't rightly tell you, Samuel."

"Do you think it's like Mama says, with angels and harps and all that if you're good, and hellfire and brimstone if you ain't?"

Frank wrestled with that one. I could tell he came close to lying and saying that Mama was right, and that our Pa had gone to the good place, but at last he just shook his head and said, "I don't know what it's like, or if it's anything at all, but I reckon it's not at all like the preachers say."

"Good," I said. "I don't think Pa would much like any place without whiskey or horses."

Frank laughed.

"I'm going to enjoy having you around," he said.

We were riding out the next morning for Fort Smith.

That night, I snuck out of the house and felt my way in the dark over to the Williamsons'. I shinnied up a tree beside Johnny's room, slipped the blade of my knife under the window and raised it up, then stepped inside. Johnny was a pretty sound sleeper, and it took me a spell to rouse him.

"I'm up, Pa," he said. "I'm awake."

"It's me, Sammy."

"Huh? What're you doing here?"

"I snuck in the window," I said. "I've come to say goodbye."

Johnny rubbed his eyes.

"What do you mean?"

"I'm headed down to Fort Smith to help my brother Frank with his farm. I'm leaving in the morning. I'll be back, though. And I want you to give your sister something for me."

"Jane? What for?"

"Never you mind what for." I handed him a piece of paper, folded down to a square with Jane's name written on the outside as neat as I could get it. He started to unfold it, but I grabbed his wrist.

"Don't you read it."

"Why not?"

"Swear to me that you won't read it and won't let anybody but her see it."

"I swear."

"Cross your heart and hope to die?"

He made the sign and said, "Hope to die."

"Thanks," I said.

"You're sweet on her, ain't you?"

"Maybe."

"Jesus, Pa would have a fit."

"Not a word, you hear?"

"You know I won't say nothing."

We sat there in the darkness for a spell, and Johnny looked kind of worried. Finally, he asked me, "Does our deal still hold?"

When we were little, we'd struck a deal and sealed it like blood brothers; whichever one of us got rich first, he'd share the wealth with the other. That way, we reckoned, we were twice ahead of everybody else. Besides, we shared just about everything anyhow.

"You know the deal still holds," I said.

Johnny nodded, satisfied.

"I'm gonna miss you," he said.

"No you won't," I said. "It'll mean more pumpkin pie for you."

We both laughed, then we shook hands and said a proper goodbye. I was feeling pretty low when I crawled back out on the roof, because Johnny and I had been friends since I was old enough to have a best buddy.

I crept along the side of the house and looked in through Jane's window. The moon was high and shone right inside to where she was sleeping. Her hands were clasped over her breast, on top of the covers, and her long hair was undone and spread out around her face on the pillow. She must have felt being watched, because she gave a little start and propped herself up on one elbow. I ducked back real quick so she wouldn't see me, and when enough time had gone by that I reckoned she was asleep again, I scooted across to the tree and made my way to the ground.

The moon was big and bright, and somewhere in the woods an owl was asking "Who, who?" over and over again.

The stars were like diamonds in the sky as we saddled the horses and filled our saddle wallets with Mama's biscuits wrapped in cheesecloth, salt, beans, and Arbuckle's coffee. Behind his saddle Frank had tied a regular bedroll, canvas covers, and a soogin or two, with their possibles bags stuffed inside. All I had was an old tarp and a quilt, but it would have to do. I hung the Navy in the grain sack from the horn, not having the sand—or Frank's permission, yet—to strap it on.

Grat was bleary-eyed and a little unsteady as he swung up in the saddle. He and Bob had been out all night. They were headed to Pawhuska, where Bob had an appointment as chief of the Osage tribal police.

Mama came out to bid us farewell, clutching her shawl around her but still shivering in the cold. She kissed each of us before we wheeled the horses and urged them down the lane. There were lights showing in the Williamson place as we passed; I thought I saw Jane's shadow watching from an upstairs window. The air was still and the steam from our breath hung like smoke, mingling with the locomotive-like gusts from the horses. Cimarron was already used to my weight, and my scent. I held the reins loosely in my left hand and let him take his stride from Frank's horse.

The dawn was real pretty, like God had taken all the warm colors in His palette—the reds and yellows and golds—and thrown them up in the east to chase away the stars. My brothers didn't seem to notice, but I kept turning and craning my neck to see. Mounted on Cimarron, riding with my brothers, I felt like I was ten feet tall.

About mid-morning Frank passed around the cold biscuits and bacon. I had hoped that we would stop to eat, but when my brothers were in the saddle they seemed kind of single-minded, so I didn't complain. Truth was, my butt was getting sore. I hadn't done much long-distance riding before because I didn't have a horse. And the old army saddle I was using was a mite thin, hard, and dried out. But I didn't say anything, just shifted around from time to time. Soon there wasn't a comfortable position anywhere on that saddle, which was beginning to feel more like wood than leather.

After a spell the road forked, and Bob and Grat took off down the whiskey trail to the west, while Frank and I went east. Bob slapped me on the back before leaving, then waved before they went out of sight. I hoped it would not be long before he came to visit at Frank's farm.

By that afternoon every step Cimarron took felt like somebody was jabbing a knife into my rear. By the time we made camp, at a little creek, my butt was just one throbbing blister. I removed my boots and peeled off my breeches and waded out into the shallow water. I crouched down, letting the freezing water cool my scalding hide.

"Not a little tender, are you?" Frank asked.

"I'm all right," I allowed. "Just felt like a little swim."

"I'll bet you did," he said.

A few minutes in the water was all I could stand, because my private parts ached from the cold. Dripping, I waded back to shore and carefully dried my butt with a rag.

"Don't worry," Frank told me. "That'll only last about a week."

"A week?" I nearly fainted on the spot.

"Yeah, it'll take that long for your hide to get toughened up. You should be just about over it by the time we reach Fort Smith. Be careful with those blisters, though, and don't let them get infected. Why don't you sit down and rest while I get supper started?"

"If it's all the same to you," I told him, "I'll stand."

Six

WE CROSSED THE ARKANSAS RIVER by ferry, which was just a big wooden raft pulled across on a rope thick as a man's forearm, stretching from one bank to the other. The river was muddy, and the brown water slapped and gurgled at the side of the ferry. The rope was taut like an arrow in a bowstring.

"What do you do when a steamboat comes along?" I asked.

"The line's weighted," the ferryman said as if it were the most common fact in the world. "We just give it some slack and let it sink to the bottom."

"Has the rope ever broke with folks out in the middle like this?"

"Yep," he said. "If it does, and we don't swamp in the bargain, we'll be lucky if we don't sail all the way down to Little Rock in a current like this. More rain comin', too."

"Rain's here," Frank said as we felt the first drops land cold and wet on our faces. The rain swept across the river as if thrown from a giant scattergun, and the ferryman cussed and began winching faster. A flock of mallards dropped out of the sky and wheeled close to us, so near that we could hear the wind whistling through their set wings. They skimmed a few feet above the water, then flared and circled high once more before settling near some canebrake downriver.

I was anxious for a glimpse of Fort Smith, but a big sandstone bluff hid our view of the city. We were finally deposited on the Arkansas side, and we made our way up the bluff. When we reached the top the first building we saw was Parker's courthouse. It sat at the far end of the grassy area that used to be the parade grounds for the old army fort. The building itself was a barracks back in the forties. It looked more like a big brick barn than anything else, because of the way the roof came down low on either side. Columned porches ran the full length of both sides, and each of the ends was capped by a pair of chimneys. The foundation was made of stone and came up seven or eight feet, and a flight of wooden stairs got you to the first floor. Frank and I bounded up the stairs, and we stayed under the protection of the porch while we tried to shake the water off.

Across the grounds to the south, next to the wall that surrounded the fort, was an enclosure fenced in by whitewashed boards. I asked Frank what was inside.

"The gallows," he said. "A new one was put up last year. It can hang twelve at once, if Parker has a mind to."

"Why's it fenced in?"

"Parker hanged six men at one time the first September he was here. Thousands of folks came from miles around to see the event. I guess they reckoned it was free entertainment. That's when the newspapers back East started calling Parker the 'hanging judge.' They've put a fence around it to keep out the curious, but Parker keeps hanging them regular—sixty or seventy altogether, I guess. In fact, two murderers around are going to their last reward today at noon."

I followed Frank into the courthouse and down a narrow hall to an office with gold lettering on the door: "John Carroll, United States Marshal, Western District of Arkansas." That was Frank's boss. A clerk behind the counter looked up when Frank came in, then glanced at the clock on the wall.

"You're due in court in five minutes, Dalton."

"Damned if I don't know it," Frank said. "Any papers for me?"

"Got a writ here for a whiskey runner down in the Bottoms," the clerk said, thumbing through a sheaf of papers he'd taken from a pigeonhole. "Name of David Smith. Sellin' out of a tent at Moffett. Looks like an easy hour's work. Interested?"

"Yeah," Frank said. He took the paper and tucked it into his vest pocket. "Who's in town today?"

"Proctor. Wilkinson. Jim Cole."

"Where's Cole?"

"Houses on Front Street, more than likely."

"Thanks."

"Where's Grat? I thought he was your posseman."

"He is, but he ain't made it back from helping my brother Bob with the tribal police at Pawhuska."

The clerk nodded.

"This here's my littlest brother," Frank said, jerking a thumb at me. "His name's Samuel Cole."

"Lord, how many brothers you have, Frank?"

"I stopped counting at Bob."

We went back down the hall. Frank said, "You're going to see Parker's court in action today."

"It's Saturday," I pointed out. "They hold court on the weekend?"

"They say God rested on the seventh day, not the sixth," Frank said at the door to the courtroom. "I reckon Judge Parker feels that's good enough for him, too. Take a place in the back and stay put until they're done with me."

It was so crowded in the courtroom that I had to stand. I guess this was more of that free entertainment Frank was talking about.

Parker sat like a king behind his big raised bench, his white head resting on the back of his leather chair. He was a much bigger man than I had imagined, over six feet tall and better than two hundred pounds. His eyes were half closed as he directed the prosecutor to call his witness.

The prosecutor motioned, and Frank stepped through the gate that separated the court and jury from the audience. He stepped over to a hardbacked chair beside the bench, and raised his hand. The bailiff took a well-thumbed Bible and swore Frank in.

". . . so help me God," Frank concluded and sat down.

"State your name and occupation, please."

"Franklin Dalton, deputy U.S. marshal."

"Mr. Dalton, on the third of October last did you have occasion to be in the vicinity of a cabin owned by the defendant, Bill Long Feather, in the Choctaw Nation?"

"I did."

"What was your purpose?"

"I had writs for the arrest of Henry Callahan and Jasper Riddle for introducing. I had reason to believe Long Feather might know their whereabouts."

" 'Introducing,' Mr. Dalton?"

"Introducing liquor to Indians."

"I see. And why did you believe that Long Feather would know these individuals?"

"I reckon you could say he had an educated pallet when it came to spirits."

"He drank, then?"

"Like a fish."

The audience laughed and Parker used his gavel.

"When you found that Mr. Long Feather was gone—"

"I object, your honor," the defense attorney said. "The state is putting words in the witness's mouth."

"Sustained," the judge said. "Let your witness speak for himself, Mr. Clayton."

"Yes, your honor. Now, Deputy Dalton, what did you find at the cabin?"

"I knocked but there was no answer, so I tried the door and was surprised to find it open. There was a terrific mess inside—busted dishes, a table and chairs knocked over, an oil lamp on the floor. I noticed a great deal of blood."

"Did you search the cabin?"

"I didn't have to. There was only one room, and the streaks of blood led up a ladder to a loft sleeping area. There, I found the bodies of Mrs. Long Feather and Jasper Riddle. The blood had dripped from the loft and pooled on the floor, and there were bloody hand- and footprints on the ladder."

"Could you tell the manner in which they died?"

"Riddle had been stabbed three times in the chest, and he also had . . . well, he was cut between the legs. Mrs. Long Feather had been stabbed in various parts of her body. I reckoned they had been dead for an hour or less, because they both were still warm."

"What was their condition of dress?"

"They weren't."

"So the motive for the killings seemed clear?"

"It did."

"And Billy Long Feather seemed a logical suspect?"

"He did."

"What happened next?"

"Billy Long Feather appeared at the door of the cabin. Water was dripping from his hands, and his shirt front was wet, so I reckoned he had gone and washed himself in the creek. There was a butcher knife stuck in his belt. I asked him if he had killed the two upstairs, and he said he surely did. I then told him I was compelled to place him under arrest for the murder of the white man."

"Tell the jury why you had no jurisdiction over the murder of Mrs. Long Feather."

"That would be for the tribal police," Frank told the twelve men sitting in the jury box. "We only have jurisdiction over crimes committed by whites, or done to whites."

"Thank you. Continue."

"Well, Billy said he wasn't going to jail, especially not the one in the basement of this court here. No offense, your honor. I told him I didn't have any choice but to take him in, and he reached for his knife. I disarmed him."

"And transported him to this court?"

"Yes, sir."

"Thank you, Deputy," Clayton said. "That's all I have."

Frank started to get up from the chair, but the defense attorney spoke up.

"I have a few questions," the attorney said, walking over in front of Frank. He stood there a moment, reviewing his notes, while Frank fidgeted.

"Mr. Dalton," the attorney began. "You say you disarmed my client. You did that literally, didn't you?"

"I don't understand the question."

"Perhaps it would help if the defendant stood up. Billy, get to your feet, please. Come on, it's all right."

For the first time I noticed the Indian sitting at one of the green felt-covered tables. He looked slowly around him, and then struggled up to his feet. His right shirtsleeve was folded up and pinned neatly beneath the elbow.

"You blew it away, didn't you?" the attorney asked.

"Indians and Mexicans are born with knives in their hands, so to speak," Frank said. "It was all I could do to pull my shotgun and fire before he was on me."

"You meant to kill him."

"No sir, I did not. If I had done that I would have had to pay to bury him. So I aimed to cripple the arm that held the knife. Blowing it off was an accident."

"This murderous weapon of yours, this shotgun. Describe it for us."

"Well, it's a L. C. Smith," Frank said, scratching his head. "Twelve gauge, double hammers. The barrel's cut down to eighteen inches, but it throws a pretty tight pattern at the range I shot Billy there."

"You had time to go back to your horse and retrieve it when you saw my client approaching the cabin?"

"No. I carry the shotgun with me on the trail, from a sling over my right shoulder, with the barrel pointing down. I've found that the shotgun is a better peacemaker in the Territory than a revolver in a crowded room."

"Now, we all know that what my client did was wrong, Mr. Dalton. It says in the Good Book, the same one that is up there at his honor's elbow, that Thou Shalt Not Kill. But let me ask you, sir, did you feel no sympathy for Billy Long Feather's plight? What man among us would not consider the very same action? Wouldn't you, Mr. Dalton?"

"I strongly object," Clayton shot out. "The deputy is in no position to comment one way or another. My colleague is attempting to confuse the issue in the jury's minds."

Parker shifted in his chair and stroked his goatee while he thought on the matter. Finally, he said the jury was allowed to consider what a reasonable man would do in similar circumstances.

Frank remained silent.

"You were asked a question," the defense attorney pressed. "What would you do if confronted with the same situation? With your blood boiling, wouldn't murder cross your mind, however fleetingly?"

"I reckon," Frank said, eyeing the attorney like something he'd found on the bottom of his boot. "But I sure as hell wouldn't think about cutting off the bastard's pecker and stuffing it in his mouth."

A gasp rippled through the gallery. I have to admit my jaw dropped a few notches. The jury was buzzing, too, and Parker pounded his gavel again to restore order.

"This court will not tolerate distractions from spectators," the judge said. "The next man who makes a sound will be fined fifty dollars. Is that understood? Good. Counselor, please continue."

"Nothing further, your honor."

The defense attorney walked back to his table and sat down with his chin resting on his chest.

"Mr. Clayton?" Parker asked. "Redirect?"

"Thank you, no."

"Very well. Deputy Dalton, you may step down. A word of advice, however: watch your language in this court, young man. I will not tolerate gutter talk. There are ladies present from time to time."

The rain had stopped temporarily and the sun was trying to peek through the clouds, with little success. Frank loosened his collar and leaned on the porch railing of the courthouse.

"I hate court," he said. "I can't breathe in there."

At the bottom of the steps I noticed a door in the massive stone foundation. Frank said it was the entrance to the jail. He led me down a couple of steps into it, so my eyes could get adjusted to the gloom. A big iron door was at the bottom of the steps, and when my eyes got used to the dark, I could see that the basement was just one big room, with big wooden pillars spaced every so often to hold up the floor above. There were men everywhere, some sitting on the floor, some lying, and a few chained to the stone walls. One was making water in a bucket.

"They call it Hell on the Border," Frank said.

"How many men are in there?"

"Sometimes as many as two hundred."

"It must be horrible," I said.

"Jail's not supposed to be a picnic," Frank said.

The smell was sickening, like a cross between a sickroom and a latrine. We left the basement and went back into the sunshine, but the sight and sounds stayed with me.

Crossing the lawn, we met a tall man in black, carrying a wicker basket. His face was long and gaunt, with eyes set far back into their sockets. When he smiled his eyes didn't smile—they just stayed the same, blue and hard. On his left hip was a big horse pistol.

"Good morning," he said with a German accent.

"Carrying your work with you today?" Frank asked.

"Yes," the man said softly, nearly whispering, and opened the lid to the basket. Inside were two ropes coiled like snakes, with thirteen-knot nooses at their ends. He pulled the nooses out of the basket and fingered the knots.

"These will do a very effective job. The trick is to lay the knots against the back of the skull, here"—he touched a spot behind his left ear—"so that it breaks the neck cleanly. These are good Kentucky hemp ropes, not sisal, and they have been stretched for a week with a two-hundred-and-fifty-pound bag of sand. They will do very nicely."

The spot behind my left ear was itching.

"George, this here's my little brother. Sammy, this is George Maledon."

He held out a skeletal hand and I shook it. It was cold as ice.

He leaned over with those eyes like burning coals and said, "I wish more young men could visit us here at Fort Smith. They would learn that crime does not pay. Eh, Sammy?"

"Yes, sir."

"Will you be coming to the hanging?" Maledon asked Frank.

"Might," Frank said.

Maledon nodded and tucked the nooses back into the wicker basket. We had moved past when he called my name. I looked over my shoulder. Maledon hunched forward and he said, "Come back and see me again, Samuel."

A shiver ran down my spine.

"What's wrong?" Frank asked when we turned away.

"Nothing," I said. "Somebody must've just walked over my grave."

We missed the hanging, which was fine with me. Frank didn't seem too disappointed, either—he said if you've seen one poor bastard dance at the end of a rope and fill his pants, you've seen them all.

We struck out north, toward the docks and warehouses that ran along the river on Front Street. I was surprised to find such nice houses across the tracks, and the nicest of all was Miss Etta's. It was two stories tall, painted a peculiar shade of lavender. I started to follow Frank inside but he put a hand on my chest.

"You better wait out here," he said. "Ma would have my hide if I let you in here. You're too young to know about bawdy houses."

I sat down on the steps, holding my chin in my hands. I was hungry and worn out from the trip. After what seemed like an eternity, Frank came out with a red-haired man. A girl dressed in practically nothing was close behind them.

"Who's the kid?" she asked. "He looks delicious."

"That's my little brother, and you'd better leave him alone for now."

"Too bad," the girl said and made a face. "He's just like a little Frank. I can't have you, so I might have to settle for the next best thing. Come back and see me in a year or two, honey."

"Thank you, ma'am. I will. I mean—"

Frank pulled me along.

We stopped at a saloon that appeared to offer the best free lunch. While Frank and his friend Jim Cole drank a couple of mugs of beers and picked at the food, I was stuffing myself with boiled eggs and corned beef. When the bartender complained that I wasn't a paying customer, Frank bought me a beer, but Cole ended up drinking it.

"Boy, there's nothing like this in Coffeyville," I said.

"All them sandcutters can think about is having somebody else's soul," Frank said. "There's just as many drunks in Coffeyville making the drugstores rich, but damned few places a working man can get a bite to eat."

Afterward, Frank and Cole decided they would serve the writ at first light in the morning. Attempting to take in a whiskey runner on a busy Saturday night was not advisable, they said.

Frank and I bedded down at the stables where our horses were. Frank was asleep in a minute or two, but even though I was dead tired, I couldn't manage it.

Once my head was down, I imagined I could hear the sounds from the jail coming up through the floor—a dull lowing sound like cattle make, but mixed with the clank of iron on iron, and whispers and cussing and crying. My mind told me it was probably just the horses in their stalls, but when I closed my eyes all I saw was the hole beneath the courthouse. When I finally did drift off, it was all mixed up with my dreams. I woke up once and bolted upright, but was too scared to cry out. There, at the foot of the bed, I could have sworn the hangman's burning eyes were drawing a bead on me.

Seven

THE NOVEMBER SKY hung close to the ground, and the rain and wind whipped through the canebrake, carrying with it the stench and camp smoke from Moffett. The sun was up, but nothing stirred in the shanty town except a pack of dogs. Frank slung the double-barreled shotgun over his shoulder and dismounted onto the moist, sandy soil. Jim Cole was already on the ground, Winchester in hand, water running off the brim of his hat and down his old yellow Fish slicker.

They handed me the reins to their horses. Frank allowed me to come with him to serve the writs, and then we would head out to the farm, a few miles outside of Fort Smith. After all, I was mighty curious about his job as a riding deputy.

"Stay put," Frank said, breaking open the breech of the Stevens and comforting himself with the sight of the twin brass shell casings. "If there's any shooting, lay low and keep ahold of the horses."

Frank made me leave the old Navy in its burlap sack, which hung from a nail in the stall where he kept his horse back at the stable.

We were in the Bottoms, just across the river from Fort Smith. Moffett was an ugly-looking place, mostly tents and lean-tos, and Frank said it was populated by the "baggage" of society: cowboys who had gone bad, gamblers, drunken Indians, white squatters, whores that were too sick or used up for the sporting houses. Moffett lived up to its nickname of "Little Juarez," Frank said—you could get anything for a price.

I watched from the edge of the brush as they walked down the muddy path toward the tent where Smith had been selling whiskey. A wisp of smoke curled from the stovepipe sticking through the canvas roof, but the flaps were pulled down, and if anybody was inside, they had to be asleep. Cole cradled his rifle in the crook of his arm and walked around to one side, where he could see anything that ran out the back way.

Frank walked up to the front, spat tobacco, then bellowed, "I am Deputy Marshal Frank Dalton. Wake up, Dave Smith. You are under arrest for introducin' liquor to Indian Territory."

He didn't wait for an answer, but proceeded to kick the flimsy wooden door to pieces. The tent started to quiver with activity at that point, and I could hear men cussing and a woman scream, and Cole got the drop on one gentleman as he tried to make his way beneath the canvas in the back. Frank had his boot caught between two of the planks, and he was hopping to keep himself up on one leg, and trying to shake what was left of the door off the other.

I couldn't help but laugh.

I was still snorting when Smith—a long-haired, skinny fellow in red flannel underwear—struggled to get past the door. I think I saw the revolver in his hand about the same time Frank did, because the barrel of his shotgun came up just as I shouted, but it snagged on a piece of the door. The .45 boomed and Frank fell backwards with one of his legs tucked up beneath him at a peculiar angle. His shotgun was still stuck beneath the door. Frank had no more than hit the ground when Cole's rifle spoke, carrying the back of the whiskey runner's head away.

Three other men and a woman piled out the front door, tripping over Smith's body and trampling Frank. The men were all shooting at Cole, and I could see places on his clothes puff where the balls hit. At the same time, he was cranking the lever on the Winchester and firing just as fast as he could. He killed one of the men outright, wounded another in the leg, and killed the woman with a ball through her throat—by accident, he said later. By the time he pulled the trigger on his last round in the magazine, Cole was pretty well shot up, including a good-sized hole in his shoulder. Somehow he clawed his way behind a tree.

That left one man standing in front of the tent. He was bald, and blood was trickling down his face from where a bullet had dug a bloody furrow across his bare scalp. He held a smoking Winchester. He screamed in rage and, seeing my brother still alive, kicked the remains of the door away. He pointed the barrel of the rifle down at Frank's head.

Frank coughed and blood flecked his lips.

"Don't," he managed. "I've got a wife. Child's on the way."

It was the only time I ever heard Frank beg.

"Oh, you sonuvabitch," the man said, and rammed the barrel into Frank's mouth. I could see the hammer was drawn back. I let go of the reins of the horses and broke through the brush, but it was like I was moving underwater, in slow motion. I screamed as I watched the hammer fall and the Winchester jump upward. Frank's head bounced on the ground like a melon.

The bald man reached down and took Frank's watch from his vest pocket. The watch, which had a hunting scene engraved on the case, was a wedding present from his wife, Naomi. The bald man held the watch to his ear, grinned, and slipped it into his own pocket.

"Much obliged, Marshal."

I flung myself down next to Frank and clawed for the shotgun, but the bastard got to it first and threw it over his shoulder. He knocked me down with the butt of the Winchester, put his foot on my chest, and cranked the lever. The spent brass casing that had killed my brother flew out. He pressed the muzzle against my forehead and pulled the trigger.

The hammer fell with a click. His rifle was empty.

"Boy," he said, "this is your lucky day."

Frank's horse was wandering aimlessly, trailing its reins. The bastard jumped up into the saddle and wheeled off to the south, toward the Choctaw Nation.

Eight

THE SOUND OF HOOFBEATS faded in the distance, but the smell of gunpowder lingered in the clearing like a bad memory. It was unnaturally quiet. Even the small birds that lived in the canebrake—the ones that generally made such a racket in the morning—were hushed. I took off my coat and placed it over what was left of Frank's head.

I reckon Mama would have wanted me to say a prayer for his soul, but I couldn't bring myself to do it, knowing how Frank felt about such truck. I closed my eyes tight to keep back the tears. I would act like a man from hell on out. If I had only been a mite closer, and could have gotten my hands on a piece of iron, Frank wouldn't have been sprawled there with his brains steaming in the chill air. I knelt down on both knees and placed my hands on Frank's chest. It was still warm.

"If you can hear me," I said, "I want you to know I'll settle the score with the bastard who done you in. I won't let you down again."

I unpinned the star from Frank's vest and held it in both hands for awhile. It was silver, six-sided, and smudged with a blackish-green tarnish. I put it in my pocket. Then I pawed at my eyes and got to my feet.

I went over to where Deputy Jim had dragged himself. I had expected to find him dead too, but his eyes were bright with pain. There were holes in his pant legs and one in his vest, and his right hand was clamped tight over his shoulder, with blood seeping from between his fingers.

"Frank?" he asked through clenched teeth.

"He's gone."

"I'm sorry, boy. He was a good man."

"Yessir. How bad you hurt?"

"Took a ball in the shoulder, and got a leg busted up. Would have bagged one in the gut, but the stock of my Winchester stopped it. I'll live."

"What can I do for you?"

"Get me something to use for a crutch."

I fished around and found a good-sized Y-shaped branch on the ground, and busted it to the right length with my boot. Jim took it and struggled to his feet, ignoring my outstretched hand.

"Can you make it back across the river on your own?"

"Where're you going?" he snorted.

"After him."

"Hell, you don't even know what his name is or where he's headed. And if you do find him, you'll end up like your brother mighty quick."

"Maybe so."

"Look here, partner, you can't be serious."

I walked away. I found Frank's shotgun, took a handful of shells from his pocket, and slipped two fresh ones into the breech. I walked over to the wounded whiskey runner who was laying near the tent and pressed the L. C. Smith against his chest.

"Lord Jesus," he pleaded, "don't kill me."

"What's the name of the bastard that killed my brother?"

"Towerly."

"What's his Christian name?"

"William."

"William Towerly," I repeated, burning the name into my memory. "Where's he headed?"

"Swear to God, I don't know."

I thumbed both hammers back on the scattergun.

"Guess," I suggested.

"South, I reckon. South to the hills." He began coughing, and blood flecked his lips. "More than likely he'll cross the Arkansas and stop at Scullyville to fix him up with supplies before making the wilderness."

"Where will he hole up?"

"Who knows?" he wheezed. "The Cookson Hills are one rough son-uvabitch from soda to huck, and there are a thousand and one hiding places."

I nodded and turned the shotgun skyward before lowering the hammers. I walked away, pausing at the two other dead on the ground. The man was facing down, but the woman was sprawled face-up, a bloody hole where her throat had been. She was in her nightdress, and one shoulder strap was ripped away, exposing a creamy breast from which all flush of life had fled. Her eyes were open wide. I'd never seen a dead woman before. I felt sorry for her, and wondered what her name was and why she came to be a whore here in the Bottoms. I covered her up with a blanket I found near the remains of the tent.

"You can't leave me like this," the wounded man called behind me. "I'm bleeding to death. You've got to fetch a doctor."

Jim hobbled over and said, "I'd stop jabbering and lie still if I were you, you worthless piece of shit. You just might live if you save your strength and keep your mouth shut."

"Deputy Jim, can you get yourself and this sorry piece of trash fixed up without me? My brother's blood is on the ground and I've got some business to the south that won't wait."

"You'll get yourself killed. That man has murdered a United States deputy marshal, and he's not aiming to be taken alive, especially not by any kid."

"It ain't a matter of what he wants."

"Then do it smart, like a man," Jim spat. "When you've shot a deer, do you start right out after him, and keep him running for miles? Or do you wait a spell, and let him pick the first brush pile he comes to to lay down in?"

"This buck ain't wounded, at least not yet. When he is, I'll remember your advice."

Now that the shooting was over, the residents of Moffett began to cautiously emerge from their tents. Jim got a couple of the men to put the wounded bootlegger on a heavy plank, so they could transport him across the river to Fort Smith.

"I'm headed for the sawbones," Jim said. "Come with me and we'll get a posse together to chase that bastard down. Don't do this by your lonesome, son."

"Trail will be stone cold by the time you get a posse together," I said.

Jim sighed. "I'm sure as hell not going to argue with a kid carrying a sawed-off shotgun and bleed to death to boot."

He unhitched his gunbelt, and his arm sagged as he held the rig out to me. His Winchester lay on the ground, the stock broken to pieces by the rounds it had stopped.

"Take this," he said.

"I've got the scattergun."

"Take it," he commanded. "You're going to need it. Don't try anything fancy. You're only going to have one shot; he'll kill you if he gets one off first, or if your aim is bad. Shoot him from behind if you have to, or if you can catch him sleeping. Don't meet him face-to-face. You know how to use a Colt, don't you?"

"I've busted a few bottles with one."

"Bottles don't shoot back."

Jim gave me his Fish slicker and cussed because he didn't have any food in his saddlebags to give me. Then he gave me three silver dollars —all he had—but said it was unlikely I'd find anywhere to spend them south of Scullyville.

"Buy victuals," he said. "It's going to get damned cold nights from now on. It's going to snow two, maybe three days on. Eat plenty of chuck to keep warm. Go get your coat off Frank's body. You need it and it won't help him a bit." He was leaning heavily on the branch now, and swaying slightly.

I buckled the gun belt around my middle and tied the holster to my right leg with the leather strap. The rig carried a .45 caliber single-action Colt with a five-inch barrel, blue, with walnut grips. It was the kind of iron I had drooled for back in Coffeyville, but now it didn't seem nearly as pretty. I drew the gun and thumbed the gate open, ejected the shells Jim had spent during the gun battle, and fitted the cylinder with five shiny brass cartridges from the belt. I left the chamber beneath the hammer empty, lest I blow off my own foot.

I retrieved the coat and threw it across Cimarron's saddle, trying not to notice the bloodstains that had soaked clear through. Then I slung the shotgun over my shoulder by the leather thong that Frank used to carry it under his coat with. It was loaded, and I had the three other shells that I took from Frank's pocket.

Cimarron's nostrils were flaring because of the blood on the ground, and I had to hold his reins fairly tight as I thanked Jim for his help. I asked him to make sure Frank got a proper burial, and to look after Naomi until my brothers got to Fort Smith.

"You know I will," Jim said. He started for the ferry, followed by the two carrying the prisoner on the makeshift litter. "I'll ask the undertaker to leave a plot for you beside Frank. If I ever see you alive again, it'll be a goddamn miracle."

The sun remained hidden behind a wall of low-sailing gray clouds for the rest of the day. Every so often it would rain—not a good, honest rain, but just a cold mist that seemed to seep into my bones. I finally pulled the canvas coat around my shoulders, and tried not to think of the dark stains that spotted the back.

The Arkansas River flowed southwest; I urged Cimarron along at a fast trot down the muddy path that wound along the riverbank. The river itself was dark and rolling. It was too wide and deep, and the bottom too muddy, to attempt crossing on horseback. Beyond it lay the territory where Towerly was bound: the wild and rocky heart of the Choctaw Nation.

I met no others on the path that Sunday morning. The trees on either side were winter-bare, and their branches brought the blood to my face, but I kept Cimarron at a steady pace. I watched the ground with a wary eye as I rode, glancing at the bare places for signs that Towerly had indeed passed this way. It was easy enough to read, most times; the bastard had ridden hard, and leaves and dirt were thrown back a yard or so from every group of hoofmarks that Frank's horse left.

The path widened as I approached a ferry crossing. A line stretched from the trunk of a big old oak to another on the other side. The ferry was hitched at the boat dock on the far bank, but there wasn't a soul in sight. Up a ways from the water was a squat little cabin with a wide porch and smoke curling from the chimney.

I dismounted and waved my arms and shouted until I was red in the face, but nothing moved across the river—except for that lazy wisp of smoke from the cabin. I considered firing a round in the air to attract attention, even had the Colt above my head with the hammer back, but reckoned that would be a foolish thing to do, seeing as how I wasn't exactly lousy with ammunition.

I kicked rocks, swore to high heaven, and paced up and down, but the Arkansas kept rolling by as if nobody was waiting to cross her. Finally I wore myself out and sat down on a rock, chin in hand. I thought about the river and how it was like a wall that separated me from where I knew I had to go. Although I was peeved I had to wait, in another way I was relieved, because Towerly was on one side of the river and I was safe on the other. I could still go back, back to Mama and the green clapboard farmhouse at Coffeyville, and let my older brothers track Towerly down. I could make up a story about catching him on this side of the river, trading shots until I had spent my last round, and barely escaping with my life. Funny how your mind spins out these little fairytales when you have time to think. There was nobody but me on the riverbank. Who could contradict me? Damned if I didn't want both; I wanted to kill Towerly, and I wanted to stay on the safe side of the river and go back to my own bed. Thing was, life doesn't work that way. I had to choose one or the other. It was easy enough to talk in front of Deputy Jim about what I was going to do. I was half crazy anyway, what with seeing Frank's head blown off right in front of me. And I meant what I said, too. But now, sitting alone on the river-bank a few hours later, watching the river roll by as if nobody's brother had been killed earlier that day, it was different—like it didn't really matter what I did, so I might as well wheel Cimarron around and go back.

I sat on that rock until it started raining again, and I got the Fish slicker from the saddle and put it on and went back to the rock and waited some more. The rain made it twice as cold; I started shivering, and before long my nose was running. I had decided to turn back when the rain let up and somebody stepped out the door of the cabin to fetch in some firewood.

I stood up and waved.

The ferry was a simple raft. We moved slowly across the water, powered only by the elbow grease of the grizzled old half-breed who winched the thick hemp line across the heavy wooden spool. The old buzzard wasn't too happy about crossing the river to get me in the first place, and he kept a bloodshot eye on me as he worked.

I stood at Cimarron's shoulder, keeping a hand on the side of his neck as a comfort. Cimarron disliked river crossings, and I could feel the muscles twitch beneath his coat. Truth be told, I felt more than a little uneasy myself.

"Would there have been another fellow cross this morning?" I asked, as casually as I could.

"There would have."

"How long ago was that?"

"Hour or two, I reckon. He was in one helluva hurry."

"Did he happen to say where he was headed?"

"Nope," the old man said and spat, staining the deck with tobacco juice. "Why are you so damned curious? You're too young to be the law, although you're toting enough artillery for two marshals. That rascal owe you money?"

"No, he doesn't owe me any money."

I hesitated before I said anything else, even though I wanted to tell him I aimed to make the bastard pay for my brother's life. But there was no point announcing I was after revenge. The old fool might be a friend or even kin of Towerly's.

"Just curious," I said. "Thought I might catch up with him and talk some business."

"Business, eh?" The old man spat again. "Only businesses Will Towerly's interested in are blacksmithing, bootlegging, and cattle rustling. You hanker to learn those trades?"

"Might." Blacksmithing was another name for pimping.

"Startin' a little early, ain't you?"

"I'm older than you think."

"What are you? Fifteen? Sixteen?"

"You're three years off," I said.

"If you're eighteen, I'm one hunderd."

I let him think what he liked. "You know much about Towerly?"

"Know enough to stay clear of him and his gang. You'd best do the same. Go back to the farm and do some growing up. Stop reading them dime novels."

We pulled up and I walked Cimarron onto the dock. The old man tied off the ferry. I fished two bits out of my pocket and held it out, but he just jammed his hands in his pockets and shook his head.

"Don't know much about the owlhoot trail yet, do you?" he asked, looking out over the river. "The law don't pay no fare. Neither do the men they chase."

"Don't seem right," I said.

"Got nothin' to do with it," he barked. "You just keep your trouble away from here. That shotgun you got slung across your saddle is good for only one thing, and that thing ain't hunting ducks."

"Which way is Scullyville?"

"Follow the road south five miles. You'll find it."

"Much obliged," I said.

"Shouldn't be," he said and spat. "It won't be long, child, before you wish to hell you never set foot on this side of the river."

Scullyville, capital of the northern district of the Choctaw Nation, was a barren-looking town with mud streets. In its center was the administrative building, a big log structure on a stone foundation whose rough-hewn walls showed signs of having survived a fire sometime before. Other buildings hadn't fared so well, and many were just piles of charred timbers fallen on blackened foundations. Federal troops had burned much of Scullyville during the war.

There were Indians sitting on the porch of the administrative building, talking and passing the time, but they all fell silent and watched as

I rode past. I ignored them and hitched Cimarron to a post outside the only general store in town. I rolled the shotgun inside the slicker, and tied it behind the saddle.

The bell above the door jangled as I stepped inside, and the clerk behind the counter brightened up. He asked me how he could be of service, but I didn't have an answer right off. I had never cared for clerks, at any rate; they were always fawning over you when they thought you had money, and didn't have the time of day when you were broke. It was late in the day and I was already powerful hungry, and I couldn't make up my mind about what I needed. I finally stammered something about supplies.

"Salt pork? Beans? Coffee?" he asked.

"I reckon," I said.

"How much do you need?"

His smile was like a ferret's.

"A can of Arbuckle's, a slab of fatback, and two pounds of beans. Salt. Cornmeal. A box of lucifer matches. Oats for my horse."

While he gathered up the chuck, I walked over to the potbellied stove near the back of the store and held my hands over it, drinking in the warmth. There were three men sitting on crates around the stove—an Indian of middling age and an old white man in a worn campaign hat—and I acknowledged their stares with a nod. There was a pot of coffee simmering on the stove top.

"How much for a cup of coffee?" I called over my shoulder.

"Free to paying customers," the clerk said.

I filled an enamel cup and sat down on an empty crate. The coffee was weak but warmed my insides just the same. The veteran sucked on his pipe and eyed me through a cloud of tobacco smoke. One of his sleeves was empty and pinned up near the shoulder.

"Name's Samuel Cole Dalton," I said, resting the soles of my boots on the bottom of the stove to warm my feet. "My folks were driven out of their home in Cass County, Missouri, by General Order Number 11, and I am pleased to meet a soldier of the Confederacy."

"Sonny Gravette. Lost my arm for Price at the Battle of Elkhorn Tavern," the veteran said, revealing a mouthful of tobacco-stained teeth. "Who'd your father fight with, son?"

"He was too old for the unpleasantness," I said, choosing my words carefully. "He'd already served his time under fire with General Zachary Taylor at the Battle of Buena Vista." Actually, Pop had only been a fifer in Company One of the Second Regiment of the Kentucky Foot

Volunteers during the Mexican War, but there was no need to let on he'd never personally carried a musket.

The old Indian didn't say anything during this exchange, just sat there staring at me with his marble-black eyes set deep in his old, leathery face. From deep inside his vest he pulled a cloth bag of tobacco and papers; he rolled himself a cigarette, then offered the bag to me.

I took it, clumsily poured some tobacco into a paper, and twisted it shut rather than rolled it. I stuck it in my mouth and accepted the match he offered. The tobacco was strong, and mixed with some peculiar ingredients, such as sumac leaves and such truck. Now, I'd smoked some before but this concoction scalded my lungs and laid waste to my windpipe. I stifled my cough and took a quick drink of coffee.

"Ole He-Who-Dances-at-Night here smokes some mighty potent stuff, don't he?" the veteran asked.

I could only nod.

"Never did care much for that Choctaw mixture myself," the veteran said. "One thing I always did like was to watch their ballgames. They are dandy. Go all day, from dawn to dusk, swatting that ball around with them sticks with the baskets on the end. They take it serious as death. Ever seen one?"

"Only in the pictures by Catlin," I said, and attempted another drag on the Choctaw cigarette. Another round of coughing followed.

"Come back this way in summer, and you'll get an eyeball full," the veteran chuckled. "Samuel, what the hell are you doing in the nation anyway?"

"I'm looking for a man by the name of William Towerly. Heard of him?"

The veteran nodded.

"Has he been through here today?"

"I ain't seen him. Have you, Dances-at-Night?"

The Indian shook his head.

"What kind of business do you have with a lizard like Towerly?" the veteran asked. "You're sorta young to be riding the owlhoot trail, ain't you?"

"I thought the bastard might stop here and buy supplies," I said, ignoring his question. "You know where Towerly might hide out for a spell?"

"South, toward the Winding Stair Mountains, I reckon," the veteran said. "It's rough country down there."

"I'll remember that," I said, and drained the last of the coffee. "I'm much obliged to you and your friend."

The Indian nodded while I shook the veteran's hand.

I went back to the counter, where the clerk had my sack of goods waiting.

"That'll be a dollar fifty," he said, chipper as ever.

I took two of the silver dollars and put them on the counter.

"How much for a box of cartridges?" I asked.

"What caliber?"

"Forty-five Colt."

"A dollar."

I nodded and he put the ammunition on the counter. I was more than a fair shot with a wheel gun, and with any luck at all I could bolster my provisions with some wild game. It would have been easier with a Winchester, but I didn't have that option. Besides, I would feel better with all the loops in the cartridge belt filled out.

I paid and he gave me four bits change. I shoved the coins into my pocket, gathered up my things, and buttoned my coat against the cold outside. I placed the chuck in Cimarron's saddlebags and led him over to the covered well in front of the administration building, where I filled my canteen with fresh water. The Indians on the porch watched me as before, and I waved at them, but they didn't wave back. I guess they had had their fill of whites, and I couldn't blame them, especially if the bastard William Towerly was any example.

Nine

CIMARRON AND I followed a path no bigger than a deer run through the woods until it got too dark to see, then made camp in the first clearing we came to. I felt a mite guilty about stopping the pursuit of Towerly, but I was tired and there was no sense plunging through unknown territory at night. It was blacker than pitch already, and the country was getting progressively rougher; I couldn't risk breaking my neck or one of Cimarron's legs by tumbling down an unseen ravine.

I unsaddled Cimarron and poured some oats in his bag, then took my cooking gear from the saddlebags, which were still loaded from the trip to Fort Smith: a can for boiling coffee, another for beans, and a small iron skillet for frying some fatback. I gathered up some wood and started a small cooking fire. There was a stream nearby, and I scooped up some water to cook with. The stream was cold; my hand was still stinging from it as I hung the cans over the fire.

I put the skillet on some rocks at the edge of the fire, and laid some fatback down to fry while the beans warmed. It was getting colder, and my breath mingled with the smoke from the fire. The aroma rising from the food and the brewing coffee was heavenly.

It soon became apparent that I wasn't the only one who thought so.

Something was moving through the brush. I moved out of the firelight and cocked my Colt, trying to figure out what—or who—it was.

"Howdy," a voice called. "I heard you hammer back your gun. No need for that, friend. I'm just a traveler looking for a little company and a warm fire to pass the night."

At the edge of the firelight appeared a man on foot, toting a saddle. He was huge, more of a bear than a man, six foot tall and at least two hundred and fifty pounds. He wore a buckskin coat and a tattered hat, and it looked as if a razor hadn't touched his hair or beard in at least a year. There was no gun in his belt, but there was a wicked-looking knife. He clasped his hands in front, where I could see them.

"What's your business?"

"I'm Arkansas Charlie Harris, and I'm on my way to California," he replied.

"Where's your horse?"

"She twisted a gut and died two days ago," he said. Judging from the size of him, it's a wonder the animal didn't die of simple despair. "Could you spare some chuck? I'd be willing to pay."

I holstered the revolver and moved into the firelight.

"Pull up a log," I said. "No need to pay. What good's money in the wilderness, anyway?"

He broke into a wide grin and put one of his paws out, and it felt like he was going to crush the bones in my hand when we shook.

"Sorry about sneaking up on you like that," he said, "but I wanted to see what you was about before introducin' myself. Sometimes, it's just better to move on."

I scooped up the beans, putting half on a plate and the other half in the skillet. Then I divided the fatback and poured the coffee.

"I got two cups but only one plate," I said. "I like it better out of the skillet, anyhow."

He nodded his thanks as he took the plate of food and one of the tin cups.

"Where the hell are we?" he asked between mouthfuls. "I'm not too good at navigatin' on foot."

"Sullyville's due north about ten miles. You can buy yourself a horse there, if you got the scratch. Fifty should get you a decent cow pony, but ten would fetch a nag."

"That would suit me just fine," he said. "Anything but walkin'."

"All you got is that knife?" I asked. "Ain't packing no firearms?"

"I was born in Arkansas," he grinned. "I don't need nothin' else."

"Say, you haven't seen anybody today, have you?" I asked, anxious to change the subject.

"One rider. He was going after it hard, and his horse was lathered up something fierce. I tried to pass the time with him, but he wouldn't even look at me, much less stop."

"Did you get a good look at his face? Did it have a scar running from the corner of his eye down behind his ear?"

"I believe he did."

"Where'd you run across him?"

"A ways back, maybe five miles. It was a couple of hours before sundown."

I would have to aim toward the southeast in the morning.

"It ain't considered polite to ask a man his name or his doings in these parts," Harris said, "but you've got blood in your eyes and my curiosity's up. What's this rider to you?"

"He killed my brother," I said, reckoning that since this fellow was a stranger in these parts and sharing my chuck, it was safe enough to be plain.

"My brother Frank was a riding deputy for Parker's court," I said, and briefly described the scene in the Bottoms. "Towerly—that's the bastard's name, William Towerly—stood over Frank and shot him in the head with a Winchester. I didn't reckon it was wise to wait until they formed a posse to go after him."

"Well, you have some sand," Harris said, scratching his beard. "Have you figured out what you're going to do when you catch the bastard?"

"I aim to take him back to Fort Smith."

"What if he don't want to go?"

"Then I'll have to kill him."

"Look here, boy," Harris said, pouring some more coffee into his cup, "I don't mean no disrespect, but I can see things others can't—I'm the natural-born seventh son of a seventh son—and on your head I can see a heap of misery. I know you have a fair chance of killing this man Towerly, because I've been studying the callouses on your right hand. Only gunfighters have palms like yours. But I can also see you're headed down a dark and miserable trail, filled with blood and women crying over their men. Let me see your hand."

"What for?"

"I want to get a better look at what you're in for."

I held out my hand, and he turned it palm-up toward the firelight. Even though I had big hands for my age, his were huge, making mine seem like a baby's. He rubbed his thumb over my palm a couple times and gave a grunt.

"What's the matter?" I asked.

"Boy, your hands is as bloody as Lady Macbeth's. You got so much death around you it makes me nervous just sitting with you. You buried somebody besides your brother recently, didn't you?"

"My Pa."

"There are other graves ahead in the next few years, some of them kin. Others, you're gonna plant there yourself. I see wealth from time to time, but not happiness. Love, but not marriage. Fame, without a name. The number six means something special. It gets cloudy right quick. I can't tell how you're gonna end, but it ain't gonna be in your sleep. If I was you, son, I'd throw that cannon away and go back to Kansas right away. Otherwise, you'd better plan on never goin' back."

"How'd you know I'm from Kansas?" I asked, and jerked my hand back. "And what does 'fame without a name' mean? What kind of trash is that?"

"I told you, I see things sometimes."

"I think you're just tryin' to booger me," I said. "Hell, you're probably a friend of Towerly's sent to scare me off or kill me."

"Think what you want," Harris said. "You don't have to take my advice. But I thought I was obligated to tell you what I knew, seein' as how you shared your chuck with me. And if I was a friend of the bastard Towerly, why didn't I kill you when I first seen you?"

"Maybe you had to make sure who I was, first."

"Ain't that many thirteen-year-old white boys travelin' alone and packing iron through the hills of the Choctaw Nation."

I hadn't told him how old I was, either.

"All right, I'm sorry," I said. "I'll give up the gun as soon as I kill Towerly."

"Do what you have to do, son, but if you wait till then, it'll be too damn late," Harris said. "Well, I've talked too much and damn near ruined our supper. Forgive me."

I shrugged.

"What about you?" I asked. "What're you running from?"

Harris laughed, so loud it nearly shook the ground.

"You're not stupid, are you?" he asked. "Listen, I'll be straight with you. I'm a smith by trade, and had a little forge near Calico Rock in the White River country. Trouble was, I liked sportin' a helluva lot better than blacksmithin'. A banker fella came home unexpected and caught me making a deposit, if you know what I mean, and I had to break his neck to keep him from shootin' the missus."

"He didn't try to shoot you?"

"He shot me all right. Took a ball from his .32 in my shoulder." Harris worked his left arm in a circle, wincing with pain. "I'm gonna have to find a doc to take it out, soon as I get to California. I can't blame him much for trying to kill me, and I would have been lucky to get away with a ball in the shoulder, but I couldn't just run away and let him kill his wife for being human."

"What'd you do then?"

"Well, I didn't stick around long enough to see if the sheriff was going to swear out a warrant to stretch my neck. Reckoned it was time to leave Calico Rock."

We finished the last of the coffee and I spread out my bedroll. My brothers had showed me how to make a proper bedroll, with a soogan— a kind of heavy quilt—and a blanket or two wrapped up in a canvas tarpaulin like a warm enchilada. It was more than Harris had. He pulled his coat tight around him and propped himself up on the saddle.

I hadn't realized how tired I was, and was asleep nearly as soon as I had pulled my boots off and slipped into the bedroll. I still had enough of a sense of preservation, however, to sleep with the Colt tucked under the covers with me.

It was damned cold when I woke, and it took a few minutes for me to gather the courage to throw the covers off and sit up. When I did, another world confronted me; it had snowed during the night, and everything was covered with white. Harris was nowhere to be seen, and I cursed until I saw that Cimarron was still hobbled where I left him. I reckon Harris found it warmer walking as soon as it was light, instead of lying on the open ground waiting to freeze. He'd left a few coins in the tin cup he'd used the night before.

I saddled Cimarron as quickly as I could make my fingers work, pausing only long enough to cut a strip from the end of my blanket, which I wrapped around my head in order to keep my ears warm.

It was slow going because the ground was as featureless as a fresh-made bed, and I let Cimarron pick his own way through the snow for fear of driving him and making him stumble. The sky was clouded and gray, and the sun was just a smudge of brightness. Early in the afternoon it began to snow again, hiding the smudge that was the sun—and my principal means of navigation. Soon I was thoroughly lost, but I pressed on until dark because it was too cold to stand still. I made camp at a rocky bluff. I built a good-sized fire near the base, where it would reflect off the rocks and warm my backside as well as the front. I bedded down soon after supper and slept through the night.

It was bright and clear in the morning. After a breakfast of beans and fatback—which I was getting earnestly tired of—it was back in the saddle and head south again. The countryside was blanketed in snow and ice. It was as if Cimarron and I were the only living things for miles and miles. We rode on like that all day, not stopping for lunch because we were making such good time in the clear weather, and not knowing what the night would bring. Late in the afternoon we came to a shallow river, and beyond a ridge on the far side I spied a column of chimney smoke rising in the still air. I led Cimarron across the river at what appeared to be the shallowest spot. In a couple of places we broke through the thin layer of ice, and I found myself in knee-deep water while Cimarron thrashed wildly for his footing. By the time we got to the other side my trousers were glazed over and I couldn't feel my feet. I swung back up in the saddle and urged Cimarron on to where the smoke was coming from.

Crossing the ridge a half mile yonder, I saw that the smoke was issuing from the stone chimney of a little country store situated in the valley. There was a wagon and team hitched out front along with a couple of saddle horses, and up over the porch was fixed a big rack of antlers. The sign said "Potter's Station," but there weren't deep enough ruts out front to indicate the Texas stage had stopped there anytime recently.

I left Cimarron's bridle on and hitched him out front, but took the saddle off and carried it in with me. It was wonderful warm inside; the big stone fireplace was crackling, and a cookstove in the corner glowing orange. There were a couple of wooden tables near the fireplace. I walked stiff-legged over to the one nearest the fire and sat down, while a couple of Indians at the other table watched me.

"Cold?" one asked.

"Damn near frozen," I said, tugging off my boots and placing them on the hearth to dry out. "Where's the storekeeper?"

"Potter's tending the livestock," the talkative Indian said, and jerked a thumb over his shoulder.

I took off my trousers and placed them near my boots, then hesitated a moment, realizing the rest of me was just about as wet as my boots and pants. I finally decided modesty wasn't worth freezing to death, so I pulled the rest of my clothes off and laid them on the warm stones as well. I wrapped myself in the blanket from my bedroll, taking care to hide the Colt in the folds when I thought the Indians weren't looking.

My feet and my hands and my face started itching and burning something fierce as they warmed up, and I was rubbing my ears when the storekeeper emerged from the back room, taking off his coat.

"What happened to you?" he asked.

"Kind of fell in the river," I said.

"Saw you ride up," he said. "Got money?"

"Some."

"Supper? Four bits."

"Done," I said, "if I can have my coffee now."

"I think you need a shot of whiskey more," Potter said. "You look downright blue." He took a brown jug and a couple of glasses down, and set them on the counter. I moved over to the counter as he poured an inch or so into each glass. I downed mine in one swallow, not really liking the taste but relishing the fire it started in my chest. It also sort of crossed my eyes for a minute.

"Local brew," he explained.

"It'll do," I said.

Grinning down on us from a shelf behind the counter was a row of human skulls, and I jerked backwards a little when I saw them. Potter laughed.

"Found 'em in the woods around here," he said. He reached up and took one down, and placed it on the counter by the jug. "Keep them as a reminder of how dangerous travel can be in this country. Found this one last summer, this side of the river about two miles down." He shoved a finger into a hole above the left eye socket. "From the size of it, I'd say he was done in with a slug from a Sharps 50. Sure would like to know his name, and what he was doing in these parts. But I guess we'll never know."

"Where's the rest of him?"

"Quien sabe? Animals, you know, scatter things about."

He placed the skull back on the shelf and took another, yellower one down.

"This one is kind of interesting," he said. "It's an old Indian. Look here, there's a flint point wedged right in the cheekbone. Might have been from an old battle between the Choctaw and the Caddoes, who used to live around here. Could be a couple hundred years old. Leastways, that's what Small Bear here tells me."

The talkative Indian nodded. "When the Choctaw lived in Mississippi, we would come far west on the big hunts," he said. "Killed many Caddoes, left them lie."

"Things ain't changed much, from the look of that shelf."

"No, it's white men do most of the killing now," Potter said, as he put the old skull back on the shelf, "and they sure as hell don't use bows and arrows. Look, son, you're either real excited to be here or you're packing a pistol under that blanket of yours. Either way, you're making me damned nervous."

The Indians laughed.

I took the Colt out and laid it on the counter.

"Sorry," I said. "Didn't know what kind of place this was when I came in."

Potter took it and laid it beneath the counter.

"Don't worry, it'll be there when you're ready to leave. I've been robbed too damn many times, and I have this rule about packin' while you're in the store. Going to spend the night?"

"What'll it cost me?"

"Two bits if you got it, but I reckon I couldn't send a dog out in weather like this, especially a wet frozen dog."

"You'll get your two bits," I said.

"You'll get a quilt and a pillow, then," Potter said. "Supper's about ready. Rabbit stew, biscuits, coffee. Would have been a lot fancier, if Blue Quail hadn't taken the cramp cholera and died last year."

After supper, I asked Potter if anyone else had come through during the last couple of days, and he said nobody but his regular customers. I asked him if he knew William Towerly, and he said no, but I thought he was lying.

Along toward ten o'clock, after the Indians had left and Potter and I were sitting at the counter talking about nothing in particular, a couple of white men came in. They were pretty woolly-looking, with wild beards and hair down to their collars, and they asked for whiskey. My clothes still hadn't dried, and I was sitting at the bar with the blanket draped around my shoulders.

They were the Bingham brothers, I learned after a spell. They were whiskey runners who were smart enough not to drink the trash they sold. It didn't seem to bother them in the least talking about their business, and how much they made, and how some of the Indians would beg. I guess they reckoned they were far enough away from Judge Parker and his deputies to brag about what they did, and how some Indians got so desperate they'd rent out their squaws for a drink.

I could tell Potter didn't like them much, but he served them anyway and took their money. I noticed he didn't ask them for their guns like he had me. They smelled terrible. I know I stunk too, because I'd been on the trail and hadn't had a bath in God knows how long, but these fellows absolutely reeked, like something turned rotten. The more they drank, the louder they got, and the smaller the store seemed to be. Sooner or later, I knew they would get around to me, so I reckoned it would be best if I struck up a conversation with them first.

"Say," I said, "you fellows haven't met up with Bill Towerly lately, have you?"

Right off, I could tell the hair was in the butter; they stopped their laughing and gave me a look like I was a snake that had crawled out from under some rock. I glanced over at Potter, but he looked away quick.

The older—and bigger—brother got off his stool and walked over to me. He leaned down, and his breath nearly knocked me off my seat.

"Now, what in blazes would a runty little bastard like you want with Bloody Bill?"

"I met Bill in the Bottoms across from Fort Smith," I said as fast as I could make it up, "after I lit out from home. He said it was my lucky day, because he could always use good men in his operation."

This struck the bootlegger as funny, and he thumped me on the back. "So Bill thought you was a good man, huh?"

"Wait a minute, Daniel," the other one said from the bar, "if Bill wanted this pistol here in on the operation, then why didn't he join him up right there in the Bottoms?"

"Yeah," Daniel said. "How come you're down here in the wilderness askin' about him?"

"When I got back down in the Bottoms, they told me Bill had lit out after some kind of trouble with a couple of federal officers," I said. "I couldn't hang around Smith, because my Pa was after me, so I took off for the Choctaw Nation, hoping to find Bill as best I could."

The big one grunted.

"Well, you rode a far piece for nothin'," he said as he walked back to his stool. "Bloody Bill don't need no help. And why in hell are you wearing nothing but that blanket?"

"I fell through the ice into the creek," I said.

Douglas, the younger one, slid off his stool and strolled over, grinning like an idiot. He flicked his hand out and knocked the blanket off my shoulder. It slid to the floor, leaving me sitting there unshucked.

"Goddamn," he said and whistled between his teeth, "this one's near as pretty as a girl."

I reached down for the blanket and he kicked the stool out from under me, leaving me sprawled on the floor, with splinters in my knees.

"That'll do," Potter said low.

"Aw, we was just funnin' him," Douglas said. "We were just funnin' you, pard. No hard feelings, right?" He held out his hand, but I got up on my own. As casually as I could, I picked up the blanket and put it around me.

"I know how you like to fun boys," Potter said, and then to me, "I reckon your clothes are dry enough by now."

I walked over to the hearth, where I pulled on my long underwear and my trousers. Potter then told the Bingham brothers that he was about to close up for the night, and they hemmed and hawed and got another round out of him first.

While the Binghams were finishing their drinks, Potter told me it would be best if I moved my horse around to the stable out back and got him settled in for the night, because it was too cold to leave an animal outside. He was really telling me to put Cimarron up so he wouldn't get stolen. I pulled on my boots and my coat and led Cimarron around back, got him some oats, and bid him good night. By the time I got back inside, the Binghams were gone.

After Potter had retired upstairs, I retrieved the Colt from beneath the bar and slipped it under the covers with me. I was getting pretty used to its cold barrel sticking me in the stomach while I slept, and don't think I could have without it.

Potter woke me after dawn the next morning. I paid him what I owed and he shared his breakfast of hoecake and eggs with me. He allowed that he could use a hand around the place if I'd care to stay on a few days, and I thanked him—it was mighty tempting, considering the cold trail that lay ahead—but I told him I had business to take care of. He just shrugged and said he hoped I wouldn't become the sixth skull up on his shelf for him to talk about.

Ten

I KNEW I WAS BEING FOLLOWED after leaving Potter's Station, but I rode all day without catching sight of anyone. It was just a feeling that I had, but I was learning to trust my feelings more and more. I reckoned it might be the Binghams, but I couldn't be sure. And because I was also getting a little low on food, I rode with the L. C. Smith slung across the saddle.

About midday I had a sign that I was indeed on "Bloody Bill" Towerly's trail. I found Frank's horse, dead, its eyes open wide. It was frozen solid, but I reckon that had happened after the bastard had ridden him to death. The saddle was gone, but I couldn't be sure that Towerly had taken it—anybody that might have come later would have undoubtedly picked it up.

Frank loved that horse, and I had to pinch myself hard to keep from crying. I sat on my haunches and studied the dead animal for a spell, to see if I could decipher anything else about Towerly's actions, but there was little else to learn; it must have snowed again since the horse died, because there were no tracks to be found anywhere around.

There was smoke on the horizon, not chimney smoke but something blacker and thicker, and lacking any other clue, I rode toward it. I was hoping it would be a homestead, where they were making soap or burning some stumps or trash, someplace where I could ask if they had seen anything. Unfortunately, Towerly seemed to have paid a visit ahead of me.

It was a cabin, half burned. Things were a mess inside; the cupboards had been turned out, drawers emptied, even the bedding had been gone through. Part of the roof had fallen in, and there was a horrible stench, something foul but sweet-smelling at the same time. I had inspected the interior for some time before, in the smouldering half, I noticed a brown leg protruding from the embers, and soon discerned there were two corpses thrown into the fire. I reckoned they had been a Choctaw couple. The peculiar smell I had noted was that of burning flesh.

I staggered outside and emptied my breakfast onto the snow until there was nothing left but the dry heaves, and then sat on my heels for a spell, wondering what to do. The cabin was miles from anywhere. It would take days to contact the authorities. Not even the Choctaw Tribal Police could render assistance in tracking the bastard Towerly. Towerly was a white man and tribal police had no jurisdiction, even if Indians had been killed; it was strictly a job for federal marshals from Fort Smith. And since I didn't know if there were neighbors or relations close, it was clear the first thing to do was to bury the dead.

The fire had been set to hide the murders and the robbery, and although it had only done half the job, it was still pretty hot in some places and I had to put it out with buckets of snow. Then I found a shovel and a pickax and chose a spot in the yard where I dug the graves; the first foot or so was mighty hard, but it got easier the deeper down I got. The worst part was hauling the bodies out of there. I found a couple of good blankets to wrap them in, then drug them out to the graves. The man was burned pretty much beyond recognition, but the woman was pretty much intact, except for her head, which had been split open, probably with an axe. Of course, the little corral and lean-to in back of the cabin were empty, and the gate was wide open. Towerly had gotten himself another horse in short order, and he was still a couple of days ahead of me. Whichever way he had gone, the snow had covered up his tracks.

I smoothed the graves with the shovel and tried to say a prayer, but couldn't, so satisfied myself instead with marking the graves with a couple of crosses I fashioned from some tree branches and string. I didn't know if these folks were Christian or not, but at least it would serve to mark the graves if kin came looking for them. Still, something needed to be said, so I stood over the graves and said aloud how I was sorry what happened to them and how I aimed to bring Towerly down. What I didn't say was that I wasn't feeling very brave at the moment, and wished I was back home at Coffeyville with my Mama. Before I could help myself, tears started to roll down my cheeks, but I wiped them away quick. I still had the spooky feeling I was being watched.

Last thing I did was take a piece of charcoal and write on a plank how I found the cabin with their bodies inside, and how I reckoned it was Towerly that done it, and signed my name. I left the plank in the doorway.

I thought about taking some clothing from the cabin, maybe a pair of gloves or some socks, but I had a funny feeling about wearing things belonging to dead folks. In the end, I just let things be.

I swung up in Cimarron's saddle and sat there for a spell, looking at the ruined cabin and the empty corral and the two fresh graves with their spindly crosses showing dark against the blanket of snow. The sun was a bloody ball dipping beneath the tree line in the west, and blue haze from the cabin fire hung like evil itself over the valley. It was spooky as hell, and I was quailed something fierce. I shivered, though not from the cold.

An owl hooted from the tree line, deep and searching.

Who? it asked. *Who, who?*

"Not me," I said, and pulled hard on Cimarron's reins, heading him back around north. I touched my heels lightly to his flanks and he bolted, sending snow flying behind us.

We rode hard for a mile or so, putting a good-sized ridge between us and the cabin, and it was completely dark when I reined him to a stop. As I made camp for the night beneath a rock outcrop, I turned over in my mind the easiest way to get back home. If I followed the Texas Road, it would lead me to Baxter Springs, but if I could aim west and pick up the Katy railway, it would take me directly to Parsons, just thirty miles or so from Coffeyville. Either way, I would be in country I knew. I had had enough of Fort Smith and the Indian Nations, and of killings. I wanted to go home.

That night I dreamt, not for the last time, that I was under the covers in my own bed while Mama was starting breakfast downstairs. It was so real I could feel the warmth of the sheets, and smell the hoecakes cooking, and hear my brothers calling for me to wake up, wake up.

When I finally did wake, long after the sun was up, Cimarron was gone.

Not only had they taken my horse and saddle, but most of my gear, too, leaving me only with what was in or beside my bedroll. I reckon the empty holster beside my head was the only thing that might have kept them from slitting my throat. I didn't think it was Towerly that did the stealing, because he would have surely recognized me and not left me breathing.

Now, I was in one helluva predicament—alone, in the wilderness, with snow on the ground and not a shred of food. As best I could reckon, Potter's Station was some forty miles away, and it would take me two, maybe three days to make it there, if I didn't freeze or starve along the way. I could have gone back to the dead Choctaws' cabin, but there was no guarantee that anybody would find me there before I froze or starved. It seems strange to think back on it now, but I didn't panic when I realized how dire my predicament was. I just thought about what my brother Bob would do; he would calmly strap on his Colt, roll up his bedroll, and start off as quick as he could; and that's just what I did.

As bad as riding through that rough country in winter was, walking was worse. I hadn't gone a mile before my feet felt like they was frozen plum through; my boots were old and the snow came in through the seams like water through a sieve. I had to stop every so often, take my boots off, and rub my feet to warm them up before going on. The soles of my feet were cracked and bloody, and I had to sort of walk pigeon-toed, on the sides of my feet, to stand the pain.

It was getting colder all the time, too. The air was so cold it burned my nostrils raw so that it hurt to breathe through my nose, and pretty soon I was breathing through my mouth, which burned my throat so bad I couldn't take it. I had to stop and cut some more of the blanket up to make a muffler to breathe through.

By noontime I was so tuckered out from trudging through the snow and fighting the cold that I had to stop and rest, and damned if I didn't fall asleep for a little while. Just closing my eyes from the whiteness all around was a relief. It took quite an effort to make myself get started again.

In the afternoon it started snowing again, so hard you couldn't see where you were going. It was useless to try to make it any farther. I decided to hole up in a crevice beneath some big old rocks until it quit. But it didn't. It kept coming down heavier and heavier until it was a regular blizzard, with the wind howling and the snowflakes swirling every which way.

I dragged some brush and piled it in front of the crevice, which helped some, and then just stayed huddled in a little ball inside my bedroll. Without walking and working up at least a little heat, it was colder than ever, and I began shivering out of control. No amount of rubbing my hands up and down my ribs could warm me up, and I couldn't make a fire because all my matches had been stowed in Cimarron's saddlebags with my cooking stuff. I got sleepy again and dozed throughout the afternoon, rousing every once in a while to peer outside and see that the storm hadn't let up. Eventually the snow piled up against the brush in front of my hole, and I let it, because it cut off the wind.

I slept the night that way, curled up in a hole in the rocks, and in the morning I punched a hole through the snowbank to look outside. Everything was quiet and still now. The deep snow glistened blue and pink in the light from the sun, which was just peeking over the hills to the east. It was so beautiful I just lay there looking at it all, taking it in, watching the sunbeams shimmer over the snow like it was some sparkly blanket thrown over the whole earth. I couldn't feel my hands or my feet. When I rubbed my nose it was like I was using a stick instead of my fingers, but I was so damned sleepy it didn't worry me much. I had been dreaming about home, of course, lying in a warm bed and smelling Mama's cooking, and that was so nice that I just went back to sleep.

Only, when I started dreaming again I wasn't in bed anymore. I was downstairs at the kitchen table late one night with Bob and Grat and Frank, and they're taking nips from a bottle they've hidden from Mama. I'm having a hard time staying awake because it's way past my bedtime, but I'm fighting it because I really like sitting at the table with my brothers. They're swapping stories and Frank starts talking about an old-timer he found frozen to death out on the prairie a few years back. Bob says, "Yeah, that's the way they say you go, you just drift off to sleep and never wake up. Some that have come mighty close to freezing say the peculiar thing is that you don't feel cold at all, that all at once you feel warm and your mind gets soft and all you want to do is sleep." I've laid my head down on the table, and Bob gives me a shake. Grat punches me on the shoulder for good measure. "Wake up, Sam," Bob says, and I jerk upright with a start.

But I wasn't at the kitchen table, I was curled up in a hole in the rocks in the snow, and somewhere in my mind added, *freezing to death.*

Can't go to sleep, I told myself. *Can't sleep.* I started rubbing my hands together, and before long the circulation starts coming back, needles and pins at first, and then like they're on fire. I clamp them under my armpits and force myself to think about what to do.

I hadn't slept long that last time, only half an hour or so, because through my peephole in the snowbank I could see the sun was barely over the hills; seven o'clock, maybe seven-thirty. I knew I had to start moving, get the blood circulating again, but I had to unthaw my feet. As I tried to tug off my boots to get at them, I saw a wisp of movement at the edge of the timber across the clearing. I fixed my eyes at a middle distance, hoping to see something move again. In a minute or so I saw a flash of gray, and knew it was an animal. I was hungry, and the thought of meat made the hunger even sharper, so I moved my right hand down to rest on the butt of my Colt, and stayed still. Then, at the edge of the clearing, I could make out the shape of one deer's head, and then another, bobbing through the brush. Two yearlings, one a little bigger than the other, strolled out in the clearing, about sixty yards away. They were meandering around, chewing on branches here and there and nosing in the snow at the ground, looking for salt, maybe.

They were still too far away for a good shot, considering I only had a revolver and my hands were still numb, so I remained as motionless as possible. My heart was up in my throat and my breathing was ragged. A part of me was screaming to shoot! shoot! but another part said no, it's too important to rush the shot. Let them get closer.

In my head, I started to say a prayer: *Oh Lord, let me kill one of these deer and I'll never ever smoke or cuss or choke the snake again.* But somehow it didn't feel right. So I switched in my head and talked to the deer instead. *Forgive me for having to kill you,* is how it went, *but if I don't it's me that's gonna die.*

The deer moved slowly across the clearing in my general direction, taking their time, pawing at the ground. They were some thirty yards away when I moved the Colt as slow as I could from my side to where it was clear in front of me, but still hidden under the edge of my peephole. I pressed the trigger down while I hammered back, to keep the revolver from clicking loudly as the cylinder locked in place. But the gun still made a metallic noise. The deer's ears went up and they both started sniffing the air. The wind was with me that morning, and they didn't flag. They knew something wasn't quite right, and one began moving off toward the timber again, while the bigger one hung back and turned in a circle. I could see now that the bigger one was a little spike buck. His eyes were staring right at me. A tremor ran through his flank and he got ready to run, but I was already sighted on the lung area, just behind the shoulder. I squeezed off a round.

His front legs folded and he dropped to the snow. I could hear the other deer crashing through the woods on her way to the next county. The little buck got unsteadily back to his feet—he was finished, it would just take a matter of minutes—but I didn't have the strength to track him to a brush pile and drag him out, so I put another round where I had sent the first. This time he dropped and stayed.

I knocked the snow away from my hiding place and crawled out. My legs felt like stumps, and I fell a couple of times before I got some feeling back into them. Kneeling beside the little buck—he was seventy-five or eighty pounds—I took my knife and slit him open from bung to brisket. I shoved my hands deep inside and coils of intestines spilled out onto the snow. I cupped some blood out of the cavity, steaming in the cold, and drank. It was salty and coppery, and the warmth spread inside like the very taste of life itself.

I ate the liver raw, then butchered the deer, noting with some vanity that my first shot had pierced the heart. I laid several good-sized roasts out to wrap later in my bedroll, after they had drained of blood, then took the time to carefully skin the animal. I made a pretty neat job of it, taking the hide off in one piece with very little flesh remaining. I separated the cape from the rest of the hide, then split it in two, and wrapped the halves around my boots. They came up nearly to my calves, and I tied them up using some tendons from the hind legs. I cut a hole in the center of the hide and put it over my head like a poncho, then put the gun belt over it to cinch it up tight. There was plenty of hair on the outside of the hide, considering as how the buck had already grown its winter coat, and it was very warm. I must have been quite the sight, what with blood up to my elbows and dripping off my chin, and wearing a fresh fur coat, but my spirits had picked up and my mind had cleared.

Inside my bedroll was my war bag, which I used as a pillow at night, and inside it were a few odds and ends, such as Frank's marshal's badge, that picture Tackett took of us boys, a deck of playing cards, a pair of dice, and the box of cartridges I had bought back in Scullyville. Before continuing on, I reloaded the Colt. I saved the casing from the shell I had first shot the deer with, throwing it in the bag with the other stuff.

Then I wrapped the meat up and slung the bedroll over my shoulder, and said thanks aloud over what was left of the little buck before I started on. Already, buzzards were wheeling overhead, and in a few days there would be no trace of what had happened there. But I would remember.

That evening I found some good flint rock, and used the blunt edge of my knife to throw sparks into a pile of wood shavings and start a fire. Not only did I have warmth for the night, but I had roast venison for supper.

Eleven

I WANDERED ON FOOT for three more days in the wilderness. Even though the weather warmed enough to reduce the snow to scattered patches in shaded valleys and the lee sides of rocks, my situation was still serious. I was sick and lost—hopelessly lost—and even though I tried to navigate with the sun by day and the stars at night, the country was so rough that making a straight line was difficult. I probably could have managed it if I hadn't been so feverish, but putting one foot ahead of the other was hard enough. I wasted much time picking my way through the low country, avoiding the stair steps of the mountains that hemmed me in, searching in vain for the road that would take me back to Potter's Station. My meandering in the valleys had unwittingly taken me farther south, deeper into the rough country, until at last I decided I would have to shoot a straighter course—over the hills, instead of around them.

So I began climbing.

I scrambled over rocks and through the cedars, running the ridges where I could. But I always faced more dips and grades when the ridges ran out or strayed too far from my southwesterly course, toward where I judged Potter's Station to lay. On the afternoon of the third day, bleeding from brush cuts and bruised by rocks where I had fallen, I crested a particularly steep ridge and found myself staring down into a box canyon with a shallow stream running along a grassy bottom. At the end of the canyon, wedged tight against the cliff face, was a shack.

The creek curved around to hug the eastern wall of the canyon, then ran to within a few yards of the shack before seeming to disappear into the cliff. Next to the shack was a split-rail corral penning a pinto pony; nearby was a stump and an axe and a pile of logs waiting to be reduced to firewood. A cooking fire smouldered only a few paces from the front door. Although a stovepipe stuck up out of one end of the cabin, I imagined it was a mite tight inside and easier to cook out-of-doors in fair weather.

It made a perfect hideout, hidden from the outside world and offering good water. The mouth of the canyon to the north was the only way in or out of the place on horseback. Just a few men could hold off a posse for days. Only trouble I could see was that there was no way out once they had you pinned down.

The place was messy, even by backwoods standards: the door hung unevenly on its leather hinges, pots and dishes from the last meal lay in the dirt near the cooking fire, and scattered about the yard were brown jugs and liquor bottles. On a fence rail was a row of shattered glass, where bottles had obviously been used for target practice. It seemed the shack's inhabitants were uncertain shots, for one green bottle stood untouched among the shards.

As I watched from my hiding place in the cedar break, a pair of riders entered the mouth of the canyon at an easy trot. They splashed across the creek and approached to within seventy-five yards of the cabin, where they halted. It was the Bingham brothers. Neither of them was riding Cimarron. Dan, the bigger one, took off his glove, put his fingers to his mouth, and whistled.

In a moment the front door slammed open and a man stepped out into the sunlight, rubbing his eyes with one hand and toting a Winchester in the other. He pulled up his suspenders and waved for the Bingham brothers to come on in. He wore no hat. Even from a distance, I had no trouble spotting the big red mark on the man's balding skull; it was the bastard William Towerly.

The Binghams dismounted and hitched their horses to the corral fence. Doug Bingham took a grain sack that had been hung from his saddle horn and handed it to Towerly, who groped inside and brought out another one of those green bottles. He pulled the cork with his teeth and took a good long pull before handing it to the brothers.

I heard Towerly ask something about food, and Dan Bingham fetched along two more grain sacks. As they entered the cabin, Doug Bingham chirped, "We got thirty dollars for that horse we stole," upon which brother Dan cuffed him soundly on the ear. Then the door swung closed and I was left to guess about what horse they meant, but I had my suspicions. Hell, I knew Cimarron was worth three times that amount.

The little brother came out of the cabin, went to the woodpile, and began chopping wood. He was cussing as he went about his chore, muttering, "It's Doug do this and Doug do that. Christ Almighty." He worked furiously until he had a good supply of firewood. Then he went back inside, cradling the bundle, and soon the stovepipe was belching smoke.

I should have hightailed it right out of there, considering the odds were three-to-one, even more taking into account the other side had Winchesters. I could have made my way back to civilization and informed a posse about the whereabouts of Frank's killer. They would have had a good chance to catch him and send him to hell via Judge Parker.

But I was right frothy about damn near freezing to death in the wilderness, and I was more than a little feverish. All I could think of was Frank a-mouldering in his grave while the bastard Towerly was drinking whiskey, and how that trash down there had stolen and sold my horse. My feet were bleeding and hurt like hell. I was damned tired of walking, and if I couldn't have Cimarron back I aimed to ride out of that canyon on one of the Binghams' horses.

So right off, my mind began churning out a plan.

First I thought I would wait until the Binghams left, and bushwhack them at the mouth of the canyon. I soon rejected that plan because it depended on me dropping them both in the open, and I didn't know if I could do it. Even if I did, it would alert Towerly that he was likely to be under attack, and he could hole up in the cabin and wait me out.

I had to get them all together in a pretty tight spot, where I was well protected and they were in the open. I also had to get down close, where my Colt would do the most good, because I didn't have enough ammunition for a long fight.

I lit upon the idea of sneaking up on the roof of the cabin and throwing my hide coat over the chimney. The smoke would back up in the cabin and flush them out the front door, where I could nail them one by one as they came out.

It was the start of a plan, but it wasn't yet complete. If I waited until they were good and drunk—and it appeared they were on their way—their confusion would help me out considerably, so I was better off staying put. Also, I needed something to throw down the chimney that would really make some smoke before I plugged it up with my deer hide, something that would make them gag for air and run for the door in spite of themselves. I reckoned strips of wet blanket would do nicely, so I set about carving up what was left of my bedroll.

I took the box of cartridges out of my war bag and emptied all of them into the pockets of my jacket, where I could get to them in a hurry. Then I opened the gate on the Colt and slipped a round into the last chamber, making it a mother dog and six pups.

I made my way farther down the cliff and closer to the cabin, going slowly so as not to break my neck or make a ruckus, but every once in a while my foot would slip and send some rocks skittering down. Fortunately, the trio in the cabin paid no mind. I made it to where I was hidden by a considerable ledge, close enough to the ground where I could drop down into the corral, but still far enough away that they were not likely to discover me by accident. There I waited, chewing my venison and rubbing Frank's marshal's star for luck.

The drunken laughter in the cabin got louder and louder, and the Bingham brothers took turns coming out of the cabin to make water, but I did not see Towerly. He either was not drinking as much as the brothers or had a bladder the size of a cow's. More wood was hauled into the cabin by Doug, and the stovepipe chimney was soon glowing.

It seemed like I hid on that ledge for hours and hours waiting for the right moment, but I knew by the sun it couldn't have been that long. There was still at least an hour of daylight left when the laughter was replaced by general snoring and I judged it was time to make my move. I pinned the badge to my coat and checked the Colt one last time.

I dropped to the ground and the horses started to snort a bit, but I whispered some nonsense words I used with Cimarron and they settled right down. I hurried in a crouch over to where the stream was, then lay down with my hands in the water as I soaked the blanket strips.

I fairly sank right into the ground when big Dan Bingham came out the cabin door to relieve himself, but thankfully he was lazy and didn't venture too far outside to take care of business. When the door slammed shut again I crawled on my belly over to the corner of the cabin and, carefully as I could, climbed the corral rails and up on top of the cabin.

All I could hear from inside was snoring.

I dumped my strips of wet blanket down the stovepipe, capped it with the hide, and jumped down. The roof was the first place they would expect somebody to be waiting, so that's the last place I intended to be. I scurried over to the log-splitting stump, about fifteen yards away, and crouched behind it to watch.

Not long after smoke began to trickle from the edges of the roof, Big Dan roused and began cussing his brother for not opening the damper on the stove, and cussed again because it was open. Smoke began gushing from chinks around the top of the cabin. There were some crashes as a table and maybe a chair hit the floor, and I could hear some glass breaking. Then the door flew open so hard it tore one of the hinges away, and Dan fell out onto the dirt on his hands and knees, gasping for air, followed by his brother stumbling over him. The little brother had a revolver in his hand.

I hesitated for a moment, hoping Towerly would be close behind, but he was smart and wasn't going to make it easy. From deep inside the cabin he started bellering about it being a trap, that they were being smoked out, couldn't the dumb bastards see that?

Doug Bingham, standing over his brother, saw me and tried to bring the revolver up, but not before I put a round into his wrist. It was a foolhardy shot to try in a mortal situation, and I'd had every intention of shooting every one of them dead when I made my plan, but in that last instant I knew I didn't want to kill him. He flew back against the doorjamb and howled in pain, clutching his useless arm. The gun fell from his limp fingers.

Dan Bingham's whiskey-soaked eyes cleared like magic as he grabbed his brother with one hand and picked up the revolver with the other, sending a wild round that thudded in the dirt ten feet away from me. I shot him between the eyes and he fell forward, dead as a doornail.

Then a volley of rifle shots began pouring out of the doorway, and I reckoned Towerly had found his Winchester. The first three just tore chunks out of the stump, but the fourth puckered the fabric of my coat over my upper left arm, and it was a second before I realized I was hit. As I hunkered down with my back to the stump, they rolled Dan Bingham's body out of the way and shut the door to the cabin. When I heard it slam I jumped back up and emptied the other four chambers of my Colt at it fast as I could, making a diamond chest-high on the planks.

After reloading, I slipped my left arm out of my jacket and tore away my shirt. The ball had passed through the flesh of the underside, not touching the bone, and although I was bleeding like a stuck hog it wasn't a serious wound. I wrapped the torn sleeve around my arm, sloppy but quick, then struggled back into my jacket and returned my attention to the cabin. They had managed to throw the stove out the door, where it lay on its side. Some of the burning embers had spilled out of it and were scorching Dan Bingham's outstretched arm.

"Who are you?" someone yelled from the cabin. "What do you want?"

"Federal officers," I shouted back, playing it as I went. "We have a writ for the arrest of William Towerly. Send him out and nobody else will die. Throw down your guns, because you're surrounded."

There followed a lot of quick talking inside the cabin, and finally Towerly shouted, "Bullshit! There's not more than two of them out there!"

"Time's up!" I shouted. "Come out or we're coming in."

"Don't shoot, I'm coming out," Doug Bingham called, and threw the revolver out the door. "I'm sorry, Bill, but I'm not going to swing for you. I didn't have any part in killing that federal marshal at Fort Smith." Hands high in the air, one sleeve dripping blood, he stepped over the body of his fallen brother and walked toward me.

"I'll see you in hell first," Towerly called, and shot him square in the back. The force of the rifle blast lifted him out of his boots and threw him on the ground, face forward, with a blossom of red spreading around him.

Bingham was hardly on the ground when I sent a round through the doorway. Towerly yelped and the Winchester clattered to the floor. I emptied the revolver as he retreated into the darkness.

I reloaded and waited. Nothing seemed to be stirring inside. After fifteen minutes of silence I began to think I might have killed Towerly with that one shot. Cautiously, I edged my way around the stump, sidled along the wall of the cabin to the doorway, and peered in. There was a lot of blood on the floor where I had winged Towerly, but the cabin was empty.

I slumped against the doorway. It was impossible. There was no way out. He was trapped. And yet, Towerly was gone. I could feel my fever coming back with a vengeance now, creeping up my spine and down my sides. My ears were ringing. What kind of demon was he, to disappear at will? I walked over to Doug Bingham, kicked him face-up with the toe of my boot, and was surprised to find him alive.

"It's so cold," he said.

I threw my coat over him and knelt down. Blood was foaming around his lips and there was a horrible gurgling sound with every breath he took. Lung-shot. It was not good.

"I am dying," he said.

"Yes."

"Daniel is dead."

"Yes."

"We made a poor fight of it."

"Not so poor," I said, indicating my arm. He smiled.

"I want you to send word of our death to our father. He has a farm at Jimtown by the Kansas border, near Baxter Springs. He will want to fetch our bodies home. He is a decent farmer and a good Methodist and I am heartily sorry for the trouble we have caused. Will you do that?"

"Yes, if you will tell me where you sold my horse."

Bingham looked confused a moment, then studied my face.

"You are the kid from Potter's Station. We should have killed you when we took the horse. It was our end that we did not."

"Where is my horse?"

"McAlester's Store. We sold him to a trader named Boudinot . . . Water. May I have some cool water, please?"

By the time I had fetched some from the stream, he was gone.

I was too damned tired to dig graves. The fever was raging now; I was seeing double, and my arm was beginning to throb. I dragged the bodies over to one side of the yard and laid them out side-by-side. Then I went inside the cabin to find a blanket to throw over them. There were a couple wadded over a pallet in the corner, and when I snatched them up I discovered an Indian girl hiding beneath.

She was not more than twenty, with bronze skin and almond eyes and long black hair. She wore a soiled beaded dress, torn from one shoulder, and no shoes. Her legs, folded beneath her, were long and slim. Around one ankle was a manacle. She was chained to a bolt in the wall. She held the shoulder of her dress up and looked searchingly at me.

"I'm not going to hurt you," I said.

She nodded.

"Where did Towerly go?"

She indicated a corner of the cabin where a couple of boards leaned against the wall. I moved the boards to one side, revealing a hole big enough for a man to duck through. It opened into a cavern in the side of the cliff, and from deep within I could hear the gurgling of water—the stream that ran along the floor of the canyon.

"He is gone," she said. "The passage leads to an exit on the far hillside. He is wounded, shot in the leg. But I believe he will live."

I had been wrong; the shack was the perfect hideout, complete with an escape route. Towerly had apparently kept this hole card from the Binghams, and killed the younger brother to buy time for his escape. If it had not been for the passageway, my plan to flush Towerly out would have worked. It was too late to follow him; he'd had plenty of time to clear out. Besides, I was unsteady on my feet.

"Thank you, Marshal," the girl said. "You have rescued me from the man that killed my sister and brother-in-law. I was visiting when the man Towerly came in the night. I have been here for more than a week, cooking and . . . pleasing him. But he was tiring of me and my days were not long. I only wish he had stayed and fought like a man, so that you could have killed him."

"Where is the key to the lock?"

"With Towerly."

"I will have to shoot away the chain, then. Cover yourself with the blankets."

I shot the chain away about six inches away from her ankle, afraid to aim any closer because of my wavering vision. The report brought dust down from the roof of the shack. The girl got slowly to her feet.

"You are a great warrior," she said. She touched the blood-soaked bandage over my arm, then brushed her hand against my cheek. "You are also very sick with the fever."

Things went black, as if somebody had pulled a bag over my head.

Twelve

I DON'T REMEMBER MUCH about my first week with Angelina because I was more out of this life than in it. She got me to her parents' home in the Winding Stair Mountains by tying me on one of the Binghams' horses, and leading me on the spotted pony that Towerly had taken from her brother-in-law. She also had the savvy to collect the Binghams' guns and other prizes and pack them out on the other horse, reckoning, as she told me later, that I had rightly won them as spoils of war. She doctored me up with poultices on the way, until the village medicine man could get down to some real business when she got me home.

She sat beside me through that long week, having first bathed me and dressed my wound, and having tucked me unshucked, so to speak, beneath a magnificent pile of Indian quilts. She mopped the sweat from my brow and fed me broth, all the while talking about herself and her family, singing songs, and telling stories. The songs were in Choctaw and were offered to call the attention of the Great Spirit to my plight—pneumonia deep in the lungs. The rest of the time she spoke English, having polished it at the New Hope Academy for Girls at Scullyville. During the day I drifted between unconsciousness and delirium, and the stories she told were the thread which kept me from floating away forever.

"There was darkness over all the earth," the gentle voice would murmur through the fog, and I would believe it was my Mama telling a story from the Bible. Except the story was always a little different. "Our mystery men searched for the daylight a long time, and the entire nation despaired of ever seeing it, until at last a light was seen in the north. There was great rejoicing. But the light was discovered to be great mountains of water, which enveloped the earth, killing all, except a few families whom the Great Spirit had instructed to build a raft, upon which they were saved."

One story would end and another would begin: "The Choctaw people believe all of our spirits live on in a future state. After death, each spirit must cross a great distance toward the west, toward paradise. In the delightful hunting grounds there is neither pain nor sickness, it is always daylight and forever summer, and there is continual feasting, dancing, and rejoicing. People never grow old but stay young forever, and enjoy always the youthful pleasures.

"But to reach the delightful hunting grounds, our spirits must cross a great ravine, at the bottom of which is a fearsome river. Over the ravine is a very long and slippery pine log, stripped of all its bark, stretching from one side to the other. On the far side of the ravine are six warriors, holding stones, which they throw at each spirit when it is in the middle of the log. The wicked ones see the stones and try to dodge them, but always fall from the log thousands of feet to the river below, which stinks with dead fish and animals. There, the wicked are always hungry but have nothing to eat, are always sick but never die. There is continual misery. But the good do not see the rocks, they do not flinch, and they cross the log safely to the rejoicing of their grandfathers."

At other times, Angelina would talk of her family, and how soldiers had forced them from their ancestral home in Mississippi to their present home in Indian Territory. She described the brutal march and their first winters in the new land. She told of how her father, John Reed—who was half white—was full of bitterness against the federal government, and how he fought with the Cherokee Stand Watie during the unpleasantness.

I didn't know where I was. But the stories, repeated over and over, seeped into my brain and became my memories. The nights were worse, and often I would dream that I was in the grave with Pa and Frank. Sometimes I was in the basement of the Fort Smith jail, or walking up the steps to the gallows where the hangman, George Maledon, was waiting with his good Kentucky ropes at the top. Once, I dreamed I was back at the shack where the shoot-out took place, only I was crossing unarmed over a big log stretched across the box canyon, with Towerly shooting at me. I fell, but never hit the ground.

Then I woke one morning and the fever was gone.

Angelina was sitting beside me, and she smiled and leaned over and kissed me. I was weak and my chest still rattled, but I felt wonderfully cool and relaxed. Without saying a word, she slipped out of her dress. She was beautiful, an Indian angel, with her long dark hair swept behind her and her body so long and brown. She got into bed so gracefully it was like she was lowering herself into a pool of water, and the places where I touched her were silky. It being my first time, I reckoned I ought to try to get on top, but she shook her head and indicated I should just lie back. It was slow and sweet and better than I ever imagined it could be. It didn't seem a bit sinful either, although my poor old Mama would have died on the spot had she seen. We didn't tell Angelina's folks either. And I reckon I was in love with Angelina, because I didn't think of Jane until long after.

When we had finished and were resting together, Angelina asked:

"What is your name?"

I told her, but dropped the "Sammy" from the front of my name because I thought it sounded childish.

"I have something for you, Cole Dalton," she said, and laid a little leather bag on my chest. The beaded bag was hung from long leather strings, and she tied the laces around my neck. "This is a charm to protect you from mortal wounds," she said.

"What's in it?" I asked.

"Things that work together for you," she said. "My grandmother showed me how to make the charms before she died. But you must never open it to find out or the charm will not work."

The Reed family (like many Choctaw, they had taken white names since before the eastern removal) lived in a two-story log home situated on a few thousand acres of land used for lumber and cotton. The valley itself was called Reed's Valley, and several families formed the community, which boasted its own school and meetinghouse. I became well acquainted with the Reeds during my long recuperation, being somewhat of a hero because I had rescued Angelina from the murderous Bloody Bill Towerly. If they wondered about my age, they did not ask.

One of the hands was sent to Potter's Station to find Boudinot, the trader, and secure the return of Cimarron. Boudinot had sold my horse to a farmer named Madison who lived near Kiamichi. Madison was reluctant to part with Cimarron, but was eventually persuaded in exchange for both Bingham horses. Cimarron was returned to me shortly before Christmas. My own saddle was never found, nor was Frank's L. C. Smith shotgun the thieves had taken.

I was recovered enough to ride by about the second week of the new year, but a natural calamity prevented my leaving. After the snow that had fallen while I was lost in the wilderness, there were a few weeks of clement weather and it seemed that winter would end soon. On the day the Big Blizzard hit—January 12—we were working outside in our shirtsleeves. I was helping some of the hands mend fences in the northern sections. The air was still, not a breath of wind, and the first sign we had that something was wrong was that our horses began to stamp and cry. Cimarron put his head down and butted me on the side, as if urging me to seek shelter. That's when I noticed an angry wall of clouds bearing down on us from the northwest. Our hair stood on end as the temperature dropped twenty degrees in three minutes. We mounted and set out for the main house, but before we reached it the storm overtook like a wave crashing to the shore. The snow was so thick and so driven by the fierce wind that I could not see Cimarron's head in front of me, much less distinguish any landmarks about us. Fortunately, the horses could navigate better than we could under such conditions, and they soon led us to the stables at the main house.

I counted myself lucky to make it back. Angelina was worried about her brother and the other children in the little schoolhouse a half mile away. Surely the storm would slacken enough so their parents could get them, I said. I was wrong. If anything, the storm gained in fury as darkness fell, and the temperature dropped below zero. The schoolhouse was drafty and poorly heated, and considering how warm it had been earlier in the day, none of the children would have the proper clothing for such conditions. It was possible they would freeze to death if they stayed in the schoolhouse, and certain if they were to leave the school and become lost in the blizzard. Angelina was all for setting out herself with food and blankets, but I tried to discourage her. The only way I could convince her to stay put was to volunteer to lead a party to the school. She said that was foolish, that I had almost died from pneumonia, but I said I was fine and insisted on doing it. You see, the burden of being a hero was pressing down pretty heavy on my shoulders about then. Of course, she was quite right in saying I shouldn't risk getting sick again, but that was not what folks expected of me. I determined not to disappoint them, but I was determined not to freeze to death out there, either.

"Does your father have a compass?" I asked.

"Yes, one used for survey work," Angelina said.

"Fetch it for me, please," I said. "We'll also need a wagon, to fetch the children back here. Load up plenty of blankets so they can have some protection on the ride back, and send some hot food from the kitchen."

The main problem with navigation in a blizzard is that without landmarks, one can't keep to a straight line, but tends to list one way or the other, making a wide circle. The school was due east on the road from the main house. By making our way to the road and then setting a course by the compass—and being careful never to waver from it—we should find the school.

Angelina wanted to ride with me on the wagon, but her father would not allow it, and sent Livingston, his foreman, instead. We set off in the blizzard from the road in front of the main house, with Livingston driving the team and me holding the compass on my lap. We often had to stop and shovel our way through drifts to allow the wagon to pass, and a few times we lost the road and had to dig for several yards on either side to find it again. Blinded by the snow, we almost passed the school, but Livingston recognized the gate out front and we turned into the yard.

The teacher and the children were huddled around the potbellied stove, which was fueled by desks and chairs that had been reduced to kindling; the last of the coal had given out an hour before. Miss Poplar, the teacher, had kept the children together and not let any of them strike out for home on their own, and she had kept them busy singing songs and telling stories. We were relieved to find seven-year-old Isaac Reed among them.

I was shocked to learn from the watch on Miss Poplar's locket that it was nigh on eight o'clock at night. It had taken us two hours to reach the school, and still the storm howled outside.

Miss Poplar must have been twenty-five or twenty-six. She was bright and had some sand, and she was the first teacher I ever met that I liked.

We fed the children first, and Miss Poplar wrote a note on a slate and left it by the front door telling that we had struck out for the Reed place to spend the night. She quickly loaded the children into the back of the wagon and threw the robes and blankets over them to protect them from the wind. It was somewhat easier going on the way back, since the storm had not completely covered the trail that we had broken. Still, I kept a close eye on the compass. We pulled up to the big oaks in front of the main house a little after nine o'clock, according to Miss Poplar's watch.

We all piled into the house while some of the hands put up the wagon, finding their way by using lines tied from the stables to the house. I was damned cold and bone-tired, but I never did get sick, so I guess the charm hung around my neck was working. Angelina hugged me, and my position as a hero was secure. Only, I didn't feel so good the next morning when we learned that the Ward sisters, who had had permission to leave school early that day to help their mother with the chores because she'd just had a new baby, had not made it home yet when the storm struck. They were found beneath the snow, huddled together in a field just a few dozen yards from a neighboring farmhouse. Both had frozen to death. Sally, the ten-year-old, was found without a coat. She had taken it off and wrapped it around her little sister in an attempt to save her.

Anything I had done seemed a trifle small.

But that's the story of how I came to stay on with the Reed family, when I had really intended to set out for home once I had Cimarron back. I hadn't heard a word about my brothers or whether Towerly had ever been captured. March brought another round of bad weather, and travel was just about impossible clear into April. By spring, I had become such a fixture around the place that Angelina's father had asked me to stay on because of the way I could handle a gun. It wasn't all that unusual in those days for successful Indian farmers and ranchers to hire white gunmen, because the federal government's laws protected whites and ignored anything done to an Indian.

It was the kind of job I had set out to find when I left Coffeyville the year before, so I took it. I had a place to sleep in a cabin not far from the main house, all I wanted to eat, and a little money besides. There wasn't much trouble—well, not much trouble I couldn't handle just by pulling back my coat enough to reveal the butt of my Colt. It was pleasant work, mostly. And I was fond of Angelina. She would often sneak out of the big house and come see me late at night. She seemed to know the right time to avoid making babies. It was somewhat of an awkward situation; her father asked me every so often whether I intended to marry the girl. I'd say I was too young. He would say that seventeen was old enough to start a family, but I never bothered to correct him about my age. Thing was, I wasn't sure I wanted to marry Angelina; she was beautiful all right and I even believed I loved her at times, but it turned out I couldn't ever get Jane completely out of my mind. Then there was the schoolteacher, Miss Poplar, and the picnic lunches we sometimes shared down by the creek.

I sat down several times during my months in Reed's Valley and started to write my old Mama a letter, but I never could figure how to start it without getting myself into a spot I couldn't explain: why I ran off, how I'd killed the Bingham brothers, or why I was living in the Choctaw Nation with an eighteen-year-old girl by the name of Angelina Reed.

Finally I worked up enough courage to write a little note saying I was in good health and working on a fine farm in the Choctaw Nation. I left out all the stuff about Frank's murder and me nearly freezing in the wilderness and the Bingham shoot-out and Angelina and such, and just said I'd be coming back home soon. I posted it at Potter's Station.

The letter came back after a few weeks. A note scrawled on the envelope by the postmaster said the Daltons had moved and left no forwarding address.

Thirteen

I LEFT REED'S VALLEY in the spring of the following year, after Angelina found the schoolteacher and me together in the hayloft. It was probably for the best. Although I had many adventures during my months as police officer for Reed's Valley, I had brothers somewhere and the bastard William Towerly was still on the loose. The scene in the hayloft set me upon the trail once more.

This time, I had little trouble picking my way through the Choctaw Nation. Not only was I starting out in fair weather, but the Frisco had just finished carving a railway across the mountains, from Fort Smith to Paris, Texas. I reckoned my best bet to meet up with members of my family was to follow the railway to Fort Smith, where I could inquire at the U.S. Marshal's Office as to the whereabouts of my brothers.

I approached Wister Junction on the Frisco the evening of my second day on the trail. It was a wide-open boomtown with bare wood buildings and mud streets. People were swarming everywhere like ants. Most of them were white people, too. It was still illegal to homestead in the Nations, but the Dawes Commission had allowed Indians to *lease* their allotments to whites. Now Wister Junction, which had been nothing but a wide spot in the trail the year before, was choked with mud and merchants and drunks, and the rest that came with civilization.

Cimarron and I made our way to a place that advertised hot meals and private rooms. I was in no humor to sleep on the ground again, especially since I had a little change in my pockets from the work I did in Reed's Valley. I put Cimarron up in a stable across the street, then strode back across the sea of mud to the ramshackle hotel. It was unpainted, like the rest of the town.

The bottom floor of the hotel was mostly a saloon, with a bar and a long brass rail and several felt-covered tables. Cowboys were drinking and playing faro or poker. I hadn't been in many saloons—there had been none in Coffeyville or Reed's Valley—and I reckon I gawked a bit as I walked across to the bar to ask for a room. A fat man at one of the tables glared at me over the top of his cards and demanded, "What are you lookin' at?"

"Nothing," I replied, and meant it.

I got me a room for a dollar, and after I had paid, the man behind the bar motioned to my Colt and said, "Sorry, mister, but you're going to have to stow that. We don't allow no shootin' trouble around here."

I unbuckled the rig and wrapped the belt several times over the holster to make a neat package to slip into the saddle wallet. The bartender stopped my hand and looked curiously at the beadwork on the holster and the belt.

"Say, where did you get this?" he asked. "This is mighty fancy work. Is it Cherokee?"

"It's Choctaw," I said. "A friend made it."

The fat man watched me climb the stairs. Without my gun, I felt like I was stripped down to my underwear.

In the room, I poured some water in the basin and pulled off my buckskin shirt to wash the dust off. There was a mirror behind the basin, and I stopped lathering long enough to study my reflection. It was like looking at one of my brothers, except my hair was long. It nearly touched my shoulders. The baby fat had gone and been replaced by the same long jawline and cheekbones, the same light blue eyes. My normally fair skin was ruddy from the elements, and my sandy hair covered the tops of the ears and hung over my collar in back. A beard of the same color was coming in, and I ran a hand over the fuzz to satisfy myself it was real.

Downstairs, I ordered a steak and sat at one of the tables sipping a glass of milk while waiting for it. I had not yet developed a taste for beer, and whiskey made me sick to my stomach.

The door opened and an Indian stumbled in and fell against the bar, asking for whiskey. His eyes were wild and his clothes looked as if he had been lying in the street.

"We can't serve Indians in here," the bartender said, wiping down a glass. "It's against the law. This saloon is for white folks only."

The Indian began to beg.

"Get him out of here!" bellowed the fat man who had given me such a wicked look when I first came. "Throw his ass out or I'll do it for you!"

The bartender came around the bar, but not quick enough for the fat man, who got up and kicked the poor Indian back outside. He kicked him so hard I was afraid he may have broke some ribs.

"Control yourself, Lafe," the bartender said.

"You control yourself," the fat man—Lafe—said. "I don't have to drink with no damn dirty stinking redskins in the room. Injuns killed my folks and I can't tolerate the sight of 'em."

"It was the Cheyenne that killed your folks," the bartender said.

"They're all the same to me," Lafe said, and he was looking at me when he said it.

I ignored him at first. My food had come and I was busy working on my meat and potatoes. But then Lafe walked over to where I sat and stood there, holding his hat with both hands in front of him. He began bouncing the table with his knee, easy at first but harder as I continued to ignore him.

"Is there something I could do for you, mister?" I finally asked.

"You can leave," he hissed, placing his hat down on the table. "Take your stinking Indian-beaded gun belt and your long hair and your buckskins and get the hell out of here. I don't like you and I don't want you in the room while I'm drinkin'."

"I'll leave just as soon as I'm finished with my steak," I said.

He bounced the table again, hard, and I had to grab for the milk to keep it from toppling over. Some of the milk sloshed out of the top of the glass, and a few big drops hit his hat. The hat was so dirty and sweat-stained that you could hardly tell where the milk hit. But Lafe began raising Cain.

"Did you see that?" he screeched. "The kid poured milk on my hat. Just up and poured milk on my hat. What is that, a Choctaw trick? A dirty Choctaw trick? I'll bet they call you the Choctaw Kid, don't they? Well, kid, it's about time someone learned you some manners."

"Take it outside, Lafe," the bartender said.

"Oh, I'd be glad to take it outside," the fat man said. "What do you say, Indian-lover? You want to go outside? You want to show me some more dirty Choctaw tricks?"

The man outweighed me by at least sixty pounds, and although he was fat there seemed to be some muscle underneath. His eyes were dark and burning and his breath was foul. My gun was in my saddlebag upstairs. I didn't want trouble.

"Look, mister," I said, "I don't know what you've got against me, but I'm sorry for whatever it is. Let's just forget it, okay? Go back to your table and I'll buy you a drink."

"Forget it, he says, after ruining my hat," Lafe shouted. "Buy you a drink, he says, after insulting the memory of my folks. What a cocky little runt!"

I had had enough.

"Stick it up your arse," I said, pushing away from the table. I meant to retrieve my Colt from upstairs and meet Lafe outside, but in my haste to get my gun I made the mistake of turning my back for a second.

He hit me in the back of the head with his fist and I fell to the floor. He followed that up with a kick that knocked the breath out of me and rolled me toward the door. I stumbled to my hands and knees and he caught me with a roundhouse on the nose. Lights exploded inside my head like someone had fired a shotgun point-blank, and I heard the *pop!* as the gristle in my nose was rearranged. I crashed backwards through the door and landed on my back in the mud, gasping for breath through my open mouth.

I was still there when the bartender appeared in the doorway and set my things outside.

"I'm the one getting kicked out?" I asked, wiping blood from my upper lip. My nose was all busted up and I couldn't get any air through it, so my voice sounded awfully peculiar, as if I had the worst cold of my life.

"Sorry," he said, "but you seen what Lafe Anderson can do."

"What about my money?"

"Somebody's gotta pay for the door."

I carried my things—saddlebags, coat, hat—over to the trough in front of the livery stable, where I cleaned myself up a bit.

"Too much whiskey," said the livery man, who had come outside to see what all the commotion was about.

"Milk," I said, washing the blood off. "I was drinking milk."

"Your nose is busted," he said. "You better go see the doc if you don't want it to be flattened like that permanent."

I put my hat on. It was black and had beadwork around the sweatband to match the gun belt. Then I took my rig out of the saddle bag, buckled it on, and tied the holster down to my leg. I drew the Colt a few times to make sure everything was right.

"Son, you better not be thinking about calling Lafe Anderson out," the livery man said. "He'll kill you."

"That's a possibility," I said. I walked out to the middle of the street and began calling his name. "There's an Indian-lover out here that wants to see you, and you better bring your gun."

In a few seconds Lafe appeared, leaning against the door frame. "I think you better go home to your Mama," he said and laughed.

"Did the Cheyenne lie with yours before they took her scalp?"

He stopped laughing and stared at me for a few seconds, breathing heavy. Then he fetched his gun and stepped outside. He carried a Remington holstered butt-first on his left hip. While he was inside I had drawn back, and now stood about fifty feet down the street.

"You're gonna regret ever sayin' anything about my Mama."

It was well past sundown, but there was a three-quarter moon in the sky and plenty of light spilling from the hotel windows, so I could see Lafe pretty good. I had the advantage because I was dressed in dark clothes and was standing in a darker section of the street, away from the hotel windows, while Lafe was wearing a white shirt. He was so mad, though, I doubt if he thought of it.

The livery man had hid inside the stable, and it was just me and Lafe on that mud street. There were folks watching from the windows of the hotel and the saloons. I just stood there with my arm loose at my side, waiting for him to make a move. He crabbed out into the center of the street with his hand hovering over his gun-butt, and his hand was shaking—from rage, I think. Then he stopped and just stood there like a statue. I knew he was trying to think something up, because anybody that would clobber you from behind and kick you in the ribs and bust your nose while you were down, would not be looking for a fair fight.

"Watch out for that shotgun," Lafe said and pointed awkwardly with his left hand, trying to make me turn. I resisted the urge and saw instead Lafe's hand flash down for his pistol. He was terribly slow, so I had plenty of time to pick my shot. I hit him in the right shoulder. The Remington fell, unfired, from his grip.

Then I whirled just to make sure there wasn't somebody behind me on the board sidewalk, and damned if I wasn't looking down the twin bores of a shotgun with the hammers back. I sprang as far as I could to the right just as the barrels roared, and I felt something hot pass through my right calf. I was firing by the time I hit the mud, and I was so damned surprised by the shotgun that I was shooting at it instead of the man holding it. I broke the stock with one round and bounced a ball off the receiver with another, and the man—who was one of the ones Lafe had been drinking and playing faro with—wasted no time scrambling back inside a doorway for cover.

I got up and turned my attention back to Lafe, who was holding his shoulder and clenching his teeth. No more than five seconds had gone by since he had drawn, and he was just now getting around to reaching down for the Remington with his good hand. I sent a round into the mud near the gun and he drew his hand back quick.

"Get it over with," he said. "Kill me."

"You're not worth the trouble," I said. "I just aim to make you stop kicking people like you do."

I aimed free-hand and blew his right kneecap off, and Lafe hit the mud screaming. It was my last round. As I was ejecting the spent shells from the gun I felt something cold being pressed beneath my hair, and my guts turned to ice water. With all the screaming Lafe had been doing, I hadn't heard anyone behind me.

"Drop the gun and put your hands in the air slow," the man behind me said. "You're under arrest."

It was a bad situation. I was holding an empty gun.

I dropped the Colt to the mud and slowly raised my arms.

"It was a fair fight," I said over my shoulder. "I could have killed him, but I didn't. Why are you arresting me?"

"Because my name is Rafe Anderson," he spat. "I'm the law in this town and you just crippled my little brother." He cracked the butt of the gun against my head and I sank to my knees.

Last thing I heard before I lost consciousness was somebody in front of the hotel asking, "Who the hell is that?" and the bartender replying, "Why, don't you know him? That's the Choctaw Kid."

Rafe Anderson, a special agent employed by the railroad to discourage thievery at Wister Junction, locked me in an iron cage at the depot. When I came to, Anderson kept asking me questions about who I was and what I was doing at the junction, but I didn't reckon there was any advantage in being conversational, so I just kept my mouth shut. By and by a wire was sent to Fort Smith requesting a deputy to come fetch "the Choctaw Kid" for trial on charges of assault with intent to kill. It appeared I was going to see the basement of Parker's courthouse from the inside at long last.

The cage was about six feet by six feet, not even enough room to lie down in, and it was the kind that riding deputies sometimes put on the back of a wagon to transport dangerous prisoners. Anderson fed me no food and little water, and I was forced to relieve myself in a bucket, but I never complained—I didn't want to give Anderson the pleasure. In fact, I never said anything at all, not even when the doc came and plucked the buckshot out of my calf and tried to reshape my nose. At least he got it to where I could breathe out of it again. A couple of days later the deputies arrived from Fort Smith to take me away, and when they walked into the depot to inspect me I said the first thing that came into my mind.

"I'll be a sonuvabitch," I said.

The deputies were Bob and Grat.

Fourteen

GRAT STOOD THERE with his hands on his hips and his head cocked to one side, as if he were trying to recall where he'd seen me before. But Bob knew. He knelt on one knee and peered in through the bars and whispered, "Samuel, is that you?"

I winked.

"I'll be a sonuvabitch too," Bob said, low so that Anderson couldn't hear. He smiled, touched a finger to his lips, then stood up and turned to Anderson. "Get him outta there so we can question him," he said.

"Won't tell you nothin'," Anderson said, picking his nose. "Besides, all you need to do is take him back to Fort Smith so Parker can lock him up."

"It ain't quite that simple," Bob said. Grat looked puzzled and started to say something, but Bob shut him up with a look. "The thing here is that you're just a special agent for the railroad. We, as deputy U.S. marshals, must do our own investigation to determine if there is just cause to haul the Choctaw Kid in."

"Of course there's cause," Anderson snorted. "He shot my brother, didn't he? Winged him first, then walked over and shot off his knee-cap."

"Yes, that would be cause," Bob allowed. "If, of course, it wasn't self-defense. Was your brother Lafe wearing a gun?"

"Of course he had a gun," Anderson fumed. "The Kid called him out."

"Then it was a fair fight."

"The hell it was!" Anderson shouted. "What the hell are you up to, Dalton? Why are you on the Kid's side of things? The sonuvabitch shot my brother. He ought to rot in jail for it, and that's all there is to it."

"You want to unlock him now?" Bob asked.

Anderson cussed under his breath, but took the keys from their peg on the wall and worked the big padlock holding the cage shut. The door fell open with a crash, and I came out and started to stretch.

"Not so fast, Kid," Bob said. "Just take it easy. Turn around and put your hands behind you."

"What for?" I asked.

"Never mind what for," Grat said, punching me on the shoulder. "Just do it." I think Grat was catching on.

I turned around and Bob clamped a pair of handcuffs over my wrist, but didn't cinch them up tight enough to hurt me.

"Do you have his outfit?" Bob asked.

"Yeah," Anderson said. "His gun and saddle wallets are over there in that cabinet. His horse is still at the livery stable. I reckoned we would auction it off to pay for my brother's doctor bills."

"We'll need his gun and things for evidence," Bob said. Anderson took my things from the drawer and handed them over to Grat. "And about the horse," Bob said, "we'll just have to see about that."

"What do you mean?"

"I mean we'll see," Bob said. "We'll take it back to Smith with us, and if the judge says we can sell it, we'll wire you the money."

"Sure you will," Anderson said. "I've heard about you Daltons. Don't think you're fooling me for a minute."

Bob tipped his hat at the door of the depot office.

After we had cleared the depot we stopped. Bob took the handcuffs off.

"You really Samuel?" Grat asked.

"I'm not Stonewall Jackson," I said, rubbing my wrists. "Damn, it's good to see you two." I grabbed Bob's hand and squeezed it hard, then slapped Grat on the shoulder.

"Everybody thought you were dead," Bob said. "The last we heard, Jim Cole said you took off after Towerly in the Bottoms. We figured you either got yourself shot to death or you froze during the blizzard."

"I came close on both counts," I said.

"Where the hell did you get that nickname?" Grat asked.

"Kind of a long story," I said.

"Damn, you've grown up," Bob went on. "Got your nose busted. I'll bet Lafe Anderson did that to you. Hell, I would have shot him, too. But listen: I don't want you tell anybody what your real name is, at least not for awhile. It's better if you're just known as the Choctaw Kid

—damn, I like that handle—because we don't want numbnuts or his brother tracking you down after we beat this writ. Remember, you're our prisoner for now. Okay?"

"You bet."

I started to ask about Mama and the rest of the family. Bob said they were all fine, but told me to save the chatting until after we got well away from Wister Junction.

Bob paid the livery man for putting up Cimarron, and made sure all my tack was still there. Grat stayed with me while I saddled Cimarron up. Bob went and chatted with the bartender at the hotel first, then paid a visit to Lafe Anderson to "take his statement." He left word for Rafe Anderson that he concluded the Choctaw Kid had acted in self-defense, but would take the Kid back to Smith to settle it up with Parker's court.

We rode out of town together. I clasped my hands behind my back like they were cuffed, but as soon as we were out of sight of the city limits I didn't have to pretend. Grat handed me my rig and I strapped it on. He also had my hat. I brushed the dried mud from it and stuck it on my head.

"So," I said, adjusting my hat. "Tell me why my letters to Mama came back."

Things never got any better for Mama at Coffeyville, Bob said. Not only was it hard to make a living, but since Bob had shot Charlie Montgomery over Minnie Johnson (the name conjured a vision of her taking her nightclothes off on the edge of my bed), things had gotten a little hot around Coffeyville. For a time, Mama and the younger children moved back to Cass County, Missouri, but when the government decided to open up the Unassigned Oklahoma Lands for homesteading, Ben and the other boys came back from California to stake a claim. A Dalton never could resist an offer of something for nothing. They made the run on April 22, 1889, got a place near Kingfisher, on the edge of the Cheyenne-Arapaho Reservation, and she had lived there since with some of the older boys. Since Bill had gotten interested in politics, he stayed on in California, aiming to run for a seat in the state legislature.

Meanwhile, Grat had taken Frank's job as a riding deputy for Parker and had hired Bob and Emmett as his posse men. They had also served on the tribal police force in Pawhuska—with Bob as chief—but that ended when some nasty rumors started circulating that they headed up a horse-stealing ring. Pawhuska kicked them out with back wages coming. Then they went to work for the Cherokees, but Bob wounded a young Indian boy in a case of mistaken identity. They also had taken oaths as deputy marshals from the Wichita court, but that got queered when they were accused of selling liquor to the Osage on Candy Creek. That left their deputy jobs as their only means of support. But they had been summoned back to Fort Smith after an incident in Tulsa Town during which Grat got seriously drunk and balanced an apple on the head of a Negro kid, ordering him to stand still while he shot it off.

"Just like William Tell," I said, but Grat had never heard of him. It's a shame that what may have been Grat's only original thought had been done better by somebody a couple of hundred years earlier, and with an arrow instead of a bullet.

"So," Bob said, "word got back to Marshal Yoes about Grat's stunt. He wired us to come back to Smith, but to stop at Wister Junction and pick up a prisoner on the way. And here we are, together again."

Bob had a way of relating things that made them sound not so bad. Although it was obvious both of them were down on their luck—their clothes were somewhat ratty and neither looked like they had had a good bath or a visit to the barber in weeks—Bob acted cheerful during the telling, as if it were the most natural thing in the world to shoot somebody by mistake, get charged with introducing liquor to the Indians, and blow apples off some innocent Negro kid's head.

"And I thought I had some troubles," I said, and boiled down my adventures after setting out in the Bottoms. Grat said he knew the Binghams, and that people ought to thank me for killing them. I left out a lot about Angelina, but described Reed's Valley pretty well. When I had finished my story, I asked, "You don't know if Towerly ever got his, do you? Did anyone ever bring him down?"

"Don't know," Bob said nonchalantly. "But I tell you what, if it had been me in the Bottoms that day, it would be Towerly six feet under instead of Frank."

That kind of talk made me mad, but I didn't say anything; Bob's trouble was that he really believed all the lies he told.

"What is that up ahead," Bob said presently, reining his horse to a stop. "Is that a wagon full of nesters?"

"I believe it is," Grat replied. "There's still some whiskey left in that bottle I have in my saddlebags."

"Well, then," Bob said, smiling like a cat, "I think it's time for us to do our duty, Deputy Dalton. Come on, Kid. We'll show you how you make pocket change in the Nations."

We rode up to the wagon and Grat hailed it to a stop, and Bob identified himself as a United States marshal and started asking questions about who they were and where they were going. The man and wife sat on the wagon seat with their three kids peering out behind them. He explained that they were on their way to help homestead a claim staked by an uncle. Grat rode his horse around to the back of the wagon, as if he was inspecting it for contraband. As Bob was lecturing the family on how careful they should be while crossing the Nations, Grat hollered "Whoa, what's this?" and held up a half-full bottle of whiskey, as if he'd plucked it from the back of the wagon.

"Where'd that come from, Henry?" the mousy little woman asked, but the man just gave Bob a knowing look and shushed her.

Bob took the bottle, uncorked it, and took a swallow.

"This is whiskey," he said, wiping his mouth. "Do you know how serious it is bringing whiskey into the Nations? Don't you know it's a federal crime? I'm sorry, ma'am, but I'm going to have to take your husband back to Fort Smith with me for trial."

"Marshal," the man said, and smiled, "I apologize for being so ignorant about these things. Isn't there some way we can settle this so we can be on our way?"

"Well," Bob said, "I reckon there is one way."

"How much?"

"I reckon ten dollars will cover the fine."

"Ten dollars!" the woman gasped.

"Absolutely not," the man said. "That is outrageous."

"Makes no difference to me," Bob said. "You can just tell it to the judge how outrageous it is."

The man sat with the reins in his hands, looking at the horizon. At last he licked his lips and said, "I can see that you're talking perfect sense. I'd be pleased if you'd accept my apology and take my money in payment of the fine." The man dug into his pocket and offered a ten-dollar bill.

Bob took the money and tucked it in his vest.

"Well, that was a wise decision," he said. "It's a smart man that avoids jail. Have a safe trip on out to your new home." Bob tipped his hat as the man flipped the reins, and the wagon started with a jerk.

"I reckon there'll be some fun at Pearl's tonight," Grat said.

Things had changed something fierce since I had seen Fort Smith with Frank. The old ferry across the Arkansas was gone, replaced by a huge metal bridge built by the Missouri Pacific and called the "Helen Gould Bridge" after the wife of the grand mucky-muck of the railroad. In between the rails were planks so that horses and wagons could get across, for a toll.

Once on the Arkansas side I could see that Parker's courthouse had been redone, with an annex nearly as big as the original building added to one end. The porches on either side of the courthouse had been removed, and the brick walls extended upward to form a second story. Bob told me that it was just a jail these days. The basement had been retired after the new cells were added in the annex building. Parker now held court in a new building, three blocks downtown.

But the biggest shock was that the whole town was rigged with electric lights, the first I had ever seen. It was close to sundown when we rode across the bridge, and the lights seemed like magic, floating in the darkness. We turned our horses to the north and proceeded along Front Street, where the cathouses were lit up like Christmas trees. Pearl's place had a big red star on the front, outlined with electric lights and draped with pearls, and that's where we hitched our horses.

Pearl Starr was the daughter of Belle Starr, and her father had been a Younger—Cole Younger, some say. Considering the family tree on my mother's side, that made us cousins, I think. But that didn't seem to bother her or Bob or Grat, the way they pawed each other when we came in. Pearl was by no means a beautiful woman, in fact some might have called her plain, but there was something about her that was striking enough. It may have been the way she held her head or the way she looked you right in the eye, but whatever it was you knew right away she was special.

"Pearl, we want to introduce you to the Choctaw Kid," Bob said, when he had torn himself away.

She put her hand out and said she was pleased to meet any friend of the Daltons. Then she got motherly and touched my nose gently and asked what had happened, and Bob told her about the scrap I'd been in. But he never did let on that I was his brother.

Rafe Anderson had stolen the poke I'd had with me at Wister Junction, so all we had between the three of us was the ten-dollar note that had been lifted from that poor nester. Pearl changed the note and Bob gave me my share. He told me to pick out a two-dollar whore and save the rest for drinking.

The residents of Pearl's "boarding house" came in a variety of shades and sizes, and all wore practically nothing as they lounged in the parlor waiting for customers. I felt peculiar around them, because I had only really been with Angelina. So while Bob and Grat ran upstairs with the girls they had picked out, I stayed downstairs and drank coffee and talked to a pretty Mexican girl.

Her name was Maria. She was about my age, maybe a year or two older. She hung on my arm and let the strap of her dress fall down, and she took her time tucking herself back in. After a spell I began to feel right comfortable with her and we went upstairs. It lasted just a few minutes, and I remember laying there feeling the trains shake the walls of the house as they chugged by. Like all houses on the row, the tracks were just outside Pearl's back door.

In the morning Bob and Grat had bad hangovers, but I felt fine. About ten o'clock they worked up enough sand to visit the marshal's office in the new building downtown. I waited outside. They didn't look happy when they came back out, and they weren't wearing their badges.

There wasn't any point in staying on at Fort Smith, and Bob said Emmett was waiting for them at a place just outside Wagoner. I spent my last four bits on the toll to get us across the Missouri Pacific Bridge. Bob shook his head and muttered about how the "goddamn Yankee railroads" couldn't resist an opportunity to bleed the common folk. Once on the other side, we reined to a stop and gave "Parker Town" one last look.

"Boys, we didn't need those badges," Bob said brightly, but it sounded like he was trying to convince himself more than us. "What was it for? Two dollars for every writ served and six cents a mile, and the damned chief marshal gets forty percent of that. Kill somebody resisting arrest and you have to bury them out of your own pocket. Get shot up and you pay your own doctor bills. You know how many deputies have died serving writs for this court?"

I said I didn't know, except for Frank.

"Sixty-five. What could any of them ever show for it besides leaving their women and kids to fend for themselves? Nothing, that's what. Well, I'm damned glad I'm not going to be one of them. There are smarter ways to make a living."

Bob exchanged glances with Grat, then looked at me.

"Samuel," Bob asked, "are you with us?"

Fifteen

WE REACHED THE FARM near Wagoner on the afternoon of the day after we saw Fort Smith for the last time. Emmett was waiting for us. He was sitting on the porch of the farmhouse with his boots up on the rail, playing "The Ballad of Jesse James" on the harmonica.

"Who's that?" Emmett asked, pointing the harmonica at me.

"That's your brother Samuel," Bob said. "He's been down in the Choctaw Nation since he ran away to follow Frank. They call him the Choctaw Kid."

I had always thought my brother Emmett was a little touched, but hoped he would eventually grow out of it. My hopes were dashed when Em, eighteen or so now, accepted this bit of news from Bob without so much as a blink. He went right on playing his harmonica.

After supper, which we shared with the family that worked the farm —my brothers had a network of friends across the Territory that the Pinkertons would envy—Bob called a meeting of us brothers out in the barn. When we had gotten comfortable, Bob asked Emmett how many broncs were out in the corral.

"A dozen," Em replied, "plus a couple of mules."

"Mules?"

"They're fine animals," Em said. "I couldn't resist."

"All right, we'll find some farmer to sell them to," Bob said. "Now, I think the four of us can handle a remuda of at least twenty. We might as well go round up another six or eight broncs. Emmett, where would you say the best pickings are?"

Chills began to play up and down my spine, but I held my tongue. I finally figured out that they had left Em behind to tend to the stolen stock while they took care of their business in Fort Smith.

"Oh, the Taylor place would be good for a couple, and then there's the Pittfield spread," Em said. "Might pay a visit to the Reynolds on the way back."

"What do you say, Grat?"

Grat took a swig out of the jug of moonshine the farmer had given us and wiped his mouth with the back of his hand. He closed one eye and acted like he was studying the situation.

"I say that if we have to drive a bunch of horses to Kansas, we might as well get the most money from our effort," he said. "Let's do it."

Bob walked over and took the jug away from him

"You get this back when we're finished," Bob said. Then he turned to me and asked, "Kid?"

They all turned to look at me.

"I reckon I've gotta hang with my brothers," I said.

"Good," Bob said and slapped me on the back. Then he added, "Of course, we'll just do this one time, to get us back on our feet."

It was a moonlit night, and no work for me and Em to slip a rope halter over a bronc and lead him out, although my heart was up in my throat the whole time. Grat and Bob stood guard while we worked, and if anybody happened to come by they would say they were on the lookout for rustlers, or some such lie. The excuse would work because even though folks might be suspicious, they were known as deputy marshals and who could really argue? But things went smooth and we didn't meet anybody who challenged us. After the night's work, we had brought the count up to seventeen broncs and a pair of mules. Before dawn, we set out for the Kansas line.

They may have been stolen horses, but since they were colts it was just as much work to drive them to sale as if we had owned them. It took us three of the hottest days in the month of July to reach Columbus, Kansas, where Bob knew a stock buyer who wouldn't ask a lot of questions. We had already sold the mules for ten dollars to a Cherokee farmer along the way, and Em was mad because he figured they were worth more, but the rest of us were just glad to be rid of them. The stock buyer paid us thirty dollars a head for the broncs, which was a good price considering we didn't have bills of sale for a one of them. That amounted to more than five hundred dollars we had made for less than a week's work. Em and I got a hundred bucks each, while Bob and Grat split the rest.

We set out for Baxter Springs, about twenty miles southeast, where Bob knew a place we could enjoy our money.

Annie Walker's was a white two-story house with wide porches along the grassy banks of the Spring River, a few miles north of Baxter Springs. It was one of Bob's favorite houses because Annie had been a mistress of the guerrilla Quantrill during the war, and had known Jesse and Frank James personally. While still in her teens, Annie had left a respectable Blue Springs, Missouri physician in favor of a more exciting life. She liked to talk about those days almost as much as the boys enjoyed hearing about them. The first thing I noticed when we hitched our horses out front was the Stars and Bars billowing from the eaves above the front steps.

The girls hung over the porch upstairs and called Bob and Grat's names as we walked up those steps, and inside Annie met both of them with a big kiss. She sent her boy to care for our horses. I was introduced, of course, as the Choctaw Kid. Bob was taken with the idea of keeping my identity secret, since everybody thought Samuel Coleman Dalton was dead. I swept off my hat and said how it was an honor to meet her. Annie was in her forties now, but I could tell she had been one dark-haired beauty in her day.

Bob and Grat went upstairs to bathe with a couple of the girls, and Em just went upstairs to sleep. I was tired, but I needed to take care of my guns first. I laid my Winchester and the Colt on a blanket spread out on the floor, and tore them all the way down until I had all the parts spread out in front of me. I ran a cleaning rod down each bore and used an oiled cloth to wipe down every part. Then I put everything back together and slipped seven shells into the magazine of the Winchester and five into the Colt.

"I used to know somebody else who would take care of his guns before he slept," said Annie, who had watched my progress from her big overstuffed chair.

"Yeah?" I asked. "Who?"

"A friend," she said. "He's now serving twenty-five years in prison up in Minnesota, and carries seventeen bullets in his body."

"Cole Younger," I said.

"Yes," she said. "He was quiet and soft-spoken and a gentleman, just like you. You can see where it got him. You know where it's going to get your brothers."

I gave her a surprised look.

"I know you're a Dalton brother," she said. "You have the blond hair and the blue eyes, true, but that's not what tipped me off; it's how you all act together. Like Cole and Bob and Jim acted together. You're cousins to the Youngers, aren't you?"

I nodded.

"They were better boys than the Jameses were, no matter what Bob thinks," Annie said. "When things got tight in the Hanska Slough after the Northfield Raid, it was Jesse that wanted to leave Bob Younger behind because Bob was slowing them down. It was the Youngers that stayed and shot it out, the Jameses that ran."

I nodded again.

"Honey, I know what old Cole would tell you if he was here," she continued, not unkindly. "He'd say to hang them guns up and go and have you a life. The world has changed since the James-Younger Gang gave the Yankee banks and railroads hell. The world is getting smaller and the lawmen are getting smarter. And it doesn't matter how good you are with a gun, because there's always somebody willing to shoot you in the back for a reward."

"Yes ma'am, ole Cole might tell me that," I said. "But I reckon he would understand after I tell him about how my brothers saved my neck down in Indian Territory."

We stayed at Annie Walker's for most of a week. Bob and Grat went through their money like grease through a goose, but since I didn't drink and went sparingly with the girls, I held on to most of my poke. I rode into Baxter Springs one day and sent Mama forty dollars and an equal amount to Frank's widow, Naomi. I just signed "the boys" to each. That still left me a few dollars to see me through, and I have to admit that where the money came from was beginning to bother me less and less. I reckoned if I had the sand to take the risks, I ought to enjoy the rewards. That made it pretty easy when Bob announced it was time to go down into the Indian Territory and steal some more broncs.

We went as deep as Claremore that second time, and gathered a herd of nearly thirty driving them up to Columbus and selling them to the stock trader as before. The only trouble we had was that a hand recognized Bob and Grat while we were in one of the pastures. We didn't take any ponies that time but lifted a couple on the way back. The idea was to just take one or two from each location, which was not enough for anybody who had any amount of stock to miss right away.

We got more than seven hundred dollars for that second trip, which held us for a few more weeks. Then Bob decided it was time to make a third withdrawal from the Indian Territory; a heist that would bring us enough money to quit rustling for a spell.

Things were tougher that third trip because everybody knew Bob and Grat weren't on the Fort Smith payroll anymore. There was a lot of talk about how they headed up a stock-theft ring. You can't go strutting around in new clothes and buying drinks for everybody without arousing suspicion. Bob never did learn the art of being inconspicuous.

We had just crossed the state line into Baxter Springs with a string of broncs one morning, when we collided with a posse of Cherokees led by Clem Rogers. We were in the middle of town, and the meeting must have been by accident because they looked as surprised as we did. There were eight of them, and when they saw Bob and Grat they drew their pistols and shouted for us to halt. A couple of shots rang out when we didn't. They were shooting into the air to get our attention, not at us— the street was too crowded to turn the encounter into a shoot-out.

It suddenly didn't feel so grand being a horse thief. My heart was pounding so hard that I thought it would leave my chest. It seemed like forever before I got Cimarron turned and going in the opposite direction. Grat was at the head of our string of ponies, and he spurred his horse to the east, toward the river. The horses reared in all directions, which temporarily halted the progress of the posse. Bob and Emmett and I made some time back toward the south, the direction we had come from.

The posse ignored Grat and chased the three of us.

I didn't feel like killing anybody over stolen property, so I just kept my head down and raced along with Bob and Emmett. Bob's horse ran neck-and-neck with Cimarron, but Emmett's nag just wasn't up to it. Em kept dropping further and further back, until after a few miles Bob said, "We have to put an end to this."

It was soon after that we met a farmer on the road into Baxter, and with guns drawn we traded Emmett's tuckered-out mount for the farmer's, saddle and all. The whole exchange didn't take more than a few seconds, and we were on our way once more. Our plan was to run a little further and then double back to a spot near the river where we had made camp with the horses the night before. We figured that's where Grat would be.

But Grat was thinking on his own. After catching a couple of the stolen broncs, he had set out to find us and relieve our tired mounts. His intentions were good, but as usual, his timing was terrible.

Grat, his hands full leading the two ponies, stumbled upon Rogers and the posse as they were examining the horse and saddle that had been left with the farmer. He found himself looking down the bores of eight cocked revolvers. He had no choice but to give up.

Because Grat was arrested across the line in the Territory, he was taken to the jail at Claremore to await transfer to the federal jail at Fort Smith, the same one to which he had taken so many prisoners as Frank's posse man. Meanwhile, according to the newspaper, Clem Rogers sent a wire to the federal prosecutor at Fort Smith.

The wire, sent from Claremore, said, "Bob and Emmett Dalton are stealing horses here by the drove. Grat is here under arrest. Have writ sent here to W. B. Killion, U.S. Marshal, for the arrest of the Daltons."

Sixteen

THE HAIR WAS IN THE BUTTER, all right. Grat was in jail at Fort Smith, and a warrant had been issued for the arrest of Bob and Emmett for horse stealing. The Daltons were now official U.S. government-certified desperadoes. The only thing going for us was that we still had plenty of money and could afford to lay low for a spell until things simmered down. Bob decided the best place to do that would be in the Cookson Hills. I knew a shack at the end of a box canyon that had a built-in escape route through a cave, so that's where we headed.

Bob was downcast about the whole thing, of course, but crazy Emmett had his wanted poster at last and he kept playing "The Ballad of Jesse James" over and over on his harmonica. But we put up with it, because Em was the only one of us three that could cook.

Bob had a lot of time to think while we hid out in the woods, and whenever Bob had time to think, trouble was never far behind. We had been hiding out almost a couple of months when, one evening after supper, Bob pushed himself away from the rough-hewn table and lit a cigar.

"Boys, I am swearing off stock stealing," he said through blue clouds of smoke. "It is altogether too burdensome and the chance of getting caught is too great."

For a moment my heart soared in the hope that we were about to renounce crime for good and take up honest occupations as farmers or ranch hands, but those hopes were dashed the next instant.

"Since it is money we are after," Bob said, "why don't we just steal *it* instead of something we have to change into money later? Holdups will be our main line of work. To do that, boys, we need to put us together a gang."

"Now, there's an idea," Emmett said and clapped his hands.

"I'll be the leader, of course," Bob said, exhaling another column of blue smoke. "We're a little shorthanded with Grat in jail, so we'll need some gang members. Let's see. Emmett, do you reckon your old pards at the XB-Bar Ranch or the Bird Creek would throw in with us?"

"I'm sure old Bill Doolin would," Emmett said. "Maybe Bitter Creek and Blackface Charley, too."

"Good men," Bob said. "After we get formed up we can go break Grat out."

"Hold on," I said, getting up from my chair and holding my hands palm-out. "I know you're my brothers and I owe you for saving my hide from the Andersons back at Wister Junction, and I helped you rustle those ponies, but you're talking armed robbery and jailbreaking here. I don't know if I'm ready for that. Maybe you reckon you don't have much to lose, since you already have warrants out for your arrest, but nobody wants the Choctaw Kid, and I aim to keep it that way."

"Samuel?" Bob asked. He hadn't used my real name in a long spell. "I've been meaning to talk to you about that warrant for assault-with-intent-to-kill back in Fort Smith."

"You took care of that," I said.

"Well, things got a little complicated that morning Marshal Yoes took our badges back. We meant to explain how you shot Anderson up in self-defense, but we never really had the time. I'm afraid that warrant's still good."

We rode out that night toward the XB-Bar and Bird Creek ranches, which butted spreads just north of Tulsa. I can't say I was comfortable about being a wanted criminal helping to form up a gang, but I was downright relieved to get out of that cabin.

Halfway to Tulsa we rode up on a farmhouse and asked the old couple there what they'd charge to share their supper and put us up in the barn for the night. The old man said they weren't in the habit of taking on boarders because of so much wickedness going around, but the old woman allowed as how they would take a chance on us.

"We certainly appreciate your kindness," Bob said after the old woman had muttered a blessing over the food. "We know how hard times are for folks."

"Son, you don't know the half of it," the old man said, spooning potatoes onto his plate. "I haven't been able to keep up with the farm by myself since our boy Johnny died. We've fallen behind—"

"Hush up, Zeke," the wife said. "These boys don't want to listen to our troubles."

"It's the truth, ain't it?" the husband asked, then turned back to Bob. "As I said, we're behind on the mortgage. The banker's coming out in the morning to collect, and since we don't have the money, I reckon we'll lose this farm."

Bob suffered a genuinely pained look.

"I'm sorry to hear that," Bob said, putting down his fork.

"I wish I was young and strong like you," the old man said. "Then I could work my way out of this fix, could get back on my feet again. But I'm just too old and stove-up to start over. This farm is all we got left in the world, and I don't know where we'll go after they take it from us."

"How much do you need?"

"Three hundred and ten dollars," the man said, "but it might as well be a million."

"I don't have no million," Bob said, reaching deep in his suit pocket for his poke, "but I reckon I could go you three hundred and some change."

"Please, we couldn't—" the old man said.

"Don't even think twice about it," Bob said, peeling off the bills and placing them under the salt shaker in the center of the table. "I can't stand the thought of our old mother losing her home, and I'm sure if the situation was reversed—if your Johnny were still here—he'd do the same for us. My brothers and I would be honored if you'd take it."

"I went to sleep prayin' last night for a miracle," the wife said, with tears spilling down her cheeks. "I reckon that the Lord sent one our way."

The wife was still bawling as she walked around the table and hugged each of us in turn, and the old man's eyes were misted up pretty good too. I have to admit mine weren't exactly dry.

"I don't know how we can ever thank you," the old man said, wringing Bob's hand.

"Just be sure to get a receipt," Bob said, "and be sure to tell folks what Bob Dalton and his gang did for you after you were good enough to feed them supper one night."

The next morning we waited down the road a couple miles, and about nine o'clock we hid in the brush while a scowling fat fellow in a black carriage rolled by. He came back thirty minutes later, only this time he was smiling, with his leather valise sitting betwixt his knees.

We pulled our kerchiefs over our faces, and me and Bob rode out in front of him on the road. The fellow saw what was up and tried to turn around, but Emmett was crowding his back. All he succeeded in doing was getting the horse and carriage so crosswise in the road that it wasn't going anywhere.

"Good morning," Bob said cheerfully as he cocked his revolver. "I hope you don't mind poking your hands in the air, 'cause this is a holdup."

"I'm sorry," the business fellow said, "but all I have on me is the cash in my wallet, about ten dollars. You're certainly welcome to it." With that last, he wet his lips and managed a smile.

"Hand it over," Bob said, "but do it slow."

He reached a hand into his jacket pocket and gently withdrew his wallet. He took out a ten-dollar note and held it out. Bob motioned with his Colt and I snatched the money away.

"Now we'd like the rest of it," Bob said.

"I told you, that was it."

Bob shot a hole in the backboard and the fellow cringed.

"It's a sin to lie," Bob said. "Hand over that bag."

The man sighed and slowly handed the bag to me.

"You can't blame me for trying to protect my livelihood."

"Shut up!" Bob commanded.

I tucked the Colt under my left arm as I unlatched the bag and dug inside. There, among the papers, was the wad of bills Bob had given the couple the night before. I tossed the roll to Bob, who stuffed it back into his pocket.

I threw the bag back at the man, who wasn't quick enough to catch it. The bag bounced off the carriage and lay in the road. Bob pulled back on the reins and his horse edged backwards.

"It was a pleasure doing business with you," Bob said, and touched a finger to the brim of his hat. Then he wheeled his horse and we all plunged into the brush.

Oscar Halsell, a Texan who became a citizen of the Cherokee Nation by marriage, was a deeply religious man and owner of the XB-Bar Ranch. Back in '80 Halsell had driven a herd of longhorns north and established the ranch on the good grass that stretched from Bird Creek all the way north to Bartlesville, and there was no question that he was the *jefe* on his spread. He allowed no drinking, gambling, or swearing among his men—at least not within earshot. It is a great mystery why some of the baddest desperadoes that ever rode the owlhoot trail got their start on his spread.

After we reached the ranch, Emmett told a couple of his old pards that the Daltons were having a recruiting meeting that night at a line shack in the north pastures. By sundown practically every hand on the XB-Bar and the Bird Creek knew about the meeting, and eight men that Emmett knew we could trust crowded into that shack to hear what the Daltons had to offer.

Emmett introduced me and Bob all around.

Bill Doolin was a big man in his thirties with a drooping black mustache and an Arkansas drawl. He was easygoing and smart, although Emmett told me he had learned to read and write while at the XB, and he was apparently what was called a "natural leader," since the other cowhands seemed to look to him for advice.

Blackface Charley Bryant was an old-timer who wore twin Colt .45s in a border rig. He was a silent and moody man, and got his nickname from the powder burns that scarred one cheek. Emmett once said that Bryant had taught him everything he knew about guns.

Then there was Bitter Creek Newcomb, who fancied himself a ladies' man, and Newcomb's friend, Texas Pierce. George Waightman and "Little Dick" West were also in on the meeting; both were orphans who had been adopted by the cowhands of the Halsell ranch.

"What's this I hear about y'all forming up a gang?" Doolin asked when everybody had got settled in.

"You hear right," Bob said. "Right now, it's me and my brother Emmett and the Choctaw Kid here. We're looking for a few other men we can count on."

"Rustlin' don't pay," Newcomb said.

"We're not talking about stealing stock," Bob said. "We're thinking bigger."

"Banks? Trains?" Doolin snorted. "That's a tough row to hoe, pardner. You go messing with the banks and you're going to find yourself sleeping with special U.S. marshals. You rob a train and you're not going to be able to make water without a Pinkerton agent shaking it dry for you."

"The James boys did it successfully for almost twenty years," Bob said.

"And look what it got Cole Younger and the bunch," Doolin said. "Look what it got ole Jesse, for that matter."

"A Pinkerton didn't get him," Emmett piped up. "It was that 'dirty

little coward' Robert Ford what done him in. Poor old Jesse thought he
was a friend." Em knew the song by heart.

"What it comes down to," Bob said, "is whether you want to starve
to death punching cattle, never being able to afford to get married or
own your own place, or whether you want to live right and have a little
money in your pocket."

Bob reached down into his jacket and pulled out his bankroll. I'll say
this for my brother Bob, he sure knew how to get a body's attention; he
made quite a sight, standing there in the fancy Eastern suit he'd bought
in Baxter Springs and holding that money up. Those cowhands' mouths
nearly dropped open as they sat there staring at that wad of government
green.

"Here," Bob said, tossing the roll to Bill Powers. "Get a feel of it and
pass it down. Don't worry, I trust you—I know every note will be there
when you hand it back."

"I'll be damned," Powers said when he finished counting the bills. He
handed them to Broadwell. "There's over three hundred dollars there."

"How long does it take you to make that kind of money punching
cows?" Bob asked.

"We make thirty dollars a month," Bryant said.

"Close to a year, then," Bob said. "A year's work, right there in the
palm of your hand. And that is just what I have left over, because I
already spent most of my money. But I promise you that there's more
where that came from."

All of them were more or less interested in joining up. All of them
but Doolin, that is; he looked kind of perturbed, like he was having a
tough time digesting his dinner.

"Where you plan on doing your first job?" he asked.

"Things are a little hot for us in the Territory right now," Bob said,
"so we reckon we'd head out west for a spell and visit our brother Bill
in California. We reckon there might be a few places between here and
California where we can withdraw a few dollars. We'll just have to scout
it out and see what feels natural to us."

Bill Doolin the big Arkansawyer, nodded.

"Are you with us or ag'in us?" Bob asked.

"Oh, I'm with you, all right," Doolin answered. "It's hard for a man
to turn down that kind of money. But what I keep wondering is, is a
man's life worth a wad of bills?"

"What's a man's life worth without it?" Bob asked back.

Doolin shrugged his shoulders.

"I don't know, boys," Doolin said. "I've been courting a minister's daughter, and I've been trying to keep to the straight and narrow. Your offer's mighty attractive, but I'm going to have to think on it some."

"We're riding out in the morning," Bob said.

"Well, that settles it," Doolin said. "I wish you boys the best. I can't ride with you tomorrow, but you can count on my help, if you need it, when you come back to the Territory."

"Well, I'm with you," Blackface Charley Bryant declared. "I'm damn tired of working for a living and having nothin' but a sore back to show for it."

Bitter Creek Newcomb said he would throw his lot in with us, and punctuated his decision by throwing his head back and singing, "I'm a lone wolf from Bitter Creek and tonight's my night to howl," drawing out the howl part.

"And you boys that can't ride out with us right away, we understand," Bob said. "You just keep us in mind and pass along any information about marshals or such that might come your way."

The Dalton gang set its sights on New Mexico Territory. Bob didn't say much about springing Grat, but I reckoned he had some kind of plan that he was keeping to himself.

We were laughing and kidding with each other like it was a Sunday School picnic as we rode west across Oklahoma Territory, and we didn't even bother to go around the towns that were likely to have telegraphs and wanted posters tacked up in their city jails. Who in their right mind, Bob asked, would ride out to confront six heavily armed men that hadn't done nothing to *their* town?

There was a sign on the opposite bank where we crossed the north fork of the Canadian River, and left Indian Territory behind. The sign, which was weather-worn and pockmarked with bullet holes, said, "Fort Smith—Five Hundred Miles."

Beneath that someone had scrawled, "—to Hell."

Seventeen

TALES OF GOLD AND SILVER so plentiful that ingots were stacked on the sidewalk to await shipment, is what lured Bob Dalton and the gang to Silver City, New Mexico. The fact that Silver City's marshal, Ben Canty, was an old friend from Missouri didn't hurt a bit.

I had never seen country as wild as those rugged hills around Silver City, which were hoary with juniper, piñon, and oak. The scrub provided cover for the grizzly bear, the mountain lion, and the coyote, and for the Gila and Mimbres Apache. Just seven years before, the Apache had kidnapped little Johnnie McComas after killing his folks, and the boy hadn't been seen since. Despite the best efforts of the army, I was convinced there were still Apache lurking in the hills. Even Bob eyed the brush on either side of the rode keener than usual.

A bunch of greaser kids crowded around our saddle skirts as we rode into Silver City, chanting *"Tengo hambre, tengo mucho hambre."* They were dirty and wore rags. Bob threw out a few coins and they scrambled for them. The ones that got them said, *"Mucho gracias, señor. Salud!"*

"I don't know why you bother," Blackface Charley said. "You know damn well they ain't hungry. You just fell for their racket is all. They'd sell their mother for the right price."

"Maybe," Bob said, looking disgusted. "But what if they *are* hungry?"

Charley spat a wad onto the street.

We didn't see no stacks of gold and silver on the sidewalk, but there was plenty of other activity in town, and most of it had to do with one form of wickedness or another. Saloons and gambling houses were common, and a street called Shady Lane promised a variety of carnal delights.

We hitched our horses in front of the Saint Vincent Saloon and took a seat at one of the tables. It must have been a popular place. The mirror behind the bar was boarded up, there were bullet holes in the floor, and the roulette table showed signs of being busted up and pieced back together—several times. Bryant brought a bottle of mescal back to the table, while Bob went out to find his old friend, Ben Canty.

There was a man at the end of the bar who had seemed to be eyeing us since we came in, but every time I looked up he would turn his head away. I began to wish that the mirror hadn't been shot to hell, so I could get a glimpse of this character's face. I couldn't tell much from behind; he was small, maybe a couple of inches below average, and the hair which peeked out beneath the hat was dark brown. Clean-shaven. Dark-colored jacket and trousers. When he put his boot up on the brass rail, the jacket fell back to reveal the butt of an American poking forward, cross-draw fashion.

I leaned across the table and said to Bitter Creek, "Look at that fellow at the bar. What do you make of him?"

Bitter Creek took a shot of mescal and studied the man.

"He's no cowboy," he said. "Doesn't look rough enough to be the law. Could be a Pinkerton, maybe."

Bob brought Ben Canty back to our table at the saloon. Canty looked to be in his late forties, with gray nipping at his sideburns and mustache. He had watery blue eyes that didn't stay in one place for long. On his shirt he wore a badge.

Bob introduced us around and Bryant offered Canty a drink of mescal, but Canty shook his head and said he couldn't stand the Mexican stuff. Bob sent Emmett to the bar for a bottle of whiskey and two glasses.

"What are you and your boys doing in Grant County?" Canty asked Bob nervously, his eyes roaming from one to another of us and his right hand drumming the table.

"Just here on a little business," Bob said. Emmett placed the bottle and glasses down, and Bob uncorked the whiskey and poured a shot for each of them. "We hear that streets are just about made of gold and silver down here."

Canty grinned, toasted Bob's health, and threw the whiskey down the back of his throat.

"Used to be," Canty said, "that they would haul the ore down from the mines in the Mogollon Mountains behind fourteen-horse teams, to the shipping offices here. I can see how those rumors got started, with all the bullion that passed through plain sight here."

"What kept folks from stealing it?" Bob asked.

"They kept hanging those who tried," Canty said, and helped himself to another shot. "But that was before the railroad came through in '81. Now, the gold and silver is shipped out directly, at least what's left. You see, the mines have begun to play out. This ain't no boomtown anymore. Most of the gold that flows in these days comes from the San Francisco mint."

Bryant cleared his throat and gave Bob a miserable look.

"All that hustle," Canty said, waving toward the street, "ain't nothin' like it used to be. A couple of years ago you couldn't find the room to walk across the street."

Bob nodded and had another drink.

"Tell me something," Bryant said, leaning across the table, "who is that little fellow at the end of the bar? Do you know him?"

"That's Tom King," Canty said. "Says he's from Cass County, but I sure don't remember him. All I know for sure is that he is one peculiar duck."

Bob looked over his shoulder; King was looking back at him. King touched the brim of his hat and Bob nodded.

"Looks familiar," Bob said, "but I can't place him."

"Look here," Canty said suddenly, his eyes quivering between the whiskey bottle and Bob's face, "I know we go back a long way, back to when we was kids. But I also know you've got a warrant ghosting you from Indian Territory. You're up to no good here, Bob Dalton."

"Ben," Bob said, and managed a hurt look. "I don't know what you mean."

"Just your being here has put me in a bad spot," Canty continued. "I just ask one thing, Bob Dalton. If you're planning to make some trouble around here, do it out of my jurisdiction. Stay out of Silver City, or I'll have to run you in."

Bob laughed and shook his head.

"At least," he said, "give us until the morning. We've ridden a long way and we could use a bath and a night's rest in a real bed. Surely you can't deny us that."

Canty's eyes danced over the table.

"All right," he said, putting his palms on the table and standing up.

"But tomorrow morning, I expect you to be out of town. And . . . well, thanks for the whiskey."

Canty left the saloon.

Bitter Creek uttered a single four-letter word and threw his head back so he was staring at the ceiling. "I feel like getting drunk," he said.

"You're already drunk," Bryant said meanly. "Look, Dalton, what is this foolishness? You—"

Tom King had walked over to the table and laid a small hand on the back of Bob's chair.

"I'm sorry to interrupt," he said softly, "but I couldn't help over-hearing. You're Bob Dalton, aren't you? I've always wondered what happened to you. We were neighbors back in Missouri, although you probably don't recognize me."

"No sir, you're right, I don't remember you," Bob said.

The stranger leaned down and said something in Bob's ear that the rest of us couldn't catch. Bob's eyes bugged out for a moment, then he looked the stranger up and down and shook his head.

"I don't believe you," he said flatly.

"You will," the stranger said. "Or don't you remember the nights we spent in Pawhuska? But we can talk about old times later. I think we have some business to discuss first. You boys came here looking for some action, and I think I know just the place for you. There's a Mex gambling house just across the gulley, outside the city limits. It's not unusual for ten thousand dollars to pass through its doors in a single night. Are you interested?"

Blackface Charley Bryant snorted.

"Why the hell," he asked, "should we trust you?"

The stranger didn't answer.

Bob tipped the bottle and poured the last of it into his shot glass, tapping the neck on the glass to get the last few reluctant drops. Squinting, he held up the glass and studied its color.

"Sometimes things ain't what they appear to be," Bob said, "but we can trust Tom King. You boys go out and have some fun while Tom and I talk business. We'll be in that hotel across the street when you get back. We'll be under the name King."

Em and I got bored and were at the hotel a long time before Blackface Charley or Bitter Creek, who decided to see if they could drink the town's saloons dry. We found out what room Bob was in, and went up the stairs and knocked. It was a little while before he answered the door, and when he did he was in his long underwear. Behind the door he held his Colt.

"Just us," Em said as Bob returned the gun to its holster, which was hanging from the bedpost. "Kind of a funny time to take a nap, don't you—"

Emmett stopped in his tracks; that fellow Tom King was sitting on the side of the bed, with his back to us, and he was also down to his long underwear.

"Goddamn, Bob," Emmett muttered, "it ain't natural. I know we been on the trail a long time, but there's houses just down the street. Jesus H. Christ, I never."

"Shut up, Em," Bob said.

Tom King moved off the bed and stood facing us, his weight on one leg and his hips cocked at a funny angle. His long underwear was unbuttoned partway down the neck. He unbuttoned a few more loops and then pulled the red material back, revealing his chest—well, I should say *her* chest, if you get my drift. No doubt about it, Tom King was a woman.

She covered back up and laughed at the expression on me and Em's face.

"This here's Florence Quick," Bob said. "We did know each other back in Missouri, and I'm happy to say we have resumed that friendship. She is now officially a scout for the Dalton gang."

"You sure look funny with that short hair," Emmett complained.

"I was tired," Flo said, "of not being able to do what I wanted just because I was a woman. This way, I can go anywhere and do anything that pleases me."

Then she smiled wickedly.

"And I like the way it makes me feel."

We cleared out of Silver City the next day, just like Bob had promised his old friend Ben Canty, but we didn't go far—just across the arroyo to the Mexican side of things. The gambling house was a big ramshackle affair, two stories, set off by itself just like Flo had said. Bob decided that she would tend the horses while the rest of the gang went inside and cleaned out tables. Six men with drawn guns, Bob allowed, should be enough to discourage the dealers or bartenders from putting up a struggle.

The worst part of the whole plan was waiting for night, when we could get on with it. I must have checked my guns a dozen times, but I wasn't nearly as nervous as Blackface Charley, who just could not leave his revolvers alone for a second. He was always twirling them or polishing them or just touching them, touching them like you would a woman. Bitter Creek kept nipping at a bottle of mescal to keep his courage up. Emmett, of course, kept playing that damned harmonica. But Bob and Flo had a great time planning how they were going to spend the money.

We moved in at twilight.

Inside the gambling house a Mexican band played one of those fast dancing tunes while cowboys and miners laid down their money at the faro tables. Here and there gold or silver flashed at one of the tables. There was no short supply of girls, Mexican and white, working the tables.

Emmett went to the bar and had a beer while the five of us went over to the faro table and bucked the tiger with some two-dollar bets. We weren't surprised when we lost our money. I don't know whether the game was rigged or not, but even at an honest table faro is a hard game to beat. But the point was to buy us a little time to study the joint. There were about forty people in there, which seemed like too many, but Bob said it was a good thing because that meant more money in the cash drawers for us.

Bob walked to the bar grumbling about losing his money, and as he went he indicated to each one of us who we should cover: Blackface Charley was assigned the bartender, who most likely had a shotgun under the bar; I got the faro dealer, Bitter Creek was to watch the door to the back room, and so on.

Bob pushed his hat back on his head and ordered a beer. He sat looking like he was beat, but when the bartender leaned forward to put the beer down on the bar, Bob pulled his gun and fired a round into the ceiling. Everyone froze in their tracks. Some of the women screamed, and the man behind the bar started cussing in Mexican, but he stopped when he had to stare down the bore of Blackface Charley's cocked .45.

I already had my gun on the faro dealer.

"This is a holdup," Bob said. "Keep your hands up and nobody will get hurt."

Some of the customers looked puzzled until the bartender translated for them, then they stuck their paws in the air.

Emmett took a sack from under his shirt and went around to all the gaming tables, scooping up the greenbacks and the coins. He was smiling like an idiot as he did it, and moving a little too slow, because Bob told him a couple of times to hurry it up. I noticed there was sweat beading on Bob's forehead as he waited for Em to finish.

Bitter Creek started lifting jewelry from some of the ladies, and the bartender objected. Blackface Charley poked the .45 into the Mexican's nose, pressing it flat. He cocked the piece.

"I always wanted to kill myself a greaser," Blackface said.

"You do and you ain't riding with me no more," Bob told him. "Bitter Creek, hand the ladies back their things. We're not here for that. Hell, it's probably glass."

Bitter Creek refused.

"Do it now," Bob said, and gave him a look that would curdle milk. Newcomb finally tossed the jewelry back on the table, and Bryant removed the Colt from the bartender's face.

"You're lucky," Bryant said.

Emmett tossed the loot sack to Bob, who stuffed it under his belt. We all inched toward the door, keeping our guns leveled. Then we bolted through and sprung into the saddle of our waiting mounts. The ground shook as we galloped around the corner of the gambling house, and above the roar of the hooves I could hear Bitter Creek howling at the full moon.

We pulled back the pace after a few miles, but rode steadily until daybreak, when we stopped to count our loot. There was four thousand three hundred and ten dollars.

Bob swooped Flo up in his arms and kissed her on the mouth, and that looked a mite peculiar because she was still dressed like a man. They were still smooching and talking about the kind of spread they were going to buy when there appeared a cloud on the southern horizon.

"What's that?" Emmett asked. "Dust storm?"

Blackface Charley spat tobacco juice on the ground.

"Hell no," he said. "That is a Mexican posse."

"We better find a place to make a stand, because our horses are tuckered out," Bob said. "Or, we could give it back to them, if you don't think it's worth fighting for."

"They better have a taste for lead," Bitter Creek said.

We staked our horses inside a steep arroyo, then spread out across the ravine lip, Winchesters at the ready. Flo took a position by Bob, and although she did not have a long gun, she had a brace of Colts ready.

We watched the dust cloud grow larger and larger on the horizon until it finally took the form of men on horseback. There were seven of them, and the sun glinted from their weapons. The posse slowed, no longer able to see the dust kicked up by *our* horses. They must have known something was up because they spread out and advanced at a walk, coming to within a couple hundred yards.

The leader, apparently some type of Mexican lawman, didn't know exactly where we were, but he knew we were close. He reined his horse to a stop, cleared his throat, and shouted in broken English that we were under arrest.

Bob shot the sombrero off his head.

The posse volleyed back with their long guns, but they were firing while going backwards, so none of their shots were really aimed. We answered fire, shooting over their heads, which made them retreat even faster and shoot wilder. Just the same, Emmett got hit in the fleshy part of his arm by a ricochet, and he howled until Bob convinced him he wasn't dead.

When the shooting was over, I reached inside my buckskin shirt, touched my medicine charm, and wondered what was inside it.

We didn't see the Mexican posse again.

Eighteen

BLACKFACE CHARLEY wasn't at all happy about the way Bob divided the loot, giving each of us five hundred dollars and keeping the rest—more than thirteen hundred—for himself. Bob said that included a share for Flo, who had held the horses, and for Grat, who deserved a share for pulling time for the gang.

Charley wasn't brave enough to criticize Bob directly about holding out so much, so he picked on me instead.

"Why does the Kid here get a share equal to mine?" he asked. "It seems that me and Bitter Creek ought to get something more because we're experienced hands."

"He's got a point," Emmett chimed, but Bob boxed his ears.

"The Kid did his part," Bob said coolly. "Or didn't you see him in there with his gun drawn like the rest of us? And, as a matter of fact, Charley, I think the Kid is a little handier with a gun than you are anyway."

"It's one thing to play-practice with a gun," Blackface said and pulled his Colts, one in each hand. He spun them around, switched hands, and slammed them back in the holsters. "It's something else to get into a real fight."

"The Kid's killed a couple of men," Bob said. "Shot up another for calling him an Indian-lover."

"Bullshit," Charley said.

"Hit him in the shoulder and then blew the poor devil's kneecap off while he was done," Bob said, and shook his head like it was one of the worst things he'd ever heard.

"That's just a bunch of corral dust," Blackface said.

I was sitting on a rock, keeping my mouth shut and trying to keep the peace, but I couldn't stand it anymore. I strode over to where Bob and Charley were talking and placed myself between them.

"Watch out, son, or you might get hurt," Charley said and knocked my hat off. I was awful fond of that black hat with the Indian-beaded band.

"Old man, I think you're the one that's gonna get hurt unless you shut your mouth," I said, standing toe-to-toe with him. A man has a harder time drawing on you if you crowd him than if you stand a comfortable distance away. "All you know is parlor tricks. Anybody that would ruin a perfectly good brace of Colts by sticking pearl handles on them couldn't have the sand to stand up to a real *pistolero.*"

"You sonuvabitch," Charley said and went for his guns, but he hadn't cleared leather before the bore of my .45 hovered an inch from his nose.

"Not so fast, are you?" I taunted.

"What do you expect, crowding me like that?" he fumed. "Let's go after it at twenty paces and see who—"

Bob pushed his way between us.

"Stop it," he commanded. "We're not going to start killing each other. Put your gun up, Kid."

"Tell him to get his palms off his butts first."

"Do it," Bob told Charley, who reluctantly moved his hands away from his guns. I uncocked mine and returned it to the beaded holster, then reached down and picked up my hat. I brushed the dust off with my sleeve before putting it back on.

"I think we ought to split up for a spell," Bob said, "at least until the heat's off."

"That suits me just fine," Charley said.

"Bob's right," Bitter Creek said. "Each of us has enough to keep us in style while we lay low for a little while. I've got a little homestead at Guthrie that could use some attention."

"Flo's headed back to Guthrie, too," Bob said. "We talked before, and there's some business she has to take care of with the express companies. I'd appreciate it if you'd keep her company on the way back."

"Okay," Bitter Creek said, "but what do I call her? Tom or Florence or what?"

"You call her Bob's girl."

"I reckon I could go down to Jim Riley's spread," Charley said. "The company's better down there, at least."

"Mind if I go with you?" Emmett asked. Like I said, he and Black-face Charley were tight.

"Hell, no," Charley said.

Bob shrugged and said okay, but that he personally was headed on to California to see brother Bill. He asked me if I wanted to ride out with him, and I allowed that I might.

Bill was twenty-eight years old, of slighter build than either Bob or Grat, with slender hands that, like Pa's, were made to hold the fiddle. Like the rest of us, he had blond hair and blue eyes and a fair complexion that flushed red when he was angry or embarrassed. The bloom spread from his collar to both cheeks when he came home one day to find us waiting in the kitchen of his farmhouse near Paso Robles, but he acted like he was glad to see us anyway. Bill was smart and knew me right off, without Bob having to tell him.

"Thought you were dead," Bill said. "Glad to see you ain't. I hope the sonuvabitch that flattened your nose paid."

"In full," I said, and let it go. I had come to hate explaining, because it either sounded like I was bragging or that I was a pretty cruel sonuvabitch.

We didn't have to worry none about busting Grat out of the Fort Smith jail, Bill said, he was already out and had come to California ahead of us. Grat had been sprung because the grand jury was forced to return a no-bill; the prosecutor had a problem getting the evidence together. The chief marshal wanted to avoid an embarrassing trial so soon after Grat had left his employ, and lawyers were always hungry for money. It was the best justice money could buy, Grat had told Bill. The boys would just have to steer clear of Clem Rogers's spread when they were near Claremore.

Grat had practically taken up residence at the gaming tables of the Grand Central Hotel in nearby Fresno, Bill said. He was doing pretty well at fleecing the greenhorns at faro and poker.

We were still sitting in the kitchen, drinking coffee and talking about the old days when Jennie, Bill's wife, said Sheriff O'Neill was at the door. Bill had been O'Neill's campaign manager when he ran for sheriff on the anti-railroad platform four years earlier.

"We'll just wait here," Bob said when Bill got up.

"Nonsense," Bill said. "Come on out and meet Ed."

"He's the law, ain't he?" Bob asked.

"Yes, but he's my friend. Come on."

Bob and I got up to follow our older brother to the dining room, but Jennie stopped us a moment and asked if we were going to the dance on Saturday night. "Bill will be playing the fiddle," she added.

"I reckon we will," Bob said, "if you promise the girls there will be as pretty as you."

"Bob Dalton, you are terrible," Jennie said, but with a smile.

In the dining room, Bill was talking to a pudgy man in a brown suit who stood with his hands in his pockets. Bill began to introduce us, but Bob cut in quick.

"I'm Bob," he said, and shook hands with O'Neill. "This here is little brother Emmett." Bob was still protecting my identity and he gave me a knowing glance, although Bill looked a trifle confused.

After O'Neill had pumped my hand, he looked down at our revolvers and scratched his beard.

"Boys, this ain't the Indian Territory," the sheriff said with a butter-wouldn't-melt-in-my-mouth smile. "I'm afraid you'll have to stow those guns away while you're in my county. You can't walk around the streets of Fresno with that kind of artillery, or you'll scare folks half to death. I've already explained that to your brother Grat."

"No problem, Sheriff," Bob said with a smile, but his eyes weren't smiling. If there was one thing Bob hated, it was a lecture, even when it was for his own good.

"Say, you boys wouldn't have been visiting these parts in January of last year, would you?"

"Nope," Bob said. "Why?"

"Just curious," O'Neill said.

"Cut that out, Ed," Bill said, getting stern. "These are my brothers and I vouch for them. They weren't anywhere near Goshen when that train got robbed."

"Of course," O'Neill said, all pleasant again. "I didn't mean nothing."

The Grand Central Hotel was a lot different than any other joint I had ever been in. It was fancy, with brass and wallpaper everywhere, and the customers were all dressed in Sunday-go-to-meeting clothes, but when you got right down to it, it was still a joint: there was whiskey, there was gambling, and there were girls. Everything just cost more, is all.

We found Grat laying the hammer on a young fellow who wore a plaid suit a couple sizes too small for him. Grat laid his cards on the table and the kid looked like he was going to slide right off the chair onto the floor.

"Full house," Grat said.

The kid threw his cards back on the pile, not even bothering to call what he had. "How about double or nothing on the next one, mister?"

"Sorry," Grat said when he saw me and Bob standing there, "table's closed. Come see me tomorrow."

"Come on, mister, you got to give me a chance to win back what I lost."

"Let me give you some advice, son," Grat said, scooping in the chips from the center of the table. "The reason gamblers can make money is because folks like you will back a losing streak quicker than a winning one. I've seen people throw away six hundred dollars trying to get back to even, but quit a winning streak after winning only sixty bucks. Go figure."

The kid left, and Bob and I sat down.

"It's a good thing they set you free," Bob said and slapped Grat on the shoulder. "We were rounding up a regular army to come bust you out."

Grat wasn't that dumb.

"Sure you were," he said, and poured a shot from the bottle at his elbow. "But you had to come to California, first."

"Come on, pard," Bob said, then leaned close. "The gang knocked over this Mex gambling house at Silver City. Things got a little warm after that, so we had to find a place to bide our time."

"Gang?" Grat asked. "What gang?"

"The Bob Dalton gang, of course," he said. "Why, there's Blackface Charley Bryant and Bitter Creek Newcomb and a couple of others. Bill Doolin's waiting to join back at the XB-Bar. And Grat, I saved you a share of the New Mexico money."

Grat's eyes brightened.

"How much?"

Bob reached into his pocket, pulled out his poke, and peeled off five hundred dollars onto the table. "There you are," Bob said. "That's a full share."

Grat looked at me.

"It is," I said. "We all got the same."

Grat grinned and punched Bob on the shoulder, and even though he was only playing it nearly knocked Bob off his chair. Then they shook hands, and Grat got two more glasses from the bar and poured us both drinks.

"About that name," Grat said. "Why can't it be the Grat Dalton gang?"

Bob winced.

"Well," he said. "You know I'm the leader. But I reckon we can just plain call it the Dalton gang, and that covers both of us."

That seemed fair enough to Grat.

I drank my whiskey—I still didn't like the taste of it, but I was kind of getting used to that warm feeling that came after a couple of drinks— and sat there listening to Bob and Grat. I had a good view of the lobby, and I enjoyed watching the people in their fancy clothes come and go, some of them clutching valises or having the porters haul their trunks.

One man who came down the stairs and stopped at the desk caught my interest in particular. He was tall and thin and wore a gray Eastern suit with a telltale budge beneath the left elbow. When he leaned on the desk as he talked to the clerk, the coat fell away a bit and I caught the glimmer of gunmetal. He looked to be in his forties, with a deeply lined face and hair that was going gray at the temples. He didn't smile.

He left the desk and, to my surprise, made for the saloon. He stopped in the doorway and put his hands on his hips as he surveyed the room for a moment. Then he spotted our table and worked his way toward us, not fast but determined just the same.

"Here comes trouble," I said and nudged Bob's arm.

"Good afternoon," the man said in an even voice when he drew up to the table. "Grat Dalton?"

"That kid lost fair and square," Grat said, drumming his fingers on the table. "It ain't my fault if he's a lousy poker player."

"I'm not here to discuss your luck," the man said impatiently, "but I would like to ask you about you and your brothers' activities during January of last year. I presume these are your brothers Bob and Emmett?"

"No, that's—"

Bob held up a hand to silence Grat.

"I don't know who the hell you think you are, mister, but you've got no right to start questioning us," Bob said.

"I'm afraid I have every right, Mr. Dalton. My name is William Smith and I am chief of detectives for the Southern Pacific Railway. My offices are upstairs in this hotel."

"Bully for you," Grat said. "Get lost."

"Wait a minute," Bob said. "The Southern Pacific? Why, Senator Leland Stamford is president of that octopus."

"Stanford," Smith corrected.

"Ain't it funny that our brother Bill has got his eye on Stanford's seat in the legislature? Kind of coincidental that you're here questioning us about a train robbery that took place when we was a thousand miles away fulfilling our duties as U.S. deputy marshals in Indian Territory?"

"You haven't been marshals since last year," Smith said. "As a matter of fact, Grat here was arrested for horse stealing and just recently got out. And, there's some fascinating stories coming out of Indian Territory about your exploits, Bob. I'm waiting right now for a wire from Fort Smith about a couple of outstanding warrants."

"The charges against me were trumped up," Grat said, "and they were eventually dropped. So were the warrants against my brothers."

"We shall see," Smith said.

"You are right in that we no longer are riding deputies," Bob said. "We are between commissions right now—there was some disagreement over back pay that led us to turn in our badges. But at the time that train was robbed, we were in the Cherokee Nation."

"There were two robberies," Smith said, "The first was at Pixley, where our express was robbed of twelve thousand dollars. The second was at Goshen and a Modesto county sheriff's deputy was wounded. More than twenty thousand dollars was taken. Both robberies were committed by two men. I'd say, Mr. Dalton, that you dress pretty well for having lived on a deputy's pay for the last few years. I couldn't help noticing, either, that you ride one of the finest saddle horses I ever did see."

Grat jumped up, spilling the whiskey and nearly knocking over the table, but Bob pulled him back down.

"That's what he wants," Bob told him, "so that he can call his good friend Sheriff O'Neill and have all of us thrown in the calaboose."

"You have me wrong, Dalton. O'Neill is your brother Bill's friend, not mine."

"I reckon the goddamn Yankee railroad is paying better these days," Bob said. "I don't know why you're looking to pin those robberies on us —you've got plenty of suspects right in your own backyard. I reckon any kin to those settlers who were killed by the Southern Pacific at the Mussell Slough massacre would be mighty eager to get even."

"Good day, Mr. Dalton," Smith said, ending the conversation. "I'll keep you posted on the wires from Fort Smith. Just remember—you're not dealing with a bunch of hicks now. The Southern Pacific owns this valley. Anywhere you go, I'll be watching over your shoulder."

"I don't like it," I told Bob after Smith had gone.

"They're bluffing," Bob said. "Don't let it worry you. They're trying to use us to get to Bill, but it won't work. They don't have a thing on us."

I found no comfort in Bob's words. If justice was cheap enough that Grat could buy his way out of a horse-stealing charge, then couldn't it also be bought to hang the train robberies on us? The way I saw it, the Southern Pacific had enough money that if it said the world was square and cows gave moonshine, the courts would naturally agree.

"And cows give moonshine," I said.

Bob asked what the hell that meant. Although it made perfect sense to me, I had had too much whiskey to explain it.

Bill took one of the law books down from the row over the fireplace and held it in his hands like a preacher holds a Bible. Bill had a knack for seeing what was possible in things and tending to overlook the realities. When he talked about the law, it was like a cowboy talking about the mug of beer and the doe-eyed girl waiting for him in the next town.

"This is what will put an end to the greed of the banks and the railroads and people like Senator Leland Stanford," he said, patting the book. "When I am elected to the legislature I will write laws to make sure of it."

"That's terrific," Bob said, "but that doesn't solve our problems right now. Ed O'Neill has sold out to the Southern Pacific and you had better watch your back."

"I can't believe that Ed would do that," Bill said. "He was one of the original members of the anti-railroad league. We made a deal, that after we got him elected sheriff he'd support my campaign for senator. Hell, he knows I aim to be governor someday."

"He's not going to bite the hand that feeds him," Grat said, "and right now, he's the SP's yellow dog sure enough. How else would Smith know so much about us?"

Bill put the law book back in its place and sighed.

"We need to clear out now," I said. "Go back to the Territory and hide out. Then they'd leave Bill alone."

"The railroad will keep after me, whether you're here or not," Bill said. "No matter how it may look, I know that Ed O'Neill will keep them from trumping up robbery charges against us. You can count on that."

Nineteen

THE DANCE IN KINGSBURG that Bill fiddled was some affair, although there were only a few girls in attendance pretty as his Jennie.

We arrived at the Brick Hotel an hour after the dance started, having stopped at a dive along the way so that Grat could quench his considerable thirst for whiskey. Grat was awkward when he was sober, and the more he drank, the bigger his feet got. He was determined to dance with some of the Swedish girls. I felt sorry for those that got their toes stomped. His dancing got wilder and wilder, and he clapped in time with the music. Every time he lifted his arms, the tail of his frock coat went up a few inches and you could get a glimpse of the Colt that was stuck down his pants.

We flagged Grat down before the next dance started. We went outside on the porch and had a few pulls from the flask that Bob carried, then when nobody was looking we hid our guns beneath the steps. It sure was a lot easier in the Territory, where you could carry your guns in plain sight and not have to sneak around with them down your pants or in your boot.

"What are you hiding?"

We turned around to find a Swedish girl of seventeen or eighteen standing in the doorway. She had come out for a breath of air and had watched us put the guns beneath the porch.

"Don't mind us," Bob said. "You see, we're deputy marshals and we have to have our guns handy. We just didn't want to frighten anyone inside."

"I see." Her expression said she didn't really understand at all, but that she was fascinated by men that needed to carry guns. I had seen the look before, and in some pretty respectable ladies, too.

Grat stumbled onto the porch.

"May I have this dance?" he asked.

Bill fiddled while Grat and the Swedish girl struck out across the dance floor. It was a miracle that Grat could even stand up, let alone dance, considering the amount of forty rod he'd swallowed that night.

Things went along right pleasant for the next hour or so, and Bob danced with some of the girls, too. I didn't because I had never really learned to dance. But it was fun watching my brothers.

About ten-thirty a man ran breathless into the hotel with news that three men had attempted to rob the Southern Pacific express at Alila. No money was taken, but the train's fireman had been shot in the stomach and wasn't expected to live through the night.

The girl Grat was with gasped and took a little step back. "You came to the dance late," she said out loud, "and you hid your guns under the porch in case you needed them in a hurry, you said." Then she fainted, or pretended to, crumpling into Grat's arms.

We could feel the eyes of the crowd boring holes into our backs as we left.

We tried to persuade Grat not to go back to the Grand Central Hotel, but he said he had to get his faro outfit and other things out of his room. Bob took off for Bill's farmhouse near Paso Robles. He told me to go with Grat to the hotel and watch out for him.

At the hotel, I waited downstairs while Grat went up to get his things. I was sitting in a leather chair in the lobby, where I could watch the front entrance and the staircase. It took Grat only a few minutes to gather his things, and he had no more than stepped off the stairs when Will Smith and Sheriff O'Neill rounded the corner, pistols drawn. Smith ordered him to put his hands in the air.

Grat looked disgusted, but set his things on the floor and slowly reached for the sky. O'Neill told him he was under arrest for the Alila holdup, while Smith frisked him and took his Colt and the knife away.

"Where's your brothers?" O'Neill asked.

"Go find them yourself, you egg-sucking sonuvabitch," Grat said.

Smith backhanded him hard across the mouth, but Grat did not cry out. Blood began trickling from the corner of his mouth. "We didn't rob that express," Grat mumbled.

"Of course you did," Smith said.

They still hadn't seen me, and Grat at least had enough wits about him not to look my way, so while they clamped the handcuffs on him I eased out of the chair and slipped through the door. I mounted Cimarron and set out for the farm.

"I haven't done anything wrong," Bill said, pounding his fist on the fireplace mantel. He had his back to us and was nose-to-nose with the row of law books.

"That doesn't make any difference to the Southern Pacific," Bob said. "They have made up their mind that we are going to burn for those express robberies."

"If I run," Bill said, "people will assume I'm guilty. Even if our names are cleared after some time, I'll never be able to run for office. I'd never be able to explain why I ran from the charges."

"That's just what Mr. Will Smith wants," Bob said.

"We better get going," I said. "They're going to ride up here any minute."

"We're not leaving without Bill."

"I can't," Bill said. "It's not just the campaign—there's Jennie and the kids. I can't leave them and take to the owlhoot trail."

"You'll have to unless you want to spend the next twenty years in prison," Bob said. "Come back to the Territory with us. You help Mama with the homestead at Kingfisher and send for Jennie and the kids later."

Bill shook his head.

"I'm not running from this," he said.

Just then there was the sound of riders pulling up to the house.

"We've gotta hide," I said, pulling my Colt. "They won't bother to knock."

"Put that thing away," Bill said sternly. "There'll be no shooting in my house. Go to the boys' room and wait there until I can get rid of them."

We had no more left the front room when boots sounded on the porch and a heavy hand thudded on the front door, followed by Smith's voice. "Open up, Bill Dalton." They kicked in the door before Bill even had a chance to cross the room.

Three-year-old Lewis was sleeping soundly but Little Frank, who was seven, gave a little start and sat up in bed. Bob put a finger to his lips and sat down on the edge of the bed, smiled, and put a hand on the boy's shoulders.

"Go back to sleep," Bob said softly, and the bleary-eyed boy nestled back into the covers and dropped right back to sleep.

"Where's Bob and Emmett?" we could hear O'Neill ask.

"Haven't seen them since they left the dance, Ed. Now see here, what's this all about, you kicking my door off its hinges? What has gotten into you? And why are you dragging this Southern Pacific man into my house?"

"Doing my job, Bill," O'Neill said. "Your brothers robbed the express at Alila tonight. A fireman by the name of George Radliff was shot in the stomach and is in bad shape."

"My brothers did no such thing," Bill said calmly. "And the way I hear, whoever did rob that train didn't shoot Radliff—he was hit by a wild shot from Harwell, the engineer."

"That's true," Smith said quickly, "but the shooting is still on the thieves' heads. If they hadn't attempted to rob the express, Radliff wouldn't have had a hole blown in his gut."

"Get out of my house," Bill ordered.

"Sorry," O'Neill said. "Can't do that. I think we'll just wait here for your brothers to show. We have business with them."

Then the conversation stopped and everyone grew silent for a long spell. Now, we had our horses hid out back, and we could have gotten away if we could have sneaked out to them, but the only way in or out of the boys' room was through the front room, and we couldn't do that without walking across Smith and the traitor O'Neill. So we sat in the dark, waiting for them to leave.

They stayed until daylight. Bob and I took turns sleeping during the night, and in the morning when Jennie came to wake the boys up, we hushed her and asked that she let them sleep for a while.

Finally, Smith said it was time for him and O'Neill to leave, but there was just one more piece of business they had to take care of.

"Bill Dalton," Smith said, "I am placing you under arrest for attempted robbery. Tell your wife and gather your things, because I'm taking you back to the Fresno jail."

"I reckoned you'd get around to this sooner or later," Bill said. "I'm going to go with you peacefully, because I know I'm innocent. You know that, too. But I have faith in the law and am confident that no jury will convict me, nor any judge abide these charges."

While Jennie cried, they put the come-alongs over Bill's wrists and led him off. After they had gone, Bob tried to comfort her as best he could, but she would have none of it.

"Go away," she said, sobbing. "Why did you have to come here? You have ruined us, with your drinking and whoring and lying. Bill is a good man and does not deserve this, and for all I know you did rob those trains. Just leave. Please, leave."

"Jennie, we'll get Bill—"

"Get out!" she screamed. "I hate you all! Out!"

We hid out in the valley, living with some of the hands that tended Bill's farm, looking for an opportunity to help Grat and Bill get free. Radliff, the fireman, died of his wounds, and the Southern Pacific filed murder charges against the engineer that accidentally shot him. It didn't make much sense to me, but Bob said the railroad was hanging its own man out to dry just so the company wouldn't lose any money if the fireman's family got a lawyer to sue for them.

It wasn't a week before the Southern Pacific posted a $5,000 reward for our arrest—actually, for Bob and Emmett, because that's who Smith still believed I was.

One of the hands we were staying with brought one of the Southern Pacific's circulars for us to read. It said the money was offered by the railroad and the Wells Fargo Company, and was payable "upon their delivery to any duly authorized agent or representative of the State of California, or at any jail in the States or Territories of the United States."

The Southern Pacific had made it too warm for us in California. Even the people we counted as our friends, the hands who worked with Bill and some of the anti-railroad leaguers, were beginning to eye us like we were Christmas dinner all wrapped up in a bow. Bob himself even joked he was thinking about turning *himself* in for the reward.

We lit out for the Territory in the middle of the night.

Twenty

FIVE WEEKS LATER—May 9, 1891—Bob and I were standing in the cold beside the Santa Fe tracks, a few hundred yards beyond the tiny depot at Wharton.

Bob had called the gang back together to make a stab against the railroads in the only way he knew how. His blood was boiling. Even though the Southern Pacific didn't run through Indian Territory, there were plenty of other tracks to choose from. The way Bob saw it, they were all just tentacles of the same beast.

There was no scheduled stop at the Wharton depot, but the train would be obliged to stop if the local express agent put out the red lantern. Tonight the red lantern was out, but the agent didn't put it there. He was bound and gagged on the floor. He didn't seem to mind after we assured him it was the safest place to be.

The Texas Express hove into sight, its big lantern glimmering down the rails. It began to slow down for the stop at the depot. Steam billowed and hissed from the sides of the locomotive, and the huge drive wheels began to groan against the rails. It was crawling by the time it reached the place where we stood.

Bob and I drew our guns and swung up the handrails into the cab of the engine.

There was a peculiar coppery taste in my mouth as Bob and I boarded that engine, and to my surprise I found it was a taste I had missed. I was nervous and excited, but not sick to my stomach like I was when we rustled horses and knocked over the New Mexico joint. With the Colt in my hand again, I felt like I had the world by the tail.

I reckon I had become thoroughly wicked.

It took a warning shot from Bob's Winchester to convince the engineer to get the train good and stopped. Blackface Charley and Bitter Creek Newcomb were already at the express car.

Emmett was hanging back, looking a little sick. I guess he still hadn't found all of his sand after getting winged by a wild shot from the Mexican posse. The only good thing about it was that I hadn't heard him play "The Ballad of Jesse James" on his harmonica since we had joined back up.

Flo Quick was there too, keeping guard over the horses with a Winchester. It had been her idea to rob the Texas Express. She had weaseled some inside information from a railroad employee at Guthrie that it would be carrying a fortune tonight. She was dressed, of course, like a man.

Bitter Creek had leaped up into the express car just as soon as the messenger had seen the red lantern and swung the door open. He now held the poor man at gunpoint.

"Open it up, goddamn it or we'll blow your head off," Blackface yelled.

"I can't," the messenger said. He was somewhere between thirty-five and forty years of age, with thin brown hair and weak eyes hidden behind thick spectacles. He was white as a ghost. "I don't have the combination. The railroad doesn't give it to us messengers; it's wired ahead to each station."

Blackface began to cuss, but Bob told him to shut up. Bob jumped outside the car and chatted with Flo for a couple of minutes, then came back to the car.

"He's lying," Bob said. "That stuff about wiring the combination ahead is just a story the railroad puts out to discourage people like us. He has the combination."

"I swear I don't, mister. Please, you've got to believe me. I got a wife and kids."

Bob took him by the collar and drug him over to a chair in front of the safe.

"You've got one minute to get that door open," Bob said, taking his watch from his vest pocket, "or I'm going to let this ugly gentleman here kill you."

Blackface cocked his pistol and held it against the messenger's temple. It was the first time I had ever seen Bryant smile. Meanwhile, Bob kept his eyes on his watch.

"You'd better get to it," Bob said. "You've got thirty seconds left to dial in the combination and get the goddamn door open, too."

"It's impossible," the messenger pleaded. "I can't do it."

"Fifteen seconds until your brains roll down your chest."

The fellow's eyes were bugging out behind their glasses, and his chest was heaving up and down. He gave one last look at the pistol thrust against his head and then reached a shaking hand out to the dial.

"Twelve seconds," Bob said.

The messenger got the last number in and turned the lever, but the door remained secure. He cursed as he twirled the dial to clear it, then tried again.

"Ten seconds."

The messenger quickly spun the numbers in again and tried the handle. It turned and the safe swung open. Blackface looked disappointed.

"I can't stand a liar," Bob told the express messenger. "Jesus, you'd think it was your own goddamn money you were trying to save. Emmett, tie this fellow up and put him with the rest of the crew while we do our business."

Bob reached into the safe and began to withdraw handfuls of greenbacks, which he stuffed into the grain sack he'd brought along. There was some silver, as well. When Bob had cleaned the last of the money from the safe, he took all the important-looking legal papers that were left and threw them into the stove. He stirred the coals with kindling until the papers caught and turned the stovepipe cherry red.

I thought the messenger was going to faint.

"Goddamn Yankee railroads," Bob said.

We jumped down from the express car to where Flo held our horses, and we were mounted and ready to go when Blackface Charley swore and pointed to the depot. The station agent had somehow got himself untied, and we could see him in his little bay window, working the telegraph key.

"Forget about it," Bob said.

But Blackface Charley already had his Winchester drawn, and before Bob could stop him, the carbine boomed. The glass of the depot window shattered and the agent slumped over his telegraph key.

Bob drew his own Winchester and, in what seemed like one motion, reached over and cracked Blackface in the skull with the butt. Blackface Charley let loose of his Winchester and fell from his horse, landing heavily beside the tracks.

Bob was down on him in a flash, hitting him with a gloved fist. Bitter Creek had to pull him off. Blackface sat up on one elbow, wiping blood from his mouth.

"I said nobody gets hurt!" Bob was screaming. "You stupid sick sonuvabitch, you've turned us into murderers. Get the hell out of here."

"I want my share," Blackface said.

Bob cocked his Winchester.

"You just blew your share," Bob said. "Get out of here. You're no longer one of the gang. I hope you die soon and burn in hell."

Emmett didn't try to stick up for Charley.

I was up beside Bob now, with my Colt drawn and the hammer back. I wanted Blackface to make a move for his grips; I reckon I had murder in my heart. He lay on the ground, and looked over to Bitter Creek for help.

"Sorry, pard," Bitter Creek Newcomb said. "We agreed no shooting, and you potted that station agent like you would a prairie chicken. I'm with Bob."

Blackface stood, picked up his Winchester, and slid it into its scabbard. Then he mounted his horse and rode off into the night.

"What if he goes to the law?" Flo asked, worried.

"He doesn't know where we're going to hide out," Bob said. "Besides, what's he going to tell them that they won't know already? That the Dalton gang robbed the express at Wharton? That Charley Bryant shot the station agent? Our express messenger saw the whole thing."

The messenger sank back into the car.

"Don't shoot me," he said. "Please."

"We're not going to shoot you," Bob said. "We're sorry about the agent. Be sure to tell the detectives how it happened. I reckon they can find Bryant if they keep on the lookout around his brother's place near Hennessey."

It wasn't the big payoff we had hoped for. After Bob divided it up, it came to only eight hundred dollars apiece. I say "only," but that was nearly three years' wages for a cowpuncher. That's how skewed our thinking was. Later, we found out that the messenger hid the real money in the stove before swinging the express door open. It burnt up when Bob stoked it with the papers.

The damn newspapers went wild with stories of the Wharton holdup. The railroad, as usual, lowballed how much was taken for fear of encouraging Dalton would-be's. The Katy reported that only $1,600 was lost.

We hid out in an old cabin near Sand Springs on the banks of the Arkansas River, and when the law came snooping around we would retire to the nearby caves. Our law-abiding neighbors—who hated the railroads as much as Bob did—would inform us of any strangers the hour they rode in. The location wasn't far from Wharton, only fifty miles or so, but it was an area Bob knew well. He intended to make the railroads bleed.

Back in California, Grat was convicted of the Alila holdup and thrown back into jail to wait for sentencing. He got his break when a file was snuck into the cell; he and two of his cellmates sawed their way through the bars. Grat played cat-and-mouse with authorities across California all that winter, living like an animal and having more than a dozen close calls, before he finally left the state on a stolen horse. It was another four months, however, until he would reach Indian Territory.

Bill, who was tried separately, was acquitted of the robbery charge, but he actually fared worse than Grat. Bill walked away from the courtroom a broken man. The farm had gone to pot during the months he was in jail and his reputation was ruined. His desire for a life in public office was gone forever.

Meanwhile, we were keeping busy in our section of the Territory. We robbed the Missouri, Kansas, and Texas line—the Katy—at a whistlestop called Lilietta, on information supplied by Flo. Blackface Charley was replaced by the cool-headed Arkansawyer we had met at the XB, Bill Doolin. Doolin proved to be worth a dozen of Bryant's kind. This time it was a big haul, more than fifteen thousand dollars, although the Katy put the figure closer to three.

It turned out that Blackface Charley Bryant didn't live long enough to turn snitch on the Daltons or feel hurt about not being in on the big casino.

The month before the Lilietta job, syphilis got the best of him and he was taken to his brother Jim's place at Hennessey. It wasn't long before U.S. Marshal Ed Short came with a warrant for Bryant's arrest.

Short captured Blackface Charley at the local hotel, where Charley was bedfast and too weak to use his guns. Short escorted Charley onto an express train to Wichita to face charges. But along the way Short became careless. Blackface Charley, in a last burst of strength, grabbed the express messenger's pistol.

Short and Blackface fired point-blank at the same time, and both of them died. I reckon that's what Blackface had wanted all along. It was too bad he had to take somebody with him. Bob should have let me kill him when we had our disagreement in New Mexico Territory.

· · · ·

Nine months after the Lilietta holdup, Bob Dalton was broke again. He had gone through more money in less than a year than the average cowpuncher earns in a decade. For Bob, it was always the best clothes, the fastest horses, the most expensive women, and he was always giving money to anybody with a hard-luck story.

Bitter Creek and Emmett and I had other plans with our money. More often than not our shares wound up buried in a kettle not far from our cabin hideout, the only kind of bank we trusted. We made no pretense of burying our shares in secret, because we observed the code of honor among thieves. We often helped each other draw maps and other ciphers of exactly where the money was, so that we could retrieve it years later, if need be. Hiding money also gave us something to do, and that helped fight the boredom; in the robbery business, it seemed that things were either tediously slow or so bloody and fast it could give you a heart attack.

Grat returned from his long flight for freedom in time for the next job. He was gaunt and haggard-looking, but we were damn glad to see him. We had reckoned long ago that he had been done in somewhere along the way from Fresno. After he fattened up a bit, Grat was excited as a kid about the prospect of striking back at a railroad.

Once more the target was the Santa Fe's Texas Express, and we planned to hit it at Red Rock, a few miles north of the Wharton stop. Bob said it was a good plan because the detectives wouldn't suspect us hitting so close to where we had before. He also said Flo was sure of her information on this one, that the express would be carrying big payrolls to Texas. For this job, two new gang members were recruited: Bill Powers and Dick Broadwell. Both were former cowpunchers at the XB who were tired of the long hours and low pay. Broadwell was a tall, polite cowhand who had come to Indian Territory to escape his gambling debts. Powers had a thick mustache he kept stroking like a cat. He didn't say much, but he had wild-looking eyes that took everything in. All told, there were now eight long riders in the Dalton army, not counting our spy Flo Quick. Bob never told us how she got her information, but I reckon it wasn't dressed in the men clothes she liked to wear around the gang.

The skinny was worth whatever she had traded to get it. We found out a decoy train, stuffed with deputies with itchy fingers, was preceding all the real express trains these days. The Daltons weren't the only ones robbing trains in Indian Territory, but we got most of the credit, or the blame, depending on how you looked at it. If you added up all the rewards that were out for various members of the gang—including the Choctaw Kid—it amounted to more than $100,000.

That made us approach the Red Rock job sort of cautious. It was a good thing, because Grat would have spoiled it by jumping the decoy train if Bob hadn't held him back. We waited in the dark and let the first train roll by, then swarmed down on the second train. The decoy train, loaded with detectives, sailed on southward without the slightest idea the money it was supposed to be guarding was under siege.

Grat jumped the engine and got the train stopped, but not before the two express messengers locked the door of their car and started pumping lead out of the gun ports the railway had added. They didn't hit anything but it proved annoying. They opened up, after they ran out of ammunition, and we threatened to dynamite the car. Even then they tried that old story about not having the combination, but they gave that up quickly enough when Grat threatened to start shooting at their toes and work his way up.

There was only sixteen hundred in the safe.

"Where the hell is the rest?" Bob demanded, peering into the stove and going through boxes and drawers.

"There ain't no more," one of the messengers said. "The railroad has advised its customers not to ship money across Indian Territory until the Dalton gang has been brought under control. Shipments have been way down."

Bob cussed and kicked at the freight boxes.

"You mean to tell me the railroad is willing to cut its own throat by turning away business and spending ten times more than we've ever stolen on extra trains and men to guard every express shipment across the Territory?"

"Yes sir, Mr. Dalton, that's about the size of it."

Because of the meager pickings at Red Rock, another job was planned just as soon as Flo could coax some information out of a randy station agent or two. And I'll be a sonuvabitch if the place she came up with wasn't Adair—twenty miles from Claremore, the town where Clem Rogers had caused so much trouble for us over a few broncs. It was too close to the county where the Daltons weren't exactly welcome. But Flo swore that seventeen thousand dollars in government cash would be in the safe in the express car. She said she had heard it from more than one source. Bob believed it, too. The gang agreed that Adair would be next.

Looking back, we were just plain stupid.

If you want to catch a mouse, you use some cheese.

If you want to catch a gang of train robbers, this was just the kind of rumor you would use to bait the trap.

Twenty-one

A STORM WAS BREWING. Lightning streaked the sky to the southwest and dark clouds were building, hiding the stars. It had been a hot night but you could feel the air cool as the storm front rolled in. I hitched Cimarron to the rail, and pulled my duster around me to hide the Colt as I jumped onto the platform at the depot.

It was nine-thirty and there were no passengers waiting for the express at the Katy station, just a couple of old men talking and smoking pipes on the spit-and-whittle bench. The station agent was busy reading a newspaper in the glow of a kerosene lamp. A cage like a bank teller's window separated him from the customers.

I walked up and cleared my throat.

"Need a ticket?" he asked, barely glancing up from his newspaper. "Where to?"

"I want to ride the express," I said, and pulled my Colt out from under my duster. I leveled it at the agent, who threw his hands in the air before I told him to.

"Have you done this before?" I asked.

"No, sir," he answered. "Is this all right?"

"Fine," I said. "I'm going to have to tie you up now, but I don't want you to take it personal. Believe me, it's for your own good."

"I understand," he said. "You're the Choctaw Kid, ain't you? I recognized you from your wanted poster. Are you really as fast as they say you are? Have you really killed seven men?"

"Nobody's as fast as some people say," I said, "and I damn sure haven't killed seven. Where do the newspapers get those lies?"

I found some rope and tied his arms and feet together, and stuffed a kerchief in his mouth to keep him from babbling. Since it was handy, I emptied the contents of the cash drawer into a sack and took the revolver I found beneath the counter. Then I lit the red lantern and strolled outside to place it beside the tracks.

Bitter Creek was up on the platform now. He revealed his Winchester to the two old-timers and asked them to behave themselves for a spell. They agreed readily enough, and then asked us if we was the Dalton gang.

"We ain't the Ladies' Temperance," Bitter Creek said. "Now, fill your pipes and stop gabbing. We have work to do."

The rest of the gang was scattered about in the shadows, some standing guard at either end of the depot and others staying close, waiting to jump onto the train. I went back inside and took a seat at the agent's bay window to make it appear everything was fine. A few drops of rain began to splatter against the glass.

We didn't have long to wait. The train pulled into the depot right on schedule and rumbled to a halt. Flo's information was that the railroad had discontinued the use of decoy trains after the Red Rock robbery. The train looked sincere enough, so Grat and Emmett jumped up into the cab and introduced their Colts to the engineer and brakeman.

Bob, Powers, and Broadwell made for the express car, but not before the messenger shoved home the lock. I came out of the depot to join them, and Bill Doolin stood guard while we tried to get the door open.

Bitter Creek's rifle boomed.

"What's going on?" Bob demanded.

"Somebody got off the train and ran to the coal shed over there. I couldn't see who it was, but I think there was a couple of them."

"What are they doing now?"

"I can't see."

"Probably some passengers that reckoned they were better off the hell away from this," Bob muttered, "but keep your eye on them." He turned his attention back to the express car.

"Listen up in there," he shouted, "We have a bundle of dynamite that we're going to use unless you open this door. All we want is the safe, and we don't care how we get it."

No reply.

"Where the hell does the railroad get these guys?" Bob asked.

"Don't know," Doolin said, spitting chewing tobacco on the ground. "Maybe they have a ranch where they breed their mamas with mules and raise 'em on shoe leather."

"They act like it's their own goddamn money," Bob fumed.

Grat marched the engineer and fireman down the track ahead of his Winchester, toward us. Both had their hands up.

"We expected you at Pryor Creek," the engineer said.

"Well, we didn't want to disappoint you," Bob said. "Listen, tell your friend inside the express car that if he doesn't open up we're going to turn it into kindling."

"You tell him," the engineer spat, which prompted a jab in the ribs from Grat's carbine.

"All right," Bob said, "tell him to open up or we're going to shoot the crew, starting with the engineer."

"Open up, Williams!" the engineer shouted.

"He's bluffing," Williams answered from behind the door.

"Let's not find out," the engineer shouted at the door.

Bob fired his rifle into the air. Grat clamped a hand over the engineer's mouth.

"The fireman's next," Bob called.

The latch scraped and the door rolled back.

"Thank you, Williams," Broadwell said, jumping up into the express car with his pistol drawn. "We do appreciate you taking the trouble to open up for us, and I'm sure you and the engineer can have a beer and a laugh about this at the next stop."

"It wasn't funny," the engineer said.

"I knew it was a bluff," Williams said, sniffing. "You don't think I'd actually let them shoot you?"

"You always did like Harry better than you did me," the engineer said, jerking a thumb at the fireman.

"Emmett, you keep an eye on these gentlemen, and if they so much as twitch a muscle, plug 'em," Bob said. "I'm tired of their chatter."

While Grat went to fetch the wagon we had brought—Bob meant to clean everything out of the express car, not just the contents of the safe —Broadwell was coaxing the combination out of Williams. Broadwell, who was a gentleman even when he was committing armed robbery, asked him politely in which order he would like to have his fingers blown off.

Williams miraculously remembered the combination.

"Damn," Bob said, "where's the money?"

While Bob was rummaging through the safe, and the other boys loaded the wagon with freight, a shadowy figure jumped down from one of the cars' smoking platforms. He identified himself as a deputy marshal, followed by three quick shots. The balls dug chunks out of the wooden side of the express car, but did no other damage. The boys outside jumped down under the wagon and returned fire, Grat and Bob took up positions at the door, and the coal shed fairly exploded with volleys from three or four guns.

"Goddamn, how many of them are there?" Grat asked.

"Nine," Williams volunteered. "There are nine special deputies riding on this train, led by Captain Le Flore."

"Charles Le Flore? Head of the Cherokee National Police Force?"

"The same."

"I'll be a sonuvabitch. We've been set up."

"What do we do now?" Grat asked.

"Boys, it looks like we're going to have to shoot our way out of here."

There was Le Flore and three others at the coal shed, and perhaps five still on board the train. When the lightning flashed I could see rifle barrels bristling out of windows, waiting for a target. Then the thunder came, and I could feel the roar telegraphed up through the floor of the express car and into the soles of my boots. The sound was mixed with rifle and pistol fire as Doolin and Bitter Creek kept the deputies pinned down.

"Maybe we should use Messenger Williams here as a hostage," Bob said over his shoulder, then fired a few rounds out the door at the shed. "But no, on second thought, he's not big enough to stop but maybe forty or fifty rounds."

The comment had its desired effect; the messenger's eyes threatened to bug out of their sockets and his hands began to shake.

Then the rain came sweeping across the plain in a sheet, drumming over the depot and the coal shed and blowing inside the door of the express car. Everything was getting drenched, and it was hard to see more than ten or twenty yards.

"This is it," Bob said. "They can't see in this downpour any better than we can. Let's get to the horses."

Bob gave a rebel yell and jumped out the door, followed quickly by Grat and Broadwell, and all of them were firing as fast as they could. Similar explosions of gunfire echoed from the windows of the passenger car and the coal shed. Although I could hear lead smacking the sides of the car and the wagon, and splattering against the rails, nobody was hit.

I touched the charm around my neck. Not that I was superstitious, but I just felt better knowing it was there. Then I drew my Colt and jumped into the storm after them, but I didn't fire my revolver for fear of wasting ammunition that I might need soon enough.

The ground was slick, and my right foot went out from under me as I hit the ground. My leg snapped with a loud *pop!* and I thought I had been shot—my knee felt like it had just exploded, and wave after wave of pain radiated from it. I landed with my leg underneath me at a crazy angle. I couldn't get up.

"Bob!" I cried.

Bob, who was already twenty yards away, stopped dead and whirled around. He ran back through the rain, firing his Winchester from the hip, and with his right hand he grabbed my shirtfront and jerked me to my feet. My knee couldn't take the weight and I collapsed, the buckskin shirt ripping away and the medicine charm going with it. I scrambled to catch it, but it was too late; the bag was torn open and the trinkets spilled everywhere.

A bolt of lightning crashed down and hit the roof of the depot, showering sparks everywhere and ringing the bells in our ears. That scene, brilliantly lit by the bolt, was seared into my mind: the lawmen standing or kneeling beside the shed, rifles at their shoulder, shell casings frozen in midair as they spun out of the top of their carbines. Bitter Creek and Doolin caught in mid-stride as they ran toward their horses at the hitch rail, Doolin shaking the spent rounds from his cylinder as he ran.

"Come on, dammit!" Bob yelled, jerking me back up and away from where the things had spilled. The bolt of lightning had torn away the screen of night and rain and shown the lawmen our positions, at least for an instant. As Bob dragged me away from the spot where we'd been, bullets nipped at my heels.

I shoved what was left of the medicine charm in my pocket as Bob tossed me over his shoulder and threw me into the back of the wagon. Then he jumped up in the seat, emptied the two last rounds from his Winchester, and cracked the reins. The wagon jerked away, and Bitter Creek jumped on as we rounded the end of the depot, bullets whizzing wildly overhead.

We made our escape down the only street in Adair, mud flying from the wheels and the other boys racing alongside on their horses. Behind us, Le Flore and his men sent a few leaden reminders after us.

"Cimarron," I gasped.

But he was running right beside us. Doolin had mounted him after his own horse was killed at the hitch rail by a lucky rifle shot.

Twenty-two

WE LEARNED FROM THE PAPERS the next day that Doolin's poor horse wasn't the only casualty of the fight at Adair. The town's two physicians, doctors Youngblood and Goff, had been sitting playing chess in the drugstore across the street from the depot when the battle started, and both had been hit by stray bullets.

Goff had died and Youngblood was seriously wounded.

"Sonuvabitch," Bob cursed, wadding the paper into a ball and throwing it into the camp fire. "It wasn't our fault. It was that goddamn wild shooting of Le Flore and his bunch."

"That's not how folks will see it," Doolin said calmly, sitting on his haunches with a cup of Arbuckle's between his palms. "If they catch us, you can bet they'll pin a murder rap onto the robbery charge."

Grat nodded.

"And for what?" Doolin asked. "A hundred and fifty dollars split eight ways?"

"Don't forget the clothes," Emmett said. "There were the clothes we stole and the thirty dollars the Kid got from the station agent."

"Right," Doolin said. "How could I forget the ladies' clothes?"

"I said I was sorry," Bob replied.

The mood was one of general, unrelieved misery. We had risked our lives in a desperate battle with Le Flore and his squad of detectives, and all we had to show for it was a few dollars. An innocent man had been killed and another shot up pretty badly. Doolin lost his horse. I had busted up my knee in the jump from the express car, and it was swollen up to twice its usual size. I could not yet stand to walk on it. Worse, I had lost my medicine charm.

The morning after Adair, I emptied my pocket and examined what contents I had managed to save. It was mostly trash: feathers and a few bones and teeth from small animals, a shiny rock, and a shell casing from a .45 pistol. I told myself it was foolish to believe that such things had been my luck, but I could not quite convince myself as I pitched the remains into the brush. There was no point in hanging on to it, since the magic was supposed to leave once I saw the charms inside. I cursed myself for being superstitious, but that did not make me feel any better about the future. My confidence had been shattered.

Doolin, who grew up on Arkansas signs and omens, made no pretense about how he felt.

"It's not good, boys," he said. "We've pissed off a witch or something. I'm going to lay out for awhile until this bad luck blows over."

"Look," Bob said, "what we need is one last job that will bring in enough money so we can retire. A bank, maybe. That's not like an express car—at least we know the big money's in there. Thirty, forty thousand dollars."

"Where?" Grat asked. "Which bank?"

"Van Buren, Arkansas, maybe. Wouldn't it be something to rob the United States marshal's own bank?"

Emmett began to perk up, but Doolin shook his head.

"Count me out, fellows," Doolin said. "I'm headed home until the signs improve."

The gang drifted apart. Broadwell and Powers took their leave until the hell from the Adair fiasco died down. Bob holed up with Flo Quick and kept watch over Grat and Emmett. The thought of living in a shack with three men and a girl for several weeks didn't appeal to me, so I begged my leave over Bob's objections. It was well past time, I told him, that I see our mother again.

Even though the others had told her I was alive, we had not met face-to-face; truth to tell, I had purposely passed up several opportunities to see her, out of fear of having her ask why I hadn't come sooner. The longer I waited, the worse the problem got and the more reluctant I became. But after the Adair robbery, I had the feeling that if I did not see her soon, I would never get another chance. There was a chill over the gang, and although I did not tell Bob this, I held no hope in my heart for our future.

So a few days after the Adair battle I saddled Cimarron and rode out of our hideout near Sand Springs. I was bound for Kingfisher, on the edge of Cheyenne-Arapaho Reservation in the west central portion of the Territory.

Bob told me to take my time and ride around the bigger towns, because there were marshals on the lookout for us everywhere. I could stop about halfway at the town of Ingalls, near the Cimarron River, for supplies, Bob said; the town was so dominated by outlaws that a marshal would be forfeiting his life if he set foot there.

He said I had to be particularly careful to visit the homestead at Kingfisher only at night. Surely the place was being watched. It was common enough knowledge that the mother of the Dalton clan lived there.

I came into sight of Ingalls on the afternoon of my second day in the saddle. The place was a favorite hangout of Bitter Creek Newcomb, who romanced a girl there by the name of Rosa Dunn. I had often heard him speak of Murray's Saloon, and so, being somewhat fond of Bitter Creek and no longer adverse to the taste of whiskey and beer, I hitched Cimarron to the rail outside. I shook the trail dust from my clothes and stepped into the saloon. None of the customers resembled Bitter Creek.

I crossed to the bar and ordered a beer. I drank in silence, reluctant to ask about Newcomb by name. Something was bothering me that I couldn't quite put my finger on. Like all saloons, this one had a large glass mirror stretching across the back bar, and while I drank I idly studied the reflection of the room in the mirror. It was hot as blazes inside and out that day. I had drank nearly half my beer when one of the men playing poker at a corner table took off his hat and wiped his head with a kerchief. Along one side of his nearly bald head was a long, angry, red scar.

It was the bastard William Towerly.

I placed the mug carefully on the bar, turned, and walked stiffly over to within five paces of the table. My knee was still so swollen it was hard to get my pants leg over it. Towerly clamped his hat back on his head with his right hand and looked at me curiously.

"Bloody Bill Towerly," I said.

"Is there something I can do for, pardner?" he asked.

"You don't remember me, do you?"

"Should I?"

"Yes, you should."

"Wait a minute," Towerly said, squinting his eyes. He had grown older, and what hair he had was turning gray. The skin on his face had turned wrinkled and blotchy. I was hoping he would go for his gun, but his hands remained on top of the table, holding his cards.

"I think I've heard about you," he said, not unpleasantly. "You're the kid that rides with the Dalton gang, aren't you? Long hair, beaded gun belt. Hat. Yeah, I've read your description in the newspapers."

"Do you remember Frank Dalton?"

His right cheek twitched, as if a bug had just crawled over it, but Towerly shook his head slowly and said he'd never heard of the man.

"You're lying," I said.

The chairs of his three poker partners scraped on the rough wood floor as they moved back. One man went clear to the other end of the room.

"I don't know what you mean, friend," Towerly said, and his hands started to shake.

"You killed Frank Dalton in the Bottoms across from Fort Smith on a Sunday morning four years ago. He had come to serve writs on your bootlegging gang. After he was down, you walked over to him and stuck the barrel of a Winchester in his mouth and pulled the trigger. You widowed his wife and orphaned his two sons. I was there, I saw you do it."

"That was a long time ago," Towerly said, and started inching his hand toward the table edge.

"Go ahead and draw," I said. "I've been looking for you a long time to kill you, but I'm not going to do it without giving you a chance to draw. You don't deserve it, because you didn't give Frank that chance, but I can't do what you did. Draw."

Towerly's hand was frozen to the table.

"You're the Choctaw Kid," Towerly said. "If I draw on you, you'll kill me."

"Won't know until we try. Draw."

"Let's work this out some other way," he said, smiling. He took off his hat again, and put it on the table in front of him while he wiped his brow. "I'm sorry if I did your brother any harm. Let me buy you a drink and let's talk, friend."

He picked up his hat with his left hand. I knew he had drawn his gun with his other hand and was using the hat to cover it. It was an old trick, and it nearly worked.

I jumped to the left as Towerly's gun spit fire and lead through the crown of his hat, but I was a mite slow because of my bad knee. The ball grazed my right shoulder and went on to shatter the mirror behind the bar. But before the bullet struck the glass I had fanned my Colt, and Towerly had toppled backwards with three bullet holes in his chest.

Not knowing how many friends he had in the place, I reloaded before struggling back to my feet. The lunge had torn things lose in my knee again and it was throbbing. As it turned out, Towerly had no friends left.

"Are you all right, mister?" the bartender asked.

"Yeah," I said, holstering my gun and cutting the sleeve away from my upper arm. "It didn't hit anything important. I just bleed a lot."

One of Towerly's former poker buddies was leaning over him.

"Dead as a doornail," he said. "Three shots—you could cover them all with a silver dollar. Damn good shooting, Kid."

I went back to my beer and finished it.

"Sorry about the mirror," I said, peeling fifty dollars from my poke. "I hope that will cover it." I hesitated, then asked the bartender if the place served steak.

"You bet," he said. "How do you want it cooked?"

"Not for me," I said and pulled another ten-dollar bill from the roll. "Drinks and steak for Bitter Creek Newcomb and his girl when they come in. Okay?"

"Thanks, Kid."

I started for the door, but then remembered something.

"Bloody Bill," I said. "Was he carrying a watch?"

"Yeah," the poker buddy said. "Nice watch on a fob. Has a hunting scene."

"It was Frank's," I said. "Let me have it."

He took it from Towerly's vest, unhooked the chain, and threw it to me. I caught it, feeling the warmth of it in my hand—the warmth of Towerly's body, now spilling into the sawdust on the saloon floor.

I slipped the watch in my pocket, touched my hat, and walked outside into the July sun.

Twenty-three

I RODE ONTO THE HOMESTEAD near Kingfisher under the cover of a new moon, and staked Cimarron in the yard. I lifted the back door latch with the blade of my knife and slipped into the house through the kitchen.

Mama was sitting in a rocker, humming softly to herself. She seemed smaller and more frail than I remembered, and she reminded me of nothing so much as a little bird perched in the chair. She stopped her knitting when she saw my shadow in the doorway to the front room.

"Who's there?" she asked.

"It's me," I said. "Samuel."

"Come into the light," she said.

I walked into the room and stopped a few paces away from her, in the circle of light thrown by the kerosene lamp. She put a hand to her face and studied my features for a moment. Her hair had all turned gray, and the lines in her face were careworn and deep.

"It is you," she said.

"Yes," I said.

She put her arms out and we embraced, her in the chair and me down on one knee in front of the rocker, like I was still a little kid.

"Why didn't you come back?" she asked. "We thought you were dead for the longest time, and then we rejoiced when I heard from your brothers that you were alive. But why didn't you come back to see me?"

"I don't know, Mama. Just couldn't," I said.

"What happened to your nose?" she asked, but before I could answer she noticed the bloodstained tear on the right sleeve of my buckskin shirt. "And this? What happened here?"

"I caught it on a fence," I said.

"A fence that leaves powder burns? Take it off and I will dress the wound and sew your shirt up for you. And please take that gun off in the house."

"I can't, Mama," I said, pulling the shirt over my head. "There's marshals everywhere. My arm is fine. I dressed it myself."

She shook her head as she gathered the shirt on her lap.

"Fetch me the sewing basket on the table," she said. "I don't understand what happened to you boys. Where did I go wrong?" She opened the basket and selected a heavy needle. "I tried to raise you right, Lord knows I tried. Why couldn't you have been like Henry or Littleton or Frank?"

"I don't know, Mama," I said.

"But you know I still love you. You know that, don't you?"

"Yes, Mama. I still love you, too."

She closed her eyes and began to cry, heartbreaking sobs that shook her small body. I tried to comfort her, but it was no use. She cried until she had no more tears left, and when she was done I asked her if she would like me to fetch her Bible.

"No, Samuel," she said. "I can find no comfort in it anymore."

It made me sick to hear her say that, because all during the time I had been in the wilderness and on the owlhoot trail with my brothers, I had this picture of Mama in my head. She was sitting by the fire in her rocker, the Bible on her lap, humming "Rock of Ages." Now, it is fine to brag that you and your brothers put no store in those Sunday-school fairytales, but it is something else when your own sweet mother tells you that she no longer has faith. I felt guilty, like me and my brothers were responsible for ruining things for her, and I wished I had not come.

"I am sorry that we hurt you so," I said.

"Men will do what men have to do," she said, "but it is the women that are left at home to mourn. Samuel, I am terribly afraid of losing you boys like I lost Frank. It doesn't matter to me what you've done—I still love you all as much as the day you were born. Why don't you give up now and turn yourself in? Marshal Thomas says that's the only way to keep yourselves from getting killed."

"Heck Thomas was here?"

"Yesterday," she said. "He is an honest and true man, Samuel, and I know he will keep his word."

"I can't leave my brothers," I said.

"You're bullheaded just like them," she said. "Here is your shirt. Do you want some supper?"

"I can't stay long, not with the marshals buzzing around," I said, pulling on the shirt. "I don't want to bring you trouble."

"It's a little late for that," she said. "Come into the kitchen and I will warm the stew and cornbread for you."

I ate with the Colt in my lap, and when I had finished I held my mother's hand for a long while, and neither of us said anything. Then I pressed my lips to the back of that gentle hand and said I must go.

"You look so tired," she said. "Can't you stay the night?"

"No," I said. "Goodbye."

"Don't say goodbye," she said. "I can't bear it."

"All right, then. Adios."

I left two hundred dollars, which had come from the Lilietta holdup, on the kitchen table, and slipped out of the house and into the shadows.

Twenty-four

BOB HAD COME UP with a plan in the weeks since the fiasco at Adair, but he was being closemouthed about it until he had the gang together. We rendezvoused one night in the cabin near Sand Springs. It was chilly that night, and a fire was popping in the stone fireplace as everyone got comfortable. Bill Doolin was there, and Grat and Emmett, of course, and the new men, Bill Powers and Dick Broadwell.

A jug was passed around. Grat was taking the biggest pulls of anybody. Broadwell nipped at it, just to be polite. Doolin passed it on to Powers, who tipped it so far back that some of the whiskey spilled out the corners of his mouth. Emmett was sitting off in a corner, turning his harmonica over in his hand.

"I heard you potted Bloody Bill Towerly at Murray's Saloon at Ingalls," Doolin commented, cleaning his fingernails with a knife blade. "Three balls in the chest."

"Three of a kind," I said, "beat what he held in his hand."

By and by Bob cleared his throat, pulled up his trouser legs, and knelt down on the wood floor of the cabin, where he started drawing with a lump of charcoal.

"Let me just show you what I have in mind," Bob said.

He drew a wedge shape, like a piece of pie, and at the crust end he wrote, "Eighth Street." Along the right side of the wedge, he put, "Union," and on the left, "Walnut."

"Must be Coffeyville," Doolin said, sticking the knife into the floor.

At the tip of the pie Bob scrawled, "Condon Bank."

"A bank?" Powers asked.

"I'm not done yet," Bob said.

On the Union Street side of the piece he sketched in a city block, and about even with the tip of the pie he drew a rectangle in the block and labeled it, "First National."

"Two banks," Bob said. "We hit them both at the same time. That means we get double the loot we would from a single robbery. It won't be like trying to stop a train, guessing whether there's money in the damned express safe or not. It's a natural fact that banks have money, lots of it. Think of it. Enough money to set us up for the rest of our lives. It will be our last job."

"It's never been done, two banks at once," Emmett said, some of the old fire showing in his eyes. "Even ole Jesse didn't try that."

"I don't like it," Doolin said. "That's your hometown. They know you there. We couldn't ride in for a stick of gum without those folks recognizing the Daltons and raising holy hell."

"We'll wear disguises," Bob said.

"Even if you aren't recognized," Doolin continued, "we don't have enough men to take down two banks at once. Emmett here seems to think this is some kind of game, where we're out to top the James-Younger gang. Hell, don't you remember what happened to them at Northfield, Minnesota? They got shot clear to hell by every nester and greenhorn that could walk into the hardware store and borrow a rifle. And they were just trying to rob one bank."

"We can do it," Bob said. "We know Coffeyville. Those folks will be too busy trying to stop their knees from shaking to give us any trouble."

"That's a dangerous way to think," Doolin said.

"How much money do you reckon we could get?" Powers asked.

"I wouldn't be surprised if we walked away with sixty or seventy thousand dollars, maybe a hundred thousand. I think I could live on my share of that for a few years, don't you?"

"Damn right," Powers said, and I knew he was hooked.

"I'm not so sure," Doolin said, "not with Bob Dalton dividing the shares. It always seems like Bob comes out with twice as much as anybody else."

"Look here, Doolin," Bob said, "as leader of this gang I have certain expenses that you men don't, such as the inside information we get."

"Like that good intelligence we got about Adair?" Doolin snorted. "It'd be cheaper if we just wired the railroads and asked them polite if they'd tell us when their next payroll shipment was going to be."

"I know what Bob spends his money on," Powers said, and made an obscene gesture.

Bob smacked him and sent his hat flying.

"That'll be enough of that," Bob said. "Flo and I are going to retire to Mexico after this job and buy us a little hacienda. That's how good this haul is going to be. Even shares, I promise."

Broadwell, who had been carefully rolling a cigarette during the last exchange, put it between his lips and lit it with a stick from the fire.

"It sounds mighty tempting, gents," he said, exhaling a blue cloud of smoke. "But let's not allow the size of the pot to lead us to ignore the odds. It sounds awful risky, and I'd like to hear how Bob proposes to pull this off."

"We'll hit them early in the morning in the middle of the week, just after they open. Neither bank hires a guard. There won't be many people on the Plaza then. The Choctaw Kid will go in first to reconnoiter the area, and stand near this well." Bob drew a circle out from the tip of the Condon Bank pie. "When the streets are clear and neither bank has any customers, he'll give us the high sign, like taking off his hat and wiping his head. That's when we'll move in. We'll have our horses tied at the rail down here on Walnut Street, where they'll be handy."

"What kind of disguises are you going to wear?" Doolin asked.

"Fake beards," Bob said. "Now, Grat and Powers and Broadwell will take the Condon Bank. Grat will be in charge of that group. At the same time, Emmett and Doolin and I will hold up the First National."

"What about me?" I asked.

"You'll go back and stay with the horses," Bob said.

"The horses will be hitched," Powers asked. "Wouldn't it make more sense for the Kid to keep standing guard?"

"I don't know," Bob said quickly. "Our horses are our lifeline out of there, and they need guarding. But I'll think about it. Now, once we get inside the banks, we need to work quickly. Grab all the cash and gold you can and hightail to the ponies."

"When do we divide up the loot?" Broadwell asked.

"We're going to have to outrun a posse first," Bob said. "Twenty miles south of the state line we'll have fresh horses waiting for us. We'll ride southwest, and avoid towns where the law is likely to wire ahead with news of the robbery. We'll also have to stay clear of places like this cabin, where they might try to ambush us. At the first opportunity to take a breather, probably along the Cimarron River, we'll divide up and go our separate ways."

"Shouldn't we split up sooner?" Powers asked.

"I'd rather have us all together if it comes down to a fight with a posse," Bob said. "Besides, this way we can divide up our shares and split clean."

"You're right." Powers grinned.

"How many hardware stores are on that plaza?" Doolin asked.

"A couple, I reckon," Bob said. "But I don't know what you're worried about. We'll be in and out and rich before those poor dumb sand-cutters realize what's hit 'em. Besides, it would take quite a bit of firepower to stop the seven of us."

"Six," Doolin said, sheathing his knife. "There's only going to be six, because I don't aim to throw my life away just so you and your brothers can play-act. Robbing your hometown is a congenital dumb idea, Bob Dalton, and I'm ashamed for you. Just what're you trying to prove to those folks?"

"I'm just looking to get rich," Bob said. "And we don't have to prove a thing. Everybody's heard of the Daltons, by God, and they'd better stand aside."

"I think you want to be recognized," Doolin said. "I'm sorry, pardner, but I can't go with you on this one. It's getting late, and I reckon I'd better ride on out."

Doolin left.

"I need to chew this one a little finer, too," Broadwell said. "Nothing personal, Bob, I just need some time."

"Take all the time you need," Bob said, "but we're riding out in the morning."

Broadwell nodded and said he'd be back by midnight.

"He's going to talk with Doolin," Bob said, disgusted, and rubbed out the drawing on the floor with the sole of his boot. "Just who the hell is leader of this gang, anyway?"

It was a crazy idea, all right—two banks at once in a town where just the mention of the name Dalton was likely to booger folks. I stared into the fire and tried to keep myself from thinking about how Doolin was right, and how Bob wanted to hit Coffeyville for all the wrong reasons. But I also knew I was in this thing from soda to huck, and I couldn't turn my back on my brothers even if it meant that hangman George Maledon was waiting for me at the end of the trail with his good Kentucky ropes. So I started lying to myself that Bob had the right idea about pulling one last big job, and retiring to a little ranch in Mexico and raising a family, and that got me to thinking about Jane.

Broadwell came back twenty minutes later and said that he was in.

He said he always was weak when it came to playing a single hand for big stakes.

We rode to near Gray Horse in the Osage Nation, waited until the dead of night, then visited the town's general store. Bob, who had been chief of police in nearby Pawhuska, still had a key to the store, and we let ourselves in.

There were ten new Colt .45s under the store's gun counter. Bob took all of them, and a hundred rounds of ammunition for each, to divide up among the gang. Bob and Grat also picked out new suits for themselves, and they tried to get me into one as well, but I told them I liked my buckskins fine. Then there were new boots, gold watches and chains, new shirts, socks, and candy.

Bob, who still had quite a poke from the express robberies, added up what we had taken and left the cash on the counter.

"Why don't we just take it?" Powers complained, loading one of the new .45s.

"We don't have anything against these people," Bob said. "Our prey is the banks and the railroads. Only a common thief would rob a storekeeper."

We drew up to the Schaefer place twenty miles this side of the Kansas line as dark was closing in the next night. Bob had known John Schaefer in the old days, and Schaefer—a cantankerous relic who had ridden with General Mosby during the war—had eagerly followed the gang's exploits in the newspapers.

"Too bad about that doc at Adair," Schaefer said coolly as Bob dismounted.

"Wasn't our fault," Bob said. "It was a wild shot from Le Flore's men."

"I knew it had to be something like that," Schaefer said, warming. "Damn Yankee railroads. To hear them tell it, you practically put the gun in the poor bastard's mouth . . . Who have you got with you, Robert?"

"You remember my brothers Grat and Emmett," Bob said. "Over there is Dick Broadwell, Bill Powers, and the Choctaw Kid. And this gentleman here is Tom King."

Schaefer's three grandchildren stampeded out the back door and gaggled around Bob's knees, begging for sweets.

"Gosh, your Uncle Bob is plumb out," he said, rummaging through the pockets of his duster. "Not a darned thing anywhere at all. Wait. What's this?"

Bob produced a handful of candy, and the trio of bandits squealed and snatched it away. Schaefer laughed and invited us inside, where his daughter-in-law was putting supper on the table. Schaefer's son had died of pneumonia two years before.

"I don't have enough for seven more men," Suzanne complained. She held a pot in the crook of her arm and a stirring spoon with the other, and brushed a wisp of hair away from her eyes with her wrist.

"Don't go to any trouble for us," Bob said.

"It's no trouble," Schaefer said. "We'll just throw another couple of birds into the skillet."

"Em, you're the cook in this outfit. Why don't you go help the lady by killing the chickens and cleaning them for her? Don't worry, John, we'll pay for what we eat."

"Your money's no good here, Bob Dalton," Schaefer said. Emmett inquired as to where the hatchet was kept and then trudged unhappily off.

"John, I have a favor to ask," Bob said.

"You usually do. What do you need?"

"I'd like to keep some broncs in your corral until we come back for them day after tomorrow," Bob said, popping some of the candy into his mouth. "It would be helpful if they were saddled and ready to go, with a sack or two of chuck packed on. And if we don't show up to claim them, they're yours."

"Now, when you come back to get them, is there any chance a posse is going to be punctuating the air with lead?"

"There's that possibility," Bob allowed. "But I reckon you can hitch the broncs to a picket line down by the creek. How were you to know the Daltons used your back acreage to stake their fresh mounts?"

"Reckon I wouldn't," Schaefer said, rubbing a hand over his jaw. "But won't you need me to tend the horses until you get here?"

"No," Bob said, "our friend Tom King will see to that. He's in charge of our remuda on this job."

"What're you going to hit?" the old man asked with a gleam in his eyes.

"You know we can't tell you, John. It's for your own good. We might be a little busy when we come for the broncs, so we'll pay in advance," Bob said, withdrawing his rolls of notes. "Here's fifty dollars for your trouble."

"I told you, your money's no good," Schaefer said.

"Take it," Bob commanded. "It's little enough for all the times you've boarded me when I needed it. Take it and spend it on your grandkids."

The old man took the bill, folded it, and tapped it into the pocket of his coveralls. After dinner, he lined the grandchildren up and made them shake Bob's hand one-by-one.

"I want them to be able to tell *their* children that they shook Mr. Robert Dalton's hand," Schaefer said.

We slept in the barn and were up at daybreak. Bob kissed Tom King goodbye and then the six of us were off. We were less than a day's ride from Coffeyville.

Twenty-five

WE MADE CAMP on Onion Creek, just south of the state line, late in the afternoon of the next day, and we spent what light was left to clean our guns and fill out our cartridge loops. I reckon we looked like a regular army encampment, with the gleaming rifles stacked up and the horses on the picket line and a sentry posted to keep watch for lawmen. Supper was cold biscuits from a sack that old Schaefer had given us, because we didn't dare light a fire and draw attention to ourselves. I drew the watch after we ate, and didn't see anything but a raccoon skulking along the creek bank.

Grat relieved me and I went back to the camp, where I lay on my bedroll looking up at the stars. All day I had been thinking how Bob had made plans to retire to Mexico with his Flo, and how long it had been since I had seen Jane, and how she had been part of the reason I set off to Indian Territory with Frank so long ago.

At about midnight I couldn't stand it anymore, so I pulled on my boots and started off for the picket line. Grat, who was still on watch, asked me where the hell I thought I was going.

"Into town," I said.

"Bring me back some whiskey," was all he said.

Cimarron and I followed the old familiar trail, and in less than twenty minutes we were at the old homestead, which was dark and overgrown with weeds. I shivered in spite of myself as I hitched Cimarron to what was left of the fence out back, and crossed over to the Williamson place. It looked just like I remembered it.

The windows upstairs were dark, which damped my hopes somewhat, but there was still light in the kitchen. I crept up to one of the windows and glanced over the sill. Jane was sitting at the table, gently rocking a baby in her arms. The baby was fussy and Jane worked patiently to calm it to sleep, singing nonsense songs and patting it gently. It was a beautiful sight, Jane with her long brown hair fallen over her shoulders and her eyes smiling at the baby. It nearly brought tears to my eyes thinking how I missed her. When the baby finally fell to sleep she went into the other room to put it down. I had lifted the back door latch with the blade of my knife, and was sitting at the kitchen table when she came back into the room.

Jane's eyes got wild and a scream started deep in her throat, and I had to clamp my hand over her mouth to keep her from waking the whole family.

"It's me," I said. "Samuel."

But she was struggling like the devil himself had got ahold of her, and she even tried to bite my fingers, so I had to hold on tighter and think of something else.

"Truly it's me," I said. "Remember how Johnny and I were best friends? Remember when I chopped the wood for you that day and a splinter cut your face? Do you?"

She nodded, but her eyes were still wild.

"I'm not going to hurt you," I said. "Promise you won't scream when I let you go. I just want to talk. That's all."

I could feel her body relaxing a bit.

"No screaming," I reminded as I lifted my hand.

She studied my face for a moment while I drank in hers. There were lines in her face, to be sure, and crow's feet beginning to form at the corners of her eyes, but it was still Jane, all right.

"Samuel, is it really you?" she asked. "You look so different. Your nose, that hair. My word, we were told you had perished in the Big Blizzard after you'd run off."

"I didn't, and I never stopped thinking of you," I said, stretching things just a bit. "I've come back for you. I want you to go away with me to Mexico, where we can buy a ranch and raise a family."

I held her face in my hands and I kissed her on the lips. She closed her eyes and kissed back, ever so slightly. Then she pulled away from me.

"Where will you get the money to buy a ranch?" she asked. "You haven't been riding with your outlaw brothers, have you? Oh, Samuel, you have—I can tell it in your eyes. You were so sweet and honest. How could you have turned so wicked?"

"I'm the same," I said. "I feel just the same for you."

I kissed her again, harder, and ran my hand over her thigh. She pushed me away.

"How can you say you haven't changed?" she asked. "The Samuel I knew would never treat me like that, never. What has become of you? You're just like your brothers. And you're wearing those awful smelly clothes. And how could you come into my house wearing a pistol?"

"I'm not like the others in the gang," I protested.

"The stories in the *Journal,*" she said. "You mean to tell me they're lies? That you've never killed, never shot a man down with that pistol, never turned a wife into a widow? Tell me that and I will believe you."

I could not lie.

"Samuel," she said, and wept. She reached out and ran a hand over my cheek. "I waited for you for so long. You were so young, but I knew you loved me and would come back for me. The note you left me was so pure. It was the only thing that saved me from my father's hatred, and for that I'll always be grateful. But it's been so long. My father passed away two years ago and I thought you were dead."

"Did your mother remarry?" I asked.

"What do you mean?"

"Well, I know that baby's not more than a year old. Did your mother remarry?"

"Oh, Samuel," she said, and tears began streaking down her cheeks like rain. "That's not my little sister. That's *my* baby girl. I married Luke Baldwin last year."

Her words made my stomach turn to ice water. What a fool I had been to come to her kitchen, wearing my heart on my sleeve like a lovesick pup. And to lose her to that Methodist Lucious Baldwin, a store clerk who had been the darling of the schoolteachers but who I remembered as being dull as dirt. What could she have ever seen in him?

"He is here for me, Samuel," she said. "You never have been."

I nodded, put on my hat, and stood.

"I'll thank you not to mention my visit to anyone," I said, then turned away so she wouldn't see the tears in my eyes. But she reached out for my hand and squeezed it.

"I won't tell," she said. "I am sorry for what time has done to us, and I'll always remember you the way you were, not wicked like this. I will pray for you."

• • • •

"Where's my whiskey?" Grat asked.

"Go get it yourself," I said, walking past him. It was almost two o'clock in the morning, but the boys were still up. The night had turned downright frosty, and they sat with their collars pulled up against the cold.

"Where've you been?" Bob asked harshly.

"To the old home place," I said.

"Did anyone see you?"

I shook my head.

"You're lucky," Bob said. "You shouldn't have taken a chance like that. You should have stayed here. What possessed you to ride out to that shit hole, anyway?"

"I honestly don't know."

"It's a good thing I'm not a suspicious man," Powers said, not looking up, "or when I noticed the Kid was gone, I'd have thought he went to turn us in for that reward money."

"Shut your trap," Bob said. "The Kid is nickel-plated. If I didn't trust you, Bill, I'd think you had to have thoughts of turning us in for the reward yourself, to say it about the Kid."

"Didn't mean nothin', boss," Powers said.

"No more yapping, then," Bob ordered.

Everybody fell silent. Bob went to relieve Grat on watch. I walked out with him, and I stayed after Grat had walked back to the others.

"What's on your mind, little brother?" Bob asked. It had been a long time since he had called me that.

"I wanted to ask you why you wanted me to hold the horses tomorrow morning, instead of going into the banks," I said. "Doesn't seem like anybody really needs to hold them. There's a hitching rail there, and our business won't take but ten or fifteen minutes. Wouldn't I be more good on the inside?"

Bob looked up at the stars.

"You're the youngest," he said. "I don't want you inside one of the banks if there is shooting."

"But I'm as brave as either Grat or Emmett, and a measure faster," I said. "If there is shooting, you're going to need me with you."

He shook his head.

"I promised Mama the last time I saw her that I'd take care of you," he said. "I got to feeling guilty about all the risks I've already let you take."

"I get a full share, don't I? Then let me take the risks."

"Look here," Bob said. "To the law you're the Choctaw Kid, not Samuel Cole Dalton. If things get crossed up tomorrow and we don't get any money to retire to Mexico on, the rest of us might as well be dead because every deputy marshal in the country knows who we are. This is our big casino. We're nothing without money. But you've got a chance even if things are shot to hell tomorrow. If you escape, cut your hair and change your name, you can live the rest of your life without looking over your shoulder. Why do you think I've forbidden Em and Grat from calling you by your real name? It's been for your own protection, little brother."

"I reckon I ain't so little anymore. I want to go in."

Bob sighed heavily and his breath hung in the air.

"We'll see, Samuel," he said.

"There's just one thing I won't do," I said, "no matter what happens. I'm through with killing, Bob. I'm not going to do it anymore."

"You know I've never tolerated killing for killing's sake," Bob said. "I don't want anybody to get hurt. But you have a right to protect yourself, don't you?"

"No killing," I said. "I'm sick of it."

Twenty-six

BOB CHANGED HIS MIND about me holding the horses, of course, and told me to go into the Condon Bank to keep an eye on Grat. That's how I came to find myself with my back to the counter and lead whizzing in through the windows, staring at the date on the calendar on the back wall and realizing it was my seventeenth birthday.

I can't say I was surprised to find us in such a desperate fix, because we had defied the odds for too long. We were due. We should have hung it up, and left the trains and the banks to them that still had Lady Luck on their side. But as Grat was fond of saying, most every cowboy will back a losing streak quicker than a winning streak, convinced that his luck will change on the next hand. It looked like the Dalton gang had been dealt its last hand right there in Coffeyville.

Dick Broadwell had already been hit and his left arm hung limp at the elbow, blood pouring down his sleeve. Powers was sitting next to me with his back to the counter, whacking the back of his head against the wood and cursing himself for letting Grat swallow the line about the safe being on a time lock. Grat was cursing and looking around as if to ask Bob what to do, but Bob and Em had their hands full across the street at the First National. Out on the Plaza, the townspeople continued to arm themselves with rifles and pistols borrowed from the hardware stores, giving every indication that murder was in their hearts.

"The horses are out that door and down the alley to the right," Grat said when there was a momentary lull in the barrage coming in through the windows. "It's the only way out of here. And if we can't make the ground, by God, let's at least die game."

Grat got a good grip on the grain sack containing the loot, and jumped over the counter into the bank lobby. The others followed. I

vaulted over the counter and found myself on the bullet-pocked floor—
my knee gave out on me again. Grat looked over his shoulder and said,
"Stay put until we're clear. We'll bring you a horse." I believe he
thought I was hit.

The three of them—Grat, Powers, and Broadwell with his shattered
arm—dashed out the door of the bank into the sunlight. I struggled to
one knee and watched from the window of the bank. The storefronts on
either side of the Plaza exploded with gunfire. They were running and
shooting wild, and puffs of dust billowed around their feet where the
bullets hit from the first volley. Even though they were caught in a cross
fire, there didn't seem to be a decent shot among any of the vigilantes
outside, and the Plaza was quickly being obscured with smoke from
dozens of rifles. I hoped that they would make it.

Grat was halfway to the alley where the horses were hitched, when
he staggered and the money sack fell to the dirt. I could tell he was hurt
bad but he kept on moving, stumbling and dragging his feet toward the
horses, spinning and shooting his Winchester from the hip. Blood was
pouring out of his nostrils and down over his new suit.

Powers was hit in the stomach and Broadwell took a ball in the back,
but both made it into the alley with Grat. Powers was terrified. He
threw himself against the back door of the furniture store and beat his
fists savagely against it, but it was locked. He left bloody smudges on
the wood.

Broadwell, though shot in the arm and the back, managed to make it
to the Long Bell Lumber Yard, where he took shelter behind a stack of
planks.

Now well down the alley, those three were sheltered from the murderous cross fire from the Plaza. Grat, still on his feet, was leaning
against a barn with his Winchester in one hand and his head thrown
back, blood running down his mouth and chin. At that moment Charles
Connelly, the city marshal, walked into the alley between Grat and the
horses. Connelly carried a rifle but must have been somewhat confused
about where the battle was actually taking place. He never shouldered
his weapon and probably never even saw Grat, who shook his head in
an attempt to clear his vision and fired off-handed. Connelly crumpled
to the ground.

Then a gaunt figure appeared at the back fence of the livery stable,
holding a gleaming Model 86 Winchester with a thirty-inch barrel. It
was John Kleohr, the German who was the crack shot of the Coffeyville
Rifle Club. He shouldered the weapon and threw down on Grat, who

was still stumbling in the direction of the horses. Kleohr aimed like he had at the rifle match—high at first, and then letting the barrel settle down to the target. I could see his trigger hand tense as he squeezed off the shot. Kleohr hit Grat in the neck. Grat took a few steps, stumbled over the body of Marshal Connelly, then collapsed with his Winchester beneath him.

"No!" I shouted and pressed myself against the window. "No, goddammit, no!"

Powers managed to mount his horse, but was knocked immediately out of the saddle into the dirt. At that moment Bob and Em emerged from a nearby yard, and saw Grat and Powers lying dead in the alley.

After robbing the First National of twenty-one thousand dollars, they had cut out the back of the bank and snuck around Eighth Street to cross a yard and reach the horses. On the way Bob had killed three people with his Winchester. George Cubine was shot in front of his mechanic's shop. He had been holding a rifle, which was picked up by the shoemaker, Charles Brown. Bob killed him too. But the casualty of the First National Bank robbery was a 22-year-old clerk who worked at the hardware store next door. His name was Lucious Baldwin.

Baldwin, holding a .32 pearl-handled revolver loosely in his hand, was sneaking around to join the action. Bob, his Winchester leveled at the hip, shouted for Baldwin to drop his gun, but Baldwin gave no sign of hearing him. I reckon Lucious, who was trotting toward my brothers, just thought Bob and Em were a couple of citizens who had armed themselves at the hardware store.

"Drop that pistol," Bob shouted again.

When Baldwin still did not respond, Bob cursed and dropped him with a shot to the left chest.

Emmett was carrying the sack of loot and Bob was providing cover fire, but neither of them had realized how desperate the situation was until they set foot in the alley.

Bob stepped into the open and I saw Kleohr shoulder his rifle again.

I stumbled to the door of the bank and cocked my Colt. It was a good hundred yards, a difficult shot with a revolver, but not impossible. I held the gun straight out, sighting down the groove-and-blade sight. But I could not pull the trigger, not even to save my brother.

Bob spotted Kleohr too late; the Model 86 boomed and Bob was thrown backwards, his own rifle firing uselessly into the air. He got up, tried to lift his rifle, and was driven down with another shot from Kleohr's rifle. He fell against a pile of curbstones.

Emmett and Broadwell had managed to reach the horses and were up in the saddles. Bright streaks of blood were pouring down Broadwell's saddle skirts. They whipped their horses and sailed out together, the sack of loot thrown over Emmett's saddle.

Then Emmett spun his horse around and came tearing back down the alley, sparks flying from his horse's hooves as they struck the cobblestones. He reined his horse in where Bob lay and reached a hand down to help him into the saddle. Bob shook his head.

Not a shot had been fired as Emmett made his desperate run down the alley, but as soon as he stopped, the artillery erupted from every side. Somewhere a double-barreled shotgun boomed. Emmett was cut down. His horse bolted, and Emmett lay in an ever-widening pool of blood beside Bob, who reached a trembling hand out to draw his brother close.

Emmett's rescue attempt was at once the bravest and most foolhardy thing I had ever seen. In at least one respect he had lived up to his ambition, because it far outshone anything the James brothers had attempted.

"Is there a back way out of here?" I demanded of Cashier Ball, pointing and cocking my revolver. "No lies this time."

"Through the office," Ball said. "Up the stairs and out the YMCA rooms to the street."

"Don't move," I barked, and ran for the back. The door in the back of the office was locked, but I shouldered it open, taking hinges and door frame with it. I found the stairs and limped up, moved through the YMCA rooms with the barrel of my Colt preceding me, then found the stairs and descended to the street. I expected to be chewed up by a hail of bullets, but not a shot was fired.

I moved easily across the Plaza, not really caring whether I was challenged or not. I did not flinch or hurry, but walked as steadily as I could manage with my bad knee. I reckon I looked like just another man with a gun among dozens of armed men. But I wasn't thinking of that at the time. In fact, I wasn't thinking at all. My brothers had been killed in front of me. I was numb, as if somebody had struck me across the skull with a piece of lumber. They had been gunned down and, rightly or wrongly, I had not busted a cap to save them. I was drawn down the alley, to the clusters around the bodies.

"Let's lynch him, by God!" somebody shouted when they discovered that Emmett's eyelids still fluttered. But Colonel Elliott, wearing his dark suit and smoking a cigar, came out of the door of the *Journal* and walked over to where Bob and Emmett lay. The newspaper office faced the alley, and Elliott had watched the battle from the desk where he wrote his editorials.

"You men get back," Elliott commanded. He was unarmed, but he brushed aside men bristling with carbines and six-guns. "Do not disgrace us by lynching a dying man. Get back, I say!"

Elliott threw away his cigar and knelt down beside Emmett, ignoring the pool of blood on the ground.

"Colonel, take my guns," Emmett said. "I can't shoot them."

Elliott took the six-gun from Em's fluttering hand and tucked it into his own belt. "It's over, son," the colonel said gently, cradling Emmett's head in the crook of his arm. "Don't try to talk. Don't worry, I'll send for your Mama."

The colonel organized the men, and they carried Em and Marshal Connelly on planks into Rammel's Drug Store to tend their wounds. I heard Elliott say sadly that neither of them would last half an hour. Bob and Grat were already turning cold.

"What a waste of courage," Elliott said.

Then someone ran in from the west and said that the other bandit that had escaped—Broadwell—had been dropped from his horse at the edge of town by a shot from a .45 fired by a seventeen-year-old kid.

I reckon it was the only thing Johnny Williamson had ever hit.

Unchallenged, I walked back to where Cimarron was hitched. Moving as if I was in a dream, I swung up into the saddle and gave one last look at the alley where my brothers lay dead, and the front of the Condon Bank, which was shot absolutely to hell. At that moment Cashier Ball appeared in the doorway, pointed at me, and yelled, "That's him!"

But nobody seemed to hear him.

I turned Cimarron and rode away.

Twenty-seven

I PUT CIMARRON on the Whiskey Trail leading south out of Coffeyville and rode for hours. The wind got colder and the shadows grew longer, but I did not stop.

At dusk I met a lone rider, headed north.

After we had passed I heard the harsh click of hammer being thumbed back on a lever gun. I froze in the saddle and slacked the reins.

"Dismount slow," a voice said behind me.

I did, and when I reached the ground I turned to find myself staring into the bore of a Winchester held by Deputy Jim Cole. He was grayer and fatter than I remembered.

"Choctaw Kid," he said, "you are under arrest. The wire from Coffeyville said there was a sixth rider that escaped the raid, and I reckon you are it."

"I thought there was something familiar about you," I said.

"You've got me mixed up with somebody else," Cole said. "We've never met. Now, hand over your gun real slow."

I took the Colt from its holster and held it out, butt-first. Cole slid down from his horse, pointing the Winchester skyward, and reached out for the gun. I twirled it around, doing a road-agent spin like Bob had showed me so long ago, and in a flash it was cocked and pointed at Cole's heart.

It was too quick for him to bring the Winchester to bear. He had no choice but to let the rifle fall to the ground.

"It would be a mistake to kill me," Cole said.

"I'm not going to kill you with your own gun," I said. "You don't recognize me, do you? Last time we saw each other was in the Bottoms. You gave me your gun."

"Samuel?"

"That's right," I said, uncocking the gun. "It's still me."

"Jesus H. Christ. I thought you were dead. I never suspected you were the Choctaw Kid, not with that long hair and that nose. Your brothers never let on. They're all dead now, except for Emmett, who's shot up bad. Got seventeen different wounds."

"I know."

"You were there?"

"Yes."

"Goddammit, what do you expect me to do?" Cole asked. "They have wired every whistle-stop and one-horse town between here and Fort Smith to be on the lookout for Dalton gang members. I was at Claremore when the news came. They're afraid there's going to be hell to pay for killing Bob and Grat and the others."

"Not from me," I said. "I'm through with killing."

"I wish I could believe you," Cole said, tugging at his whiskers. "They say you're quicker than greased lightning, you know. Did you ever catch up with Towerly?"

I reached into my pocket and withdrew Frank's watch, the one with the hunting scene, and handed it to Cole. He turned it over in his hand, looking at it close.

"I reckon you did," he said.

"Here's your gun back," I said, handing him the Colt. "Sorry I kept it so long. I didn't really plan it that way."

"Don't think I could carry it now," Cole said. "I'd always be wondering who it killed, and not sure I wanted to know. No, you keep it, son. You've made it yours."

"But you'll want it while you take me back to Fort Smith," I said. Cole shook his head.

"Don't know what you're talking about." Cole handed the watch back and stared at the sunset, blazing above the tree line. "I've got a warrant here for the Choctaw Kid. Have you seen him, stranger?"

"No," I said after a spell. "Guess I haven't."

I swung back into Cimarron's saddle and touched the brim of my hat. We rode on in our separate directions and neither of us looked back. I brushed the hair out of my face and reckoned it was time for a barber and a new suit of clothes.

• • • •

They put handcuffs on the bodies and laid them out on a hayrack in front of the city jail so Tackett could make a picture postcard. Emmett survived somehow and was sentenced to life in prison after pleading guilty to murder. Broadwell's father fetched his body back to Hutchinson, but nobody claimed Powers and he was laid to rest in potter's field.

Bob and Grat were buried at Elmwood Cemetery, near to where Frank lay, but their only headstone is part of the hitch post where they tied their horses in the alley—Death Alley, folks began calling it.

John Kleohr was elected chief of police, but for some reason he became reticent and refused to talk about the raid. He especially objected to being called a hero, and returned medals awarded to him by the local lodges.

And some say Luke Baldwin's widow is sent regular sums of money from a stranger who lives somewhere in the Choctaw Nation.